Melding Spirits

Melding Spirits

Melding Spirits

Michael E. Burge

Revised Edition: April 2019

ISBN 13: 978-0-9963098-3-7 (Paperback)

ISBN 13: 978-0-9963098-6-8 (Paperback-Large Print)

ISBN 13: 978-0-9963098-4-4 (eBook-Kindle/MOBI)

ISBN 13: 978-0-9963098-5-1 (eBook-EPUB)

Cover Design: JD&J Design LLC

For Bertha . . . and all the good spirits around us

"This is a brief life, but in its brevity it offers us some splendid moments, some meaningful adventures."

—Rudyard Kipling

"All things share the same breath: the beast, the tree, the man. The air shares its spirit with all the life it supports. There is no death, only a change of worlds."

—Chief Seattle (c.1780–1866)

Thanks to Michael Garrett
for imparting a lifetime of knowledge

Katie-Blue

See that girl with sparklin' eyes
The color of the sea
That's Katie, sweet Katie
She cast a spell on me

I can't stroll and I can't swing
So, what's a boy to do
If I can steal just one sweet kiss
I'll write a song for you

Oh, Katie, sweet Katie
Sweet, sweet, Katie-Blue

I can play, you can dance
And we will have one cool romance

Oh, Katie, sweet Katie
Sweet, sweet, Katie-Blue

— Evan Mason (1958)

1
———

Late Spring – 1958

“I'm planning to stay with a friend,” the girl said. “It'll be a bit of a surprise to her. She's not expecting me for about a week, but I don't think she'll mind. She's between boyfriends at the moment, so I won't be interrupting anything.”

“And what's your name, young lady?” the man behind the wheel of the pickup truck said.

“Rena.”

“That's a pretty name, one you don't hear every day.”

“Actually, it's Irene. My little sister had trouble saying my name, so she started calling me Rena, and it stuck.”

“Where does this friend of yours live, Rena?” he said, his eyes fixed on the open stretch of two-lane highway, the midday heat rendering illusionary sheets of water across the baking asphalt.

“Louisville,” she replied.

He glanced at her and said, "You'll be on the road for a good while, and that sun is hot today. You'd better put a shirt on over that halter-top. Nothing can spoil a good time like a nasty sunburn."

"That's what my mother would probably tell me, but whatever *she* says, I usually do just the opposite," Rena said. "She drives me crazy sometimes."

"We've got something in common," he said, tapping the pack of Luckys against the steering wheel. "My ex-wife had a way of getting under my skin like nobody else could. She had to have the last word on everything." He gingerly pulled a cigarette from the pack with his teeth, took a wooden kitchen match from the cluster stuffed in the ashtray and scratched it with his thumbnail. As he lit the cigarette the sulfur on the matchhead flared with such intensity it seemed the bushy mustache he was sporting might combust like tinder in a parched forest. He took a long drag and started to put the pack back into his pocket, but instead tapped another cigarette halfway out and offered it. "Picked up the habit?"

"No. Most of my friends from high school smoke. I tried a couple here and there, but just don't seem to have the urge, not yet, anyway."

He stuffed the pack back into his shirt pocket. "So, like I was saying," he continued, "Selma, that was my wife's name, was driving me completely nuts with her nagging. Finally had to give her the heave-ho." He looked at Rena and laughed. "To make things even worse, she wasn't the most loyal female on the planet, if you get my drift. There's only so much a man can take." Smoke was streaming from his nose and billowing from his mouth as he spoke.

Rena had been listening intently, but was now tuned-in to the man barking on the radio, ". . . pick, shell, and clean . . ." the announcer said, "a full twenty acres of corn in a day, and all in one smooth, single operation. So, stop by the showroom today and see the new model Forty-five combine. The new implement that'll get you home in time for supper . . . now, back to our regular program."

"Do you mind if I change the station?" Rena said. She glanced at the man, but before he could answer, she twisted the tuning knob.

Paul Anka serenaded them with "You Are My Destiny" as the Chevy pickup sped along Route 1. There was the smell of freshly mown hay in the air and the steady, rhythmic sound of several oil pumps laboring in the distance.

They breezed through the town of Goliath, Illinois, a name somewhat incongruous, considering the business district consisted of a bowling alley, grocery store, three saloons, and the town hall. Moments later, they were traveling through dense woodland that stretched several miles in every direction.

"I can take you another seventy-five miles, then we'll have to part company," the man said and flashed a big grin.

"That would be great," Rena said.

"I need to put a little food in me, though. I get a little light-headed if I don't eat. Got some sandwiches back there in the cooler. There's a little nook just around the bend, here. You hungry?" he said as they rounded the curve.

"I could eat. Thank you, sir."

He made a hard-right turn between two tall pine trees, drove about thirty yards, and backed the truck into a shady spot under a large oak. He stepped from the truck, grabbed the cooler from the truck bed and placed it on the ground beside the driver's door. He flipped the lid back and said, "What'll it be, ham and cheese or corned beef on rye?"

The man stood beside the pickup. The driver-side door was wide open. He popped the cap off a bottle of beer and sat on the edge of the seat, one foot in the truck, the other on the ground. "Here you go," he said, reaching across the seat with the beer.

"Oh, I don't know if I should," Rena said, "I haven't—"

"I'm bettin' this wouldn't be the first alcohol to touch those lips." He pushed the bottle toward her. "You don't have to drink it all, just a little to wet your whistle. You've got my authorization. It'll be our little secret." She hesitated for a moment, then took the beer and began to sip it. "Atta girl," he said. He opened one for himself and took a big swig. "What do your folks think about you leaving the nest?"

"I didn't tell them," she said and cringed.

"That's not good. It'll be like you fell off the face of the earth," he said.

"You're probably right. Maybe I'll send them a postcard after I find a job and get settled in." She took another swallow of beer. "Hey, this is my favorite," she said and reached for the volume control on the radio.

For the next few minutes, they drank their beer and the man watched as Rena did a sit-down version of the jitterbug.

Rena was swatting at a couple of bees circling the nearly empty bottle she had clamped between her thighs.

A gentle breeze was blowing, and Dean Martin was crooning a love song, something about Napoli and the moon looking like a big pizza.

The man was slumped back, his head resting on the edge of the seatback. He guzzled the last few ounces of his beer and dropped the empty bottle into the cooler beside the truck. He continued to stare at the roof and said, "I know why you're wearing that halter-top, young lady."

Rena stopped swatting at the bees and looked at the man. "What did you say?" she said. She was feeling a bit dizzy from the alcohol and thought she had misheard his remark.

"You're like all the rest, out to get the boys all revved up, show them who's in charge." He sprang up in the seat, turning, yelling directly at her. "You think I'm stupid? You think I didn't know what you were doing, gyrating around on that seat like a bitch in heat?"

"Please!" She was trembling, her voice loud, yet hollow. "You're scaring me, mister."

"Shut up!" He backhanded her across the mouth.

Her head collided with the window column, and blood spurted from her lower lip.

Dean continued to sing.

She was momentarily frozen, her eyes fixed on the man lurking over her. His face was flushed, his eyes full of rage. She hadn't realized what a large man he was until that exact moment.

Instinctively, she drew her leg back and kicked at him, the heel of her bare foot slamming into his chest, driving him backward toward the open driver's door. She clutched the door handle and gave a tug. The door didn't budge. She grabbed the handle with both hands, shooting sharp glances over her shoulder as she tugged frantically.

"Door doesn't open from the inside," he said in a monotone. "Little adjustment I made." He was standing just outside the driver's door, now. He bent down and pulled a towel from under the seat, reached between the folds and retrieved a hypodermic syringe. "A little surprise for you, young lady."

She screamed when she saw the needle, then grabbed the sill and threw her head and shoulders through the partially open passenger-side window. The man lunged across the seat, planting his knee against the back of her legs, pinning her there with the weight of his body. He jammed the needle through the cotton material of her shorts, into her right buttock.

Within seconds her head was swirling. She lay there on the seat paralyzed, her senses blunted. Before she lost consciousness, she heard the truck's engine start, and from somewhere high above, the shrill alarming cry of a raptor.

The man drove along the overgrown road that wound through the dense woods and stopped at a spot about a half-mile from where they had eaten lunch. He knew these woods well. He had trudged through this forest numerous times; there were a lot of good hiding places.

He carried the girl a short distance to a narrow clearing bordered by a tall, thick patch of ivy. He placed her on the ground and unfurled the blanket. Her hands and feet were bound and there was a strip of tape across her mouth.

For nearly a full minute he stood motionless, simply gazing at her. Finally, she began to stir. When she opened her eyes, he could see the look of fear in them. A feeling of power and control surged through his veins, a feeling he had experienced before—a feeling he relished.

Amid her muffled screams, he pulled the bone-handled hunting knife from the leather sheath on his belt, slid the gleaming steel blade between her skin and the fabric of the halter, and cut it away.

The killer dropped the spade and a bag of lime beside Rena's naked, lifeless body and took a long drink of warm beer. He tilted his head back and stood there stoically looking up at the sky, a cigarette hanging from the corner of his mouth and trickles of sweat tracing the deep crevices in his brow. *What a beautiful day*, he thought.

He heard a shrill cry. Cupping his hand beside his eyes, he

searched the sky, spotting the red-tailed hawk circling high overhead. He watched for a while as the bird hovered, its shrill, irritating call piercing the midday calm.

He took one last drag on his cigarette, picked up the shovel and began to dig—the shadow of the raptor crisscrossing the site as he worked.

2

———

Evan Mason sat in the back seat as Gladys Hatfield dropped the Ford Crestline into first gear, revved the engine, and lurched along the circular drive that serviced the all-in-one train depot and bus station in Chicago Pointe.

Today was Saturday, and Evan would soon be on a southbound bus headed for Laurenville, Illinois to stay with his grandmother for the summer. The thirty-three-year-old woman riding shotgun was Lila Mason, Evan's mother. On Monday, she would be in New York City for a week of training. She had worked as a clerk in the Chicago Pointe office for two years and now had a shot at becoming an agent for one of the biggest insurance companies in the world.

"Okay, Lila," Gladys said, as she double-parked near the main entrance to the station. "I'm going to drop you here. I'll park somewhere around the corner and wait for you." Gladys jumped from the car, opened the trunk, and with little effort hoisted the overstuffed suitcase and plopped it onto the ground.

Gladys was a large, sturdy woman. She wasn't what one might call homely, but she had a crooked smile and her features were plain and asymmetrical. Her lips and fingernails were painted a ruby red and her dark auburn hair was piled up on her head in a massive layer of sweeping curls. A stiff northerly breeze was blowing, but her hair remained steadfast as she went about her business.

Not long ago, Gladys had discovered the magic of those aerosol cans that had made their way from the battlefields of WW II, where they were used to dispense insecticides, to the dressing tables of women around the world. Only instead of DDT, they now were filled with a flowery smelling lacquer, a few layers of which could transform the flattest of hairdos into a high rise bouffant of staggering proportions. Gladys Hatfield had certainly done her part to keep the hairspray companies in business.

"You got a big kiss for your Aunt Gladys, Evan?" She beckoned him around to the rear of the car. He knew what was coming and tried to brace himself for the trauma that would ensue. She pulled him to her bosom, enveloping him in a fog of lavender perfume and talcum powder.

He was light-headed from lack of oxygen and the sheer devastation of the moment, and when he saw the two huge, over-puckered lips coming in for a landing, he was certain things were going to end badly. Fortunately, the sharp, instinctive reflexes of youth took over. He gave a quick twist of his neck and the two ruby red marauders landed three inches off target, splashing down high on his cheek, just below his right eye.

Gladys stepped back to arm's length. "You have a good time down south, and don't you worry about your mother. I'll be watching over her. She's going to do just fine in that new job. I just know it." She reached into her purse, pulled out several folded bills, and tucked them into his shirt pocket. "Take Grandma Bea out for a soda. Go see a movie. Buy something for yourself, whatever tickles your fancy. It's our little secret."

"Thank you, Aunt Gladys. I—"

"Hold still, honey." She yanked a flowered hanky from her pocket, wrapped it around her index finger, wet it with her tongue, and executed the *dreaded lipstick erasure*. Later in life, Evan would have Freudian nightmares related to that moment.

Incidentally, Gladys wasn't really Evan's aunt. He called her that because Lila had always considered her one of the family. It made his mother happy.

Gladys lit a cigarette and slid behind the wheel. "See you in a bit, dearie," she said to Lila, the cigarette dangling from the corner of her mouth as she spoke.

"Shouldn't be long, Gladys," Lila said, looking at her watch. "If the bus leaves on time, it'll be pulling out in the next fifteen minutes."

"Don't rush. I'll be across the street at the drugstore. Alvin is there today." She gave a little wink as she popped the clutch and humped her way down the street and around the corner. Gladys wasn't the best of drivers.

"I hope you remembered everything, Evan. Did you pack your books and the card for Grandma Bea?" Lila said.

"Yes, Mother."

She reached for the suitcase, but Evan rushed over and picked it up.

"I can carry it," he said. "Do you want to hurt your back again, right before your trip?"

"Well, if you're sure you can manage it," she said. "I don't want you to rupture something."

He rolled his eyes and said, "Please! I'm not going to get a *rupture.*"

They walked toward the waiting bus, Lila checking the list she had taken from her purse.

"Okay, do you have your good jacket, your extra belt, and—"

"Yes, Mother."

"Your new sneakers?"

He looked down at his brand-new Keds. "I'm wearing them," he said, shaking his head in mild disgust. "We went through that list an hour ago. It might be a little late now, don't you think?"

"Don't be a smart aleck, dear. I could certainly mail those things to you, now, couldn't I?" She snapped the clasp on the large purse she was carrying and pulled out two comic books. She handed them to Evan, then snatched a brand new brown leather wallet from the side pouch. "Your money is behind the little window compartment. Now, make sure you tuck this deep into your pocket so it doesn't fall out," she said as she demonstrated the prescribed *tucking technique*. Evan took it and jammed it into the hip pocket of his jeans. "And I hope you brought your harmonica. The people on the bus might enjoy hearing you play. Music helps pass the time on a long trip, you know."

At Lila's suggestion, Gladys had given Evan a top of the line harmonica for his last birthday. Evan had plenty of musical talent. His father had begun teaching him to play the piano when he was just four years old. Evan's cognitive skills and tonal awareness had been uncanny, especially for a child his age. After his father's death, Evan's interest in music had waned. Lila hoped the harmonica might rekindle it.

"Got it right here, Mother." He pulled the instrument from his pocket and waved it to allay any doubt.

They sat on a bench in front of the station and watched as the driver tossed the bags into the cavern under the bus.

Lila lit a cigarette and took a couple of puffs. "Evan, you know, I don't like the idea of leaving you with Grandma Bea all summer, but I hope you understand, it's important for both of us that I get this job and get off to a good start. It can mean everything to our future. Aunt Gladys offered to help out, but you wouldn't have been happy staying with her, would you?" She took another puff on her cigarette.

Evan looked at her and gave another roll of the eyes.

"I didn't think so. You'll have a good time at Grandma's.

She loves you a lot. She'll be grateful for the company," Lila said.

"Mother, it's okay. You know I have a lot of friends in Laurenville, probably more than I have here. You don't have to worry about me."

"Everyone headed south may begin boarding. Please be sure you have your ticket and all your belongings. Once we leave the barn, we don't look back!" the driver said as he began to assist people onto the bus.

"Now remember what I said. You give that driver a good up and down inspection as you board, and when you get off at those rest stops, you make sure you keep him in sight all the time you're there. When he gets up, you follow him. The bus can't leave without him," Lila said.

"What about when he goes to the restroom?" Evan said.

"Very funny," she said and mashed the half-smoked, lipstick-smeared cigarette into the ashtray beside her. Lila didn't have a robust sense of humor. "Now, get over here and give me a big hug."

"I'm going to miss you, Mom." He patted her on the back as they embraced.

"And I'll miss you. You're the best son a mother could ask for."

3

———

When the Greyhound turned onto Halsted Street, Evan caught a glimpse of his mother still standing in front of the station. The bus was too far away for her to actually see him, but she was waving her handkerchief like a castaway trying to flag down a passing ship.

As he looked at her, he was reminded of other times he'd been shipped off to Grandma Bea's. When he was five he spent six months with her. His father was having a difficult time finding work, and his mother was dealing with some health issues, "female problems," as she referred to them. Then, during the rough patch after his father died, he completed a full year of school in Laurenville.

One would think the interruptions and frequent changes of venue would have been disturbing to a young boy, but Evan had taken it all in stride. After all, he was an "old soul," or so his grandmother had told him many times.

Since his father died, things had become increasingly more unsettled. His mother wasn't home much, the insurance office during the day, waiting tables at night. Evan was spending a great deal of time alone. He knew she was doing her best to provide for him, and he admired her for what she had accomplished, but there were also times when he didn't understand her, times when she was angry, angry at his father for dying. That entire notion seemed strange to Evan. After all, William Mason hadn't set out to become a "valve jockey" at Vance Chemical, and he certainly hadn't expected to die in an explosion at the modest age of thirty.

He was a talented musician with a dream of a career in music. He had been attending the American Conservatory of Music in Chicago when he met Lila.

Grandma Bea had been devastated when he dropped out to marry, and even more distraught when he took the job at the factory. It wasn't exactly the life Beatrice Mason had in mind for William Joseph Mason, her only child.

Evan recalled the night he'd seen his father perform at the Copacabana, the moment he knew his father hadn't completely abandoned his dreams. He had taken to the stage and sung his heart out. Everyone had given him a standing ovation that night.

Of course, that wasn't the Copa in New York City, but the bar three blocks from the bowling alley, on Halsted Street in Chicago Pointe, the place with the neon beer sign glowing in the window, the tiny dimly lit stage, and the organist who played on Friday and Saturday nights for tips. *Sometimes, a person's dreams have to be altered a bit,* Evan thought.

Over the last year, Evan and his mother seemed to be seeing less and less of each other. Most days, when he opened the bathroom door and stepped out, a towel wrapped around him, she would be scurrying around the room, tidying up as she spoke.

"Today is a short day for me," she would say. "I'll be home by the time school lets out."

As she departed, she would blow him a kiss and, with a shopping bag draped over one arm and her purse over the other, descend the stairs from the second-floor apartment to the waiting cab on the busy street below. The last thing he would hear as she closed the door would be, "Now, don't forget your lunch, Evan. You can't keep your mind on your studies if your stomach's growling."

Each morning, probably before her eyes were completely open, she would dutifully prepare his lunch. He knew when he opened the refrigerator there would be a paper bag containing a sandwich, a Twinkie and, of course, an apple or banana, "a little something to maintain regularity," as Aunt Gladys would always put it.

The other thing he knew was that it was highly unlikely his mother would be there to greet him when he came home. She had good intentions, but it seldom happened. Most afternoons when he arrived, he would find a handful of change along with a note:

Don't forget to lock the door and close all the windows before you leave. If you go to the movies, be sure to have dinner first. You can't live on popcorn and soda pop!

Love, Mother

Dinner could usually be found on a shelf in the pantry. Most days, when he opened the door and peered in, he would see a can with Chef Boy-Ar-Dee's smiling, mustached little face looking back at him. It had become a comforting sight over the past few years, one of the more unwavering elements in Evan's capricious life.

After he ate, he would finish his homework, then scoop up the change and head for one of the two movie theaters. They were at opposite ends of town, but both within walking distance.

He didn't mind going to the movies alone. He had grown accustomed to it. The thing that bothered him most, at least when he was younger, was walking home after dark.

A couple of years ago, he'd seen a movie about alien beings that oozed from watermelon-size pods, mimicked an unsuspecting human's form, then hijacked the person's soul while he or she slept. The things would walk around like zombies, slipping those strange looking pods into people's closets, the trunks of their cars, under their beds, intent on taking over the entire planet.

It was a creepy movie, and during the walk home, against all rational thinking, he was expecting one of those aliens to slip from a doorway or an alley and follow him. Before he went to bed that night, he inspected every possible hiding place in the apartment. He even took a peek into the oven. Baking wasn't one of his mother's favorite activities, and he thought it would be the perfect place to stash one of those menacing pods.

He had lain wide awake that night until his mother arrived, finally falling asleep with visions of lifeless faces flashing in his brain.

I'd definitely been afraid that night, he thought. *Okay, let's be honest. I was scared shitless.* Surely, there were other times, but that was the only instance that came to mind.

The human brain had the uncanny ability to erase or short circuit unpleasant memories, a trait Evan would come to greatly appreciate.

All the movie theaters showed a double feature, a couple of cartoons, and maybe a newsreel. So rather than return to an empty apartment, Evan would frequently save half his popcorn and hang around for the second running.

He had seen a plethora of movies in his short life, everything from *The Ten Commandments* to a spicy little flick starring Brigitte Bardot called *And God Created Woman.*

He remembered being totally amazed when Charlton Heston parted the Red Sea. *It has to be the most exciting scene ever!* he thought. *Although, the image of Brigitte Bardot running around naked is a pretty close second . . . if dreams are any indication.*

The bus rolled under the long, tunnel-like viaduct that

ran beneath the wide span of railroad tracks at the south edge of town. When it exited, the cluttered urban setting immediately gave way to a stretch of open highway. The same feeling would invariably wash over him at that point. *Perhaps*, he thought, *the way a sailor feels when he leaves a harbor, bound for the open sea.*

Route 1, between Chicago Pointe and Laurenville, was a narrow two-hundred-mile stretch of asphalt, bordered by cornfields and farm towns. Evan and his mother had made the trip numerous times after his father died, usually with Aunt Gladys inching along at forty-five miles per hour, puffing on a cigarette and talking a blue streak. Even at that speed, the trip should have taken only about four and a half hours, but with Aunt Gladys at the helm, the voyage took a bit longer. She knew people in many of the towns along the way and would feel obligated to "stop and visit for a while." With each trip, the pool of acquaintances grew, and over time the drive from Chicago Pointe to Laurenville had mushroomed into a six-hour odyssey. Fortunately, they always got an early start. Aunt Gladys didn't like to drive at night.

Gladys had always been an eccentric woman. Some even considered her a bit overbearing. Back in 1945, at the age of thirty, Gladys met an electrician by the name of Malcolm Hatfield at a supper club in Hammond, Indiana. Shortly thereafter, the man had proposed marriage. A little over a month after they were wed, Malcolm went out one morning for a pack of cigarettes and never returned.

To this day, no one can attest to his whereabouts. Some concluded he had met with foul play, while others, those who knew Gladys well, believed he had endured her badgering for as long as he could and finally "took it on the lam."

Two years after Malcolm's disappearance, Gladys inherited a shitload of money. Everyone expected Malcolm to reappear, having risen from the dead, but there was no sign of him. Gladys never remarried.

4

____

Evan sat in an eighth-row window seat. During the first half of the trip, he had passed the time by conjuring up new knock-knock jokes and dissecting the story in his Superman comic book. Evan didn't just read comic books, he analyzed them, looking for inconsistencies in the storyline, statements that insulted the intelligence of any free-thinking twelve-year-old by completely abandoning reason.

He liked Superman because, most of the time, the storytellers threw in a smattering of scientific facts to explain certain things, like why the Kryptonian was indestructible, could fly faster than a speeding bullet, and see through anything that wasn't shrouded in lead. Evan was content with most of *that* rationale, but he still couldn't understand how the "Man of Steel" was able to hide a bulky long flowing cape under those Clark Kent duds, and completely transform himself from a dashing superhero into a mild-mannered reporter by simply donning a pair of horn-rimmed glasses. These were the little things Evan found hard to swallow.

"Say, kid, what you reading there?" the man said as he sat down in the aisle seat beside Evan, tucking the weathered canvas bag into the space between his feet. The disheveled, unshaven man had been asleep in the back section of the bus for most of the trip. Evan immediately detected the smell of alcohol, perhaps whiskey, on his breath.

"Superman," Evan replied.

"I used to read them comics when I was your age. I was a Wonder Woman fan myself. Still pick up a copy now and then. That broad is stacked like a brick shithouse. How 'bout you, kid? You like Wonder Woman?" the man said.

"Sometimes, but it's not really one of my favorites," Evan said.

The man shrugged and said, "Where you headed?"

"Going to visit my grandmother. She lives in Laurenville."

"I'm on my way to Danville. My sister lives there," the man said, leaned back, and grimaced while he assiduously reamed his ear canal with his index finger. "Never been down this way before, but people tell me I'm gonna like the town. I got a job lined up with the street and sanitation department. Not exactly sure what, though. It's probably some kind of office job. You know, white shirt and tie, something befitting my talents. A friend of mine is hooking me up. What grade you in, kid? You look like you're about thirteen or fourteen."

"I'll be in seventh grade this next year. I'm tall for my age," Evan said, feeling a bit uncomfortable with the interrogation.

"Seventh, huh? That was the year I dropped out. Learned everything I needed to know by then. Don't you pay a listen to folks when they feed you all that bullshit about book learnin'. Believe me, boy, when I tell you, it's highly overrated. Street smarts, that's where it's at. You know what I mean?"

"I think so," Evan replied.

"Say, what's your name, kid?" The man extended his hand.

"Evan, uh, Evan Mason." He reached to shake hands with the man.

"Tom Mosley. Glad to make your acquaintance." He squeezed Evan's hand for a few seconds, looking into the boy's eyes like he was trying to read his thoughts, then folded his arms across his chest, closed his eyes, and relaxed against the seat back. In minutes, he was asleep.

As the bus accelerated along the stretch of flat deserted highway, Evan turned his attention back to Superman's exploits, trying his best to ignore the high-pitched snore resonating from Mosley's half-open mouth and the thin string of saliva heading south through the forest of stubble on his chin.

"This is Danville," the driver announced as the bus pulled into the station. "We'll give you folks twenty minutes to grab a bite to eat and take care of any other pressing needs that might be on your mind. Please take all your personal items with you and note the time. The bus will depart this depot at exactly half past the hour."

The passengers began to move along the narrow aisle toward the door. As the bus emptied, Tom Mosley turned to Evan and said, "Well, kid, it looks like this is where we part company. I hope you have a good visit with your granny." Mosley fumbled through his bag, pushing aside the half-empty pint of Old Crow, and grabbing a tattered baseball cap. He yanked it onto his head as he stepped into the aisle, then reached into the pocket of his grungy jeans and pulled out a crumpled dollar bill. Mosley stretched it, smoothed it against the edge of the seatback, and snapped it a couple of times. "Here," he said and offered it to Evan. "I want you to have this. Find yourself a little country-tail down there in that town of Lawrenceville."

"Laurenville," Evan said.

"Whatever. Take her to the movies, buy her an ice cream cone, on me," Mosley said.

"That's okay, Mr. Mosley, I can't take that. Thank you, but it wouldn't be—"

"Bullshit! Now, you just tuck this away in that brand-new wallet you got there so you don't lose it," Mosley said, then mumbled, "keep those other greenbacks company."

Evan gave Mosley a quizzical look.

"I saw it back there in Watseka when you bought that candy bar. That's a fine piece of cowhide you got there. Now, you take this money. A buck don't go as far as it used to. You don't want to run out of cash midway through your summer vacation, do you? Go on," Mosley said, dangling the bill in Evan's face.

Evan stood, stepped into the aisle and gingerly took the dollar. He pulled out his wallet, tucked the bill away, and put the wallet back into his pocket.

Mosley reached for Evan, gathered him in and gave him a bear hug. "You take care now, Evan Mason," Mosley said and headed down the aisle toward the door.

A voice called out, "I believe you forgot something, Mr. Mosley!"

Mosley stopped and looked over his shoulder. A man in a Marine uniform was standing just behind Evan. The Marine's hair was cropped short. A red and gold master sergeant insignia and five hash marks were sewn onto his sleeve. There were three rows of campaign ribbons pinned to his chest. He looked to be about forty years old, stood just over six feet tall, and he was scowling.

"Say what?" Mosley said.

"Isn't there something you need to do before you go?" the Marine said.

"I'm not following you, Chief," Mosley said.

"Don't play dumb with me. You know exactly what I'm referring to," the Marine said.

"I don't have the slightest damn idea what you're talking about!" Mosley said.

The Marine rushed forward, grabbed Mosley firmly by the ear, gave it a twist, and escorted him at quickstep down the aisle toward the door.

"Well, how about I dropkick your butt across this parking lot a few times? Do you think that might shake loose a thought or two in your petrified brain?"

Mosley stumbled off the bus, the Marine dragging him along by the ear toward the side of the depot.

"Take it easy, Admiral!" Mosley shouted.

"Now, I suggest you reach into your pocket and retrieve the boy's wallet. You may think you're slick, but you're not quite the huckster you think you are! I saw you wandering off to the back of the bus for those little nips on that bottle you got stashed in your bag. You're so drunk you couldn't even remember which one of the boy's pockets to go fishing in, could you, numbnuts? You had to fork over that scroungy bill just to find out which pocket his wallet was in."

The Marine now had Mosley's left arm twisted behind his back, still pinching his ear in a vice-like grip.

"Okay . . . Okay!" Mosley shouted. He pulled the wallet out and waved it wildly. "Oooooow! Here . . . take it!"

The Marine snatched the wallet from his hand, gave the ear one last twist, and threw him into the shallow ditch running alongside the building. Mosley landed face-down in the mud.

Evan came around the side of the depot. "Mr. Mosley's," Evan said, and gestured toward the canvas bag he was carrying.

"Mr. Mosley thanks you, son," the Marine said, took it and tossed it into the ditch beside Mosley.

Mosley grabbed the bag and clambered from the ditch onto the sidewalk, clutching his ear. "I may just call . . . the cops

. . . in on this!" he shouted, spitting chunks of sod between words.

"I think that would be a wonderful idea. A few days in the brig might do you some good," the Marine shouted as he watched Mosley stumble along the sidewalk, mumbling to himself. "Good luck with your new job, dipshit!"

The Marine turned to Evan and said, "I'm Sergeant Samuel H. Gustafson, but you can call me Gus. Come on, son, I'll buy you lunch." They walked toward the bus depot. "And you might want to think about spending some of that money numbnuts gave you, get that nasty bill out of your wallet before it contaminates the rest of them. Who knows *where* that thing's been? Might be carrying Bubonic Plague. Besides, that kind of money is bad luck."

There was an improvised doorway connecting the depot to the diner. It looked as though someone had taken a sledgehammer to the wall and framed in the hole with leftover strips of molding. The diner had a half-dozen booths, several tables, and a long lunch counter. The stools, chairs, and booths were upholstered in red naugahyde, and everything was trimmed with stainless steel.

Evan and Sergeant Gus sat at a table toward the front of the diner. The teenage boy and girl who sat in a booth across from them were holding hands. The girl was wearing a poodle skirt, the boy a pair of faded Levi's. Both sides of the boy's hair were slicked back, converging in a feathery tuft to resemble a "duck's ass," a popular hairstyle aptly referred to as a D.A. The boy dropped a dime into the record selector and began quickly flipping through the song titles. The girl draped her chin over the boy's shoulder and swooned as she watched him make his selections. A few seconds later, The Platters began to sing about the girl of their dreams.

"You have to be careful who you give your name to. There are a lot of shady characters in this world," Gus said. "Sometimes, when you introduce yourself, it's best to throw out only your first name. If the stranger is sincere, he'll understand. If he's offended, he's probably not worth your time anyway. Get what I'm saying?"

Evan nodded. "How'd you know what he was up to, anyway?" Evan said as he swirled the straw around in his glass, vacuuming up the last few ounces of his chocolate malt.

"Not hard to figure out a guy like that," Gus said. "I knew the minute he opened his mouth he was up to no good. Now, I realize you were simply trying to be respectful of your elders, and there's nothing wrong with that. You're a good kid, but you got to keep your radar up to spot that type of snake. The world's full of them. If you're suspicious of someone, size him up immediately. Figure out if he's a worthy adversary who deserves your respect or just a paper tiger. You know what I'm referring to when I use the term paper tiger?"

"Do you mean like in the newsreels? The ones they carry in the parades with the fireworks and all the wild costumes?" Evan said.

"Those are the ones. The things look fierce and scary, but a bit of rain or a strong gust of wind and those monsters would be in tatters. You get the point?" Gus said.

"Yes, sir. I understand," Evan replied.

5
——

Sergeant Gus had relocated and was sitting in the seat beside Evan. He watched as Evan pulled a booklet from the pouch on the seatback and replaced it with his newly acquired Batman comic book. Written across the front of the booklet was *The Story of Hohner Harmonicas and How to Play Them.*

"What you got there?" Gus said.

"It came with the harmonica I got for my birthday." Evan reached into his jacket pocket and produced the instrument. "I'm trying to learn how to play this thing. My dad was a musician, and everyone is hoping I might have a little of his talent. I haven't made much progress with it yet."

Evan passed the booklet to the sergeant. He thumbed through it, then handed it back to Evan.

"It's hard to learn to do anything from a book. Let me take a look at that baby," Gus said.

Evan handed him the harmonica and the sergeant inspected it.

"You got yourself a good one here," Gus said. He held it against the sunlight streaming through the window, closed one eye and peered through the holes. "There's a little mouth crud in there, son. You have to keep the workings clean if you want it to perform." He pulled a handkerchief from his pocket, wrapped it around the harmonica, and slapped it against his palm several times. He showed the hanky to Evan. "See that nasty stuff? That's the sugar from all that sweet junk we eat. Corrodes the reeds. When you finish playing, give it a good dousing under the faucet, blow the water out, and you're good to go."

"I didn't know you were supposed to run water through it," Evan said.

Gus cupped the instrument in his hands and positioned it to play.

"You mind?" Gus said.

Evan smiled and shook his head.

The sergeant played a couple of quick licks, followed by a blues scale. "It has a good tone," Gus said. "Not completely broken in, though."

He handed the instrument back to Evan, stood, reached into the bag in the overhead compartment and pulled out a harmonica similar to Evan's.

"How long have you been playing?" Evan said.

"About thirty years." Gus sat down, rolled his sleeves up a

couple of turns, and said, "Pay attention, son. I'm going to show you how to pull some sweet sounds out of one of these."

When Gus wrapped up "Lullaby of Birdland," there was a group of people gathered around clapping and singing along.

"I'd like to dedicate this next tune to our recently departed traveling companion, Mr. Tom Mosley," Gus said. "He left us a few miles back and we miss his company." Gus winked at Evan and tore into a rousing version of "Folsom Prison Blues." By the time he finished, there were passengers dancing in the aisle.

"That was great. How did you learn to play like that?" Evan said.

"I had a good teacher, my granddaddy. He could bend a note with the best of them. Even played a few licks with Big Walter Horton in a little joint on the south side of Chicago late New Year's Eve back in fifty-one." He waved the harmonica and said, "A Mississippi saxophone, that's what my granddad called it . . . and where do you think he was from?"

"Mississippi?" Evan said.

"Nope, Louisiana. Go figure. Now, here's what we're going to do. Whip out that mouth organ and let me hear a little of the tune you learned. What was it?"

"*Sixteen Tons,* but I'm not very good, I—"

Gus interrupted. "I don't want to hear any quibbling. I'll be the judge of your musical ability. You can't do *anything* if you don't try. You and I are going to perform a little duet."

The sergeant ripped off a quick glissando. "Wrap your lips around that thing and do a little warm-up for me. Do you know what chugging is?"

"Drawing and blowing?" Evan replied.

"That's correct. Start slow and gradually speed it up. It's a good way to loosen up your mouth and throat. Opens up the lungs as well," Gus said as Evan began the chugging exercise. "Push that thing a little deeper into your mouth. You'll get a fuller tone from it."

As he progressed, Evan's face began turning a pale shade of red.

"Okay, son, that's probably enough warm up. I don't want you blowing a gasket before we even get started. Play your tune for me." The sergeant leaned his head back against the seat and closed his eyes as Evan began to play.

Evan finished and looked at the sergeant. "Well?"

"You know, son, that wasn't bad at all. You've got plenty of musical ability. You read music?"

Evan nodded and said, "My dad taught me. From the time I was old enough to sit still, he held me on his lap while he played the piano. I think I was learning without even knowing it. Then, when I was old enough, he gave me lessons."

"They say musical ability is passed down from one generation to the next," Gus said, "and your pop must've passed along a good size helping of rhythm sense because you definitely got the beat. You're still playing piano, aren't you?"

"Not so much anymore. I took a few lessons after he died, but it doesn't seem the same."

"Well, don't you give up on it, son. You've got a God-given talent. Don't waste it."

"I hope you're right, Sergeant Gus."

"Okay, first we're gonna perform our duet, then I'll show you how to talk to this instrument instead of simply pumping air in and out of it." The sergeant began tapping his foot, snapping his fingers, and said, "Okay, pick it up from the chorus. I'll fill in here and there, and we'll have these folks jumpin' again."

When the bus pulled into Laurenville, the boppers had all returned to their seats. Many were exhausted, having sung and danced away the last thirty miles.

"Ladies and gentlemen, you'll be tempted to wander into some of the fine establishments here in this lovely little town, but please remember this is a twenty-minute stop, so don't wander too far. Yours truly, Harold Morris, bus driver extraordinaire, is as punctual as they come, so we'll be leaving on time, with or without you. Thank you for your cooperation. If this is your final destination, please have a wonderful stay, and thanks for traveling Greyhound."

Evan was perched on the edge of his seat, forehead pressed against the window. He spotted Grandma Bea sitting on a chair in front of Maxine's Beauty Shop two doors down from the bus station.

She looked elegant as always. She was wearing a navy

blue soft jersey dress with small white split-polka-dots and white cotton gloves. Her freshly colored and permed brown hair perfectly complemented her olive complexion, and her delicate features were shaded by the white wide-brimmed hat atop her head.

Evan watched as she walked toward the bus, her shoulders held high, back erect. She had reached her sixty-ninth birthday and, for the most part, was in perfect health. Beatrice Ann Mason had led a guarded life. She had never smoked and on only a few special occasions had she indulged in alcohol.

"Is that your Grandma?" Gus said.

"Yes, sir, that's her," Evan replied. "Maybe we better not say anything about Mr. Mosley, Sergeant Gus. I don't want to upset her."

"I believe you may be right. Mum's the word." Gus pursed his lips and gave Evan a thumbs-up. "Well, you better get on out there before people start clogging up the runway! She looks like she's anxious to see you."

Evan gathered his belongings, scurried off the bus and trotted to where she was waiting.

"I can't believe how much you've grown since I last saw you, Evan," Beatrice said.

They hugged, and Evan kissed her on the cheek. "I missed you, Grandma."

"I missed you too, Evan. I want to hear all about school and what your mother has been up to," Beatrice said.

"I'm Gunnery Sergeant Sam Gustafson," Gus said as he

approached. "I've had the pleasure of traveling with this fine young man for the last several hours. He's a good soldier."

"Thank you, Sergeant. My late husband fought in the Spanish-American War. He had great respect for the military, as do I," Beatrice said. She glanced at the ribbons on his chest. "Looks like you've made a career of it."

"It's my life, ma'am. I'd be lost anywhere else."

"Sergeant Gus gave me a lesson," Evan said, pulling the harmonica from his pocket and showing it to his grandmother.

"That's wonderful, dear. I'm glad to see you taking an interest in your music. Your father would have been very happy."

"It was quite an adventure," Gus said and winked at Evan.

"I've got supper on the stove, something you're going to like. Why don't you grab your grip so we can be on our way? I'm guessing it's the one with the yellow ribbon," Beatrice said, eyeing the cluster of bags the driver had unloaded.

"How did you know, Grandma?" Evan said as he grabbed the suitcase.

"I *know* your mother. Great attention to detail," Beatrice said, then muttered, "I just wish she had a little better vision of the big picture."

Beatrice turned toward Sergeant Gus and smiled. "Thank you for watching over him." She looked thoughtfully into his eyes and extended her gloved hand.

Gus sandwiched her hand and held it briefly. "It was a pleasure, Mrs. Mason," he said, then turned to Evan and placed a hand on his shoulder. "Don't give up on the music, son . . . and remember what I told you," he said as he walked toward the door of the café.

"Let's go home, my dear," Beatrice said. Evan picked up the suitcase. "Do you think you can make it home with that thing? Mr. Garnett offered to pick us up, but I was looking forward to the walk."

"Nothing to it," Evan said, lifting the suitcase chest high to demonstrate his brawn.

Beatrice smiled approvingly. "What a beautiful day," she said, looking at the single wisp of clouds in the otherwise clear blue sky. She took a long deep breath, and they walked the five blocks home.

6

———

Evan awoke suddenly and sat straight up in bed. His heart was pounding. He'd been immersed in a strange dream, a contorted mosaic of the events of the day. Sultry air was gushing through the open window, and the light from the streetlamp filtering through the billowing white chiffon curtains gave the room a ghostly aura. There was lightning in the distance and rain was beginning to pelt the awning over the window.

It had been the thunder that had awakened him, but now there were voices. He moved to the window, sat on the floor and peered over the sill. Two men were standing at the curb behind a light-colored convertible. It was parked on the opposite side of the street two houses away. One of the men appeared older, perhaps in his sixties. The sleeves of the white shirt he wore were turned up to just below the elbow and his dark slacks were supported by suspenders. He wore a pair of wire-frame glasses. The two men stood face-to-face, the younger man listening intently, nodding now and then as the other man spoke.

There was a clap of thunder and a torrent of rain began to fall. A woman in a housecoat opened the door and stepped out onto the porch.

Evan had no idea who she was, and it occurred to him that, for as long as he could recall, he couldn't remember anyone living in that house. The property seemed generally well maintained, and there were days during previous summers when he had heard the sound of a lawnmower on the other side of the tall boxwood that surrounded the two-story brick bungalow, but until now there had been no signs of people coming and going, at least as far as he could recall.

Amidst the downpour, the younger man grabbed the suitcase at his feet and hurried toward the house. Evan saw that he moved with a limp. The other man followed.

The woman handed both of them a towel. The elder of the two sat on a bench at one end of the long porch and wiped his glasses while the woman ushered the other man to a glider at the opposite end, said something to him as he sat down, then joined the older man on the bench where they were soon engaged in conversation.

Evan continued to watch as the younger man blotted his face and arms with the towel, folded it and placed it on the table beside him. He began to rock slowly in the glider, staring out into the pouring rain, seemingly disinterested in the conversation. The light from the street lamp rippled across his face, giving it a chiseled appearance; there was something compelling about the man—mysterious. Evan was transfixed by the image.

After several minutes, the man turned his gaze toward Evan's bedroom. Instinctively, Evan recoiled from the window. *Don't be ridiculous, Evan! He can't see you.*

Evan waited a few seconds, then peeked over the sill. The man was still staring in his direction. *There's no way he can see me. It's much too dark in this room. But he knows I'm here, kneeling beside the window . . . spying on him!*

Abruptly, the thunder and pounding rain subsided, and Evan could hear part of the conversation.

"Mr. O'Malley's leaving now. Come say goodbye," the woman said.

The younger man stood and walked toward the man called O'Malley. As he moved, Evan could see that his right foot was turned slightly inward, his limp more pronounced now. He embraced O'Malley, his arms and shoulders enveloping the much slighter man.

Finally, O'Malley got into the convertible and drove away. The woman took the other man by the hand and escorted him into the house. A light on the second floor was on for a short time, then the house was dark.

Evan's mind was racing as he climbed back into bed. It would be another hour before he would fall asleep.

7
———

Ordinarily, Evan would have been up at sunrise, dressed and sitting at the table watching his grandmother prepare breakfast, but the bus ride and the middle-of-the-night interlude had exhausted him.

It was almost eight when he sat down at the kitchen table. There was a plate with three slices of French toast and several slices of bacon in front of him.

"Maple syrup or strawberry preserves?" Beatrice said.

"I think I'll have the preserves," Evan replied. He watched his grandmother scurry around like a woman half her age.

"Good choice. Effie Carrol put this up last fall. She makes the best in the county, maybe the state . . . maybe anywhere," Beatrice said, tapping the jar lid on the edge of the counter to loosen it. She stuck a spoon in the jar and placed it on the table. "I'm so glad you're here. You and I are going to have a lot of fun this summer. Effie just bought a brand-new console television, twenty-one-inch, I believe. It even has a phonograph built in. She said when she hosts Pinochle night, she'll pop some corn and you can watch your shows while we play cards. A lot of good television programs on Thursday nights. You don't mind watching them by yourself, do you?"

"No, I'm used to it," Evan said. He paused between bites, took a drink of orange juice, thought for a few seconds, and said, "I wonder if Mother thinks about me, what I'm up to, how I'm doing?"

"Of course, she does. Why would you even ask that, Evan?"

"It just seems she's gone all the time. We don't talk much."

"She's a woman with a lot on her mind and a big responsibility. Losing your father was tough on her. It was tough on all of us. She lets on like she's full of confidence, but she's unsteady just like everyone else. I think she's simply trying to find her own way in this life. I don't exactly approve of all this gallivanting, but give her some time, Evan. She'll come around."

He ate a bit more of his breakfast, then craned his neck to look through the kitchen window. "Grandma, do you know who lives in the brick house across the street?"

She stepped to the window. "The one with the hedges?" she said.

"Uh-huh. I woke up in the middle of the night and there were two men. They were talking, and there was a woman in the house."

"That would be the Phillips residence. George Phillips

passed away about two months back. The emphysema finally did him in. He suffered for several years. My mailman, you know him, Mr. Sutton, sat down for a glass of lemonade the other day and gave me all the latest news. Apparently, Mr. Phillips left the property to his niece, Wilma. Don't know her last name, but she must be the one you saw last night. I waved at her a couple of times from the yard, but she seems rather standoffish. Didn't seem to be up for any chitchat."

"What about the men I saw? I think one of them is staying there," Evan said and took another peek at the house.

"I have no idea. Maybe her husband," Beatrice said.

"I don't think so. He looked young compared to her. She's about your age, isn't she, Grandma?"

"Well, thanks a lot, you made my day," Beatrice said and smiled.

"Sorry, I didn't mean *you* were old. He just seemed a lot younger than her."

"It's okay, dear. It would take a lot more than that to offend a thick-skinned woman like me," Beatrice said.

"Eeeevaan!" The voice came from the front of the house.

"I'm guessing that's the Parker boy," Beatrice said, wiping a plate and sliding it into the corner cabinet. "Mrs. Parker telephoned me last Saturday. She said Richie was dying to see you. Seems that's all he's been talking about since he heard you were spending the summer."

Evan jumped up and ran to the window. He pulled the

curtain aside and peered through the screen. The two boys sitting on the bikes waved.

"Hey, Richie! What are you guys up to?" Evan shouted.

"We're on our way to the mound. Albert Baker found a huge arrowhead last week," Richie said.

"And a bear claw," the other boy added.

"If that goofball can find stuff like that, anyone can. Come on, get a move on!" Richie said.

"I can't go. I don't have my bike fixed yet," Evan said.

"You can ride with me. You may have to walk when we get to Sycamore Hill. I don't think I could make it to the top with you hanging on the back. You look like you grew a foot," Richie said.

The kid straddling the other bike was Donnie Jones. Both boys were a grade ahead of Evan.

"Is it okay if I go, Grandma?" Evan said. "I'll spend the whole day tomorrow helping you with the garden, promise."

"Alright, finish your breakfast first, and please, load my wheelbarrow for me before you leave." Beatrice thought for a while and said, "The two baskets, a rake, hoe, snips, and the bag of grass seed in the corner. The key is hanging on the hook by the back door."

Evan shoved the last bite of French toast into his mouth and bolted onto the porch, the screen door banging shut behind him. He leaped from the landing, flying over the steps to the flagstone walkway, raced across the yard, opened the lock and swung the rickety door open. The first thing he saw as the sunlight streamed into the shed was the reflector on the rear fender.

It wasn't his old bike, he thought as he moved closer. Even in the low light, he could tell *it was a Schwinn Phantom, the crème de la crème of bicycles.* He knew that was the correct term to describe it; he'd heard Aunt Gladys use the phrase often enough.

He grabbed the handlebars, steered the white-walled beauty into the sunlight, and knelt beside it, his blood rushing as he took in every detail. He flipped one of the pedals and watched it spin smoothly, effortlessly on its stainless-steel bearings, unobstructed by the grit and grime of age.

It wasn't brand new, and the horn tank had been removed, but the important things were there, the things that made it a Phantom: chrome fenders, front fork spring suspension, and the big tan leather saddle. There was also a rear carrier with two adjustable canvas straps and a seat pouch, probably added at Grandma Bea's request, so he could return unscathed when she sent him to McCormick's Pantry for a few items she had forgotten. *Not the coolest things to be riding around with,* he thought, *but a minor embarrassment if it gave her peace of mind.*

Evan wheeled the Phantom around from the shed. Beatrice was sitting on the back-porch swing.

He dropped the kickstand, bounded up the steps, and hugged her. "What a great surprise, Grandma. What happened to my old bike?"

"That thing had seen better days. I wouldn't have my only grandson riding around town on a clunker like that.

Just wasn't safe. Your grandfather's good friend, Al Carver, allowed me a few dollars in trade," she said, rocking on the swing while she sipped a cup of chamomile tea.

"It's perfect!" Evan said.

"I wouldn't go that far. It's used, but it has a lot of new parts," Beatrice said, "and Mr. Carver assured me it's sound. That's the important thing."

Evan climbed onto the bike.

"Aren't you forgetting something?" Beatrice said. Evan jumped off and kissed her on the cheek. "Well, I appreciate that, but weren't there some garden tools somewhere in the bargain?"

"Sorry," Evan said, disappearing briefly and returning with the wheelbarrow full of tools.

"Thank you," Beatrice said. "Now, have a good time, but be careful."

"We will," Evan said as he jumped back on the Phantom.

"Goodbye, Mrs. Mason!" Richie and Donnie shouted, almost in unison.

Beatrice sipped her tea and rocked slowly in the swing as the boys sprinted off along East Prairie for a block, then veered onto the worn dirt path that threaded its way through the display of tractors and combines at Brackston's Farm Supplies. It was the shortcut they always took on their way to the mound.

Beatrice took another sip of tea and watched as a male cardinal darted back and forth between the bird feeder and a nearby rose bush. He hopped along a branch and passed a sunflower seed to the female nestled deep in the thorny branches. Beatrice thought of Walter.

Walter Mason had been a railroad conductor and a stable provider for his family. When he died in 1948 on the operating table at Wabash Valley General, Beatrice was devastated.

If only you could have known Evan, Walter. You would have been proud, she thought, tears welling in her eyes as she descended the steps toward the yard.

8

———

The route they had taken led to a path that ran along the perimeter of the city dump. As they passed, Evan was reminded of the afternoon he and Beans Madigan had spent there the previous summer.

Beans had gotten a BB gun for his birthday and was looking to try it out. It was early morning when he and Evan invaded "ratville." They staked out a position in the front seat of an old Studebaker and picked off the residents as they went about their business, dozens of them. It seemed like tremendous fun early on, but by mid-afternoon, the temperature had reached ninety degrees, the wind had shifted, and the stench of their hunting ground had become unbearable.

For the next month, Beans spent two or three days a week there, but Evan had only tagged along on that one occasion. The smell alone would have been enough to thwart a second safari, but it was primarily the immediate feeling of remorse that had washed over him after the undertaking that discouraged him from going back. *It was, after all, the rats' domain,* he thought. *It just didn't seem right to wander in and start shooting up the place.*

Incidentally, Beans's given name was Eugene, but no one ever called him that. His family was poor, and Mrs. Madigan stretched her food allowance by serving up lots of beans: baked beans, bean soup, and chili, heavy on the beans, light on the meat. She even came up with a concoction of beans and bacon grease that she shaped into patties. When grilled and slapped onto a bun, they had a vague resemblance to a hamburger. Undoubtedly, the high-protein diet had exacerbated Eugene's propensity for flatulence and thus earned him his well-deserved nickname.

The Phantom was performing superbly on its maiden voyage, the front suspension smoothing out every bump as they breezed along Cumberland Road toward the Ghost Hill Indian Mound.

"Hey, I got an oldie. You guys remember this one?" Richie said and began singing. He sang two verses.

"*Get A Job,* by The Silhouettes," Evan said. "That's one of my favorites." He and Donnie joined in, and for the next couple of miles, they sang. It was off-key and out of sync, but it was just like the old days, way back in 1957.

It was a little past nine when they arrived at the narrow

tractor road leading to the mound. They traveled a short distance through a stretch of woods to reach Sand Bottom Creek, where the road turned west, closely following the creek for another hundred yards on a downhill grade to an open meadow. Between the creek and the meadow was a knoll. The soil was loosely compacted, and a few small trees and shrubs were growing along the perimeter.

Richie jumped off his bike, untied the burlap tool bag from the carrier, and spread it open on the ground.

"I got dibs on the kelvinator!" Donnie shouted.

"Cultivator, dipshit," Richie said and tossed it to him.

Evan and Richie each grabbed a tool, settled on a spot, and for the next twenty minutes, they dug.

"So, what you been doing up there in the big city? You seen any gangsters?" Donnie said, dumping handfuls of dirt into the makeshift sifter Richie had fashioned from a piece of quarter-inch hardware cloth.

"Gangsters?" Evan said.

Richie looked at Evan and rolled his eyes.

"My dad said he wouldn't live anywhere near Chicago for all the tea in China," Donnie said. "He said people are shooting each other right and left, and if you don't speak *I*—talian you can't even get by."

"We don't see many shootouts during the day, but there are so many bodies on the streets in the morning they have city workers driving around in trucks with big scoops on the front to clear them out," Evan said, elbowing Richie. "Then, they load them into the cargo bay of one of those big ships, take them back to Italy and bury them."

"Really?" Donnie said, wide-eyed.

Evan and Richie laughed hysterically.

"Of course not," Richie said. "You've been watching too many detective shows. What a nosebleed." He nudged Evan. "Who knows? Maybe we'll see some wild Indians out here in the woods today, huh, Evan?" Richie laughed and went back to digging.

A few minutes later, Donnie shouted, "Holy shit!"

Evan and Richie looked at Donnie; his mouth was agape and he was pointing toward the south edge of the knoll.

The man's hair was mostly gray and there was a large feather interlaced with the single braid that dangled along the side of his cheek. His face was etched with creases that seemed to crisscross his deeply tanned skin in every direction. When in full view, they could see he was fully clad in fringed buckskin, a beaded breastplate, and moccasins. He was carrying a leather bag in one hand, and some kind of canvas pouch was slung over his shoulder. He dropped the bag onto the ground and leaned the pouch against a tree. He stood fully erect, shoulders thrown back, raised his hand with open palm forward, and in a deep, gravelly voice said, "How!"

The man shifted his gaze from one boy to the next, eyes sternly fixed on each of them for a few seconds. The boys all had looks of astonishment. Suddenly, he leaned forward, hands on his knees, and let out a belly laugh.

At almost that same moment, an Airedale bounded over the top of the hill, darted back and forth between the man and the boys, circled once, and sat beside the man. The dog barked several times, a deep resonating bark. Finally, he gave a short muffled growl and, with eyes fixed on the boys, sat quietly.

"I hope none of you young men peed your pants," the man said, looking up at them, still bent over chuckling.

"We thought you were a real Indian," Richie said, seemingly relieved that they weren't going to be scalped.

"I am a real Indian, at least part of me. Just not the kind you thought," he said.

"What are you doing here?" Evan said.

"Taking photographs. You probably thought that was a bow and arrows," the man said, smiling and gesturing toward the slender canvas pouch propped against the tree. "Well, it's not. It's a tripod and camera, one of the tools of my trade. My name is Zachary Aiken, medicine man, craftsman, historian, and a direct descendant of Keokuk, great Chief of the Sauk people. This fine creature sitting beside me is Max." The dog's ears perked when he heard his name.

"Zachary doesn't sound like an Indian name," Richie said. "That's my gym teacher's name."

"Keokuk was my fourth great-grandfather," Zachary said.

"You have four grandfathers?" Donnie said.

"That means four generations ago," Evan said.

"That's right, son," Zachary said, seemingly a bit surprised at Evan's percipience. "The man's been dead over a hundred years. Passed through here in 1797 and evidently stayed long enough to produce an offspring, a daughter. I'm thankful for that or I wouldn't be standing here talking to you." He gave the boys the once-over. "And who might I be addressing in this band of explorers?"

The boys introduced themselves, and Richie followed with, "He was *really* a chief?"

Zachary nodded. "Got a town in Iowa named after him." He looked down at the trowel Richie was holding. "What in the hell are you going to do with that?"

"Digging for beads and arrowheads," Richie replied. "A kid we know found some neat stuff here, and we—"

"By *neat stuff*, you don't happen to be referring to a flint arrowhead and a bear claw necklace, do you?" Zachary said, packing tobacco into a meerschaum pipe with his thumb.

"Uh, yeah, how'd you know that?" Richie said.

"Well, don't worry. I'm not a seer. I'm not going to start dancing around in some sort of trance blowing strange smelling smoke in your face. However, I am getting a *vision* of this friend of yours. Does he have sandy colored hair and one eye that strays a bit when he's talking to you?" Zachary said, struck a match, lit his pipe and took a long puff.

"Yeah, Albert Baker. He's an eighth-grader," Richie said.

"Well, it appears Albert Baker has a vivid imagination, or maybe he just wanted to rattle your cage a bit. Finding a claw and a flint that size would be like panning in that stream down there and coming up with a gold nugget. Your friend Albert bought those items from me at the Pioneer Trading Post last week. I've gathered pieces like that from all over this country. I collected those particular items in Sioux City . . . if my memory serves me right."

"But we found a bunch of beads here last year," Evan said. "We dug up at least a dozen and—"

"Son, don't get me wrong, I'm not trying to discourage you from looking," Zachary said, "but keep in mind, this area's been combed through for a hundred years. You may find a few trinkets here and there, but chances of making a major find are slim to none . . . and *slim* just left town. Take a stroll with me, boys. I want to give you a little education."

They walked about a hundred yards to a slightly elevated circular-shaped patch of dense trees and bramble at the edge of the woods. The thicket was about thirty yards in diameter.

"Climb on up there, but don't try to venture in. That place is so overgrown, you'd come out looking like you'd been in a scrap with a wildcat. Just take a peek and tell me what you see," Zachary said.

The three boys scaled the band of scree and small boulders encircling the mound and peered through the tangled wall of gnarled trees and vines. It was dark within, except for a single column of sunlight that shone through like a spotlight, illuminating the relatively open area in the center.

"Trees, thorny bushes and . . . big rocks," Evan said, craning his neck to find something of more significance. "Can't see much else. There's a musty smell . . . and a sweet smell, like licorice."

"That smell would be sassafras," Zachary said. "The native

people used it for hundreds of years. They thought it had great medicinal power. Do you see those large flat boulders with scooped-out areas on the top?"

"Yeah," Evan replied.

"Those were used in their ceremonies, celebrations, a rite of passage," Zachary said. "They're called mortars. They used a pestle, a heavy tool with a rounded end, to pound and grind herbs and medicines. Sometimes they burned the stuff. They believed the evil spirits would be carried off by the smoke and wouldn't be able to follow them into the next world." He took a puff on his pipe. "The Lord knows there's always been plenty of evil to deal with in this world."

"What's a right Apache?" Donnie asked.

Zachary smiled and said, "Rite . . . of . . . passage. It's the celebration of a special event in a person's life. Back then it might have been killing a deer or a buffalo, maybe an enemy. The birth of a child, a wedding, all those things that make us who we are," Zachary said.

"So, what is this place?" Evan said, cupping his hands around his eyes and poking his head a little deeper into the shadows.

"What you're looking at, my boy, is the *actual* mound. When I was your age, I found all kinds of artifacts in there. Of course, that was before they had finished all their digging. It was excavated twice. A team of archaeologists came in once back in 1889 and again in 1932. They must've dug all the way to China. Scooped up everything."

"Not much room in there," Richie said.

"Not now," Zachary said, "but many moons ago this was wide open, just a big open circle in the middle of the woods with a stone wall around it. Over the years, mother nature has been closing in on it, reclaiming it. Twenty years from now it'll be completely overgrown."

"How'd you get in there?" Evan asked.

"See those two giant boulders on the far side there?" Zachary said.

"Yes, sir," Evan said.

"There's an opening between them. As far as I know, that's the only way in. It looks like it's getting tighter every year. I couldn't squeeze through that crevice today if I was coated in axle grease. Even back then it was tight."

"If this is the mound, how come people dig back there where we were?" Richie said and pointed.

"They don't know any better. It's as simple as that. They see that big pile of earth and they think it's the mound, but it's really just the dirt that was removed. Oh, those *dirt-sifters* left some small beads and shells behind, but the prime artifacts are gone. Over the years, anything that remained was probably washed down toward the stream. If you're intent on digging, that's the place to do it. You might get lucky and find something worthwhile. Not likely, but who knows?"

"What are you taking pictures of, Mr. Aiken?" Evan said.

"Myself. You'd be surprised how much someone will pay for an autographed picture of a Sauk Indian in his natural habitat, especially a descendant of one who's got a town named after him," Zachary said. "Throw in a genuine hand strung bracelet or necklace and you've got yourself a money making venture. I made a tidy little sum at this over the years." He took a couple of puffs on his meerschaum. "You know, I'm just a mile down the road, top of the hill. You're welcome to stop by sometime. I'll give you the guided tour."

"I thought that was old man Kirby's place?" Richie said.

"It *was*," Zachary replied. "The man was a good friend of mine. I was living down south when he called me and told me he wanted me to buy the place. He wasn't long for this world. He didn't have any kin, none he'd admit to, anyway. Said he would sell me the property for a song. The only thing he wanted was for Max to have someone to take care of him. It's a rundown old shack, but now it's *my* rundown old shack. It does sit on a nice little piece of land, though. There are four apple trees out back with the sweetest fruit you'll ever sink your teeth into."

While Richie and Donnie were busy gathering the tools and stuffing them into the burlap bag, Evan watched Zachary set up the tripod. He had found a piece of level ground and was focusing the camera on an area beside the stream, a spot free of litter that might tarnish the scene. Zachary peered through the viewfinder, shifted the camera slightly to negate the glare reflecting off the water, then stretched the shutter cable to the base of a moss-covered boulder at the edge of the creek.

Max darted over and sat beside Evan, nudging his hand and licking it, looking up at him, ears perked and head tilted, as terriers do. Evan dropped to one knee and rubbed the dog's neck. He pulled a burr from a spot just below Max's right ear and combed through his wiry roan-colored coat with his fingers.

"He's taken a liking to you, son," Zachary said. "Doesn't happen often. Airedales are cautious dogs, especially this one. Might even go so far as to say he's a little quirky. A month ago, I left him alone in the house for a couple of hours. On the ride home from the doctor's office, I remembered I'd left a pair of moccasins on the table next to my workbench. I stitch up a half dozen pair most every month, one of my best sellers. I expected them to be chewed to a pulp when I got home. Dogs like to chew things, you know, especially when they're alone and anxious. When I walked through the door, Max was sitting there with one moccasin between his paws, looking as guilty as sin. The strange part is, the only thing he chewed on was the very tip of one of the rawhide laces, not another spot. Now, that, I contend, is one eccentric canine."

Suddenly, Max's ears perked. He jumped up, and within seconds was in the water, wildly romping after a raccoon.

"That's the Otterhound in him," Zachary said, shook his head, and tapped the meerschaum against a tree, dislodging the smoldering bowl of tobacco. He mashed the tiny embers into the ground with his moccasin and said, "Your daddy's name William Joseph, folks called him Joe?"

"Yes, sir," Evan replied.

"Knew him. Heard him sing at the old roadhouse on Bargetown Road when he was young and full of piss and vinegar. That young man could croon a tune. Knew your grandfather, Walter, even better, railroad man, conductor. When things were tough back in thirty-three, he let me ride that run between Laurenville and Danville many times and didn't charge me a penny." Zachary thought for a few seconds, then said, "You stop by my place one of these days. I want to show you my collection, and I'm referring to *genuine* relics left here by the people who lived across this land centuries ago. You interested in that sort of thing, son?"

Evan nodded. "I'd like to stop by, Mr. Aiken," Evan said.

"I'll be looking for you," Zachary said. He snatched up the plunger, carefully draping the cable along the side of his leg to hide it from the view of the lens. He placed one foot on the boulder and gazed skyward, striking a most majestic pose.

The boys were pedaling along the tractor road and singing as he snapped the shutter.

9

——

As promised, Evan had spent the day helping his grandmother prepare the garden. Now, he sat on the edge of the porch sipping a glass of iced tea while she sketched a layout of the flower bed, using crayons to bring the design to fruition. He watched as she filled in a section of lilies with magenta and a wisp of canary yellow.

Beatrice Mason had an artistic flair. She had done numerous oil paintings, written poetry, and created some of the most interesting flower arrangements one could imagine. She had received the Laurenville Chamber of Commerce's Green Thumb Award five years running. Her flower bed was the envy of every gardener in town.

"You can't plant them just anywhere. There has to be a pattern, a plan. Otherwise, all you'll have when you're done is a bunch of plants fighting for their little patch of terra firma," Beatrice said.

"What's that?" Evan asked.

"Dirt," she said and smiled.

As Grandma Bea continued to work on her drawing, a light breeze began to blow, and Evan could smell the newly tilled mixture of black dirt and compost he had hauled, wheelbarrow by wheelbarrow, from behind the shed. *Maybe the secret to her success*, he thought.

He heard a female voice behind him.

"You have a helper, Mrs. Mason."

Evan turned and watched as she pedaled her bicycle up the sidewalk. She had blue eyes, and her light brown hair was pulled back into a ponytail. She was wearing blue jeans, turned up to mid-calf, and a sharply pressed white cotton blouse. Her slender legs tapered into bobby socks and a pair of light blue sneakers. He watched as she dropped the kickstand and walked, *no . . . floated toward him*. He felt a tingling sensation wash over his entire body.

"Hello, Katie," Beatrice said. "I haven't seen you out and about lately. What have you been up to?"

"I've been helping my mother sort through boxes since ten this morning. She finally gave me some time off. Guess she felt sorry for me." She turned and looked at Evan. "I'm Katie Dobbins. We just moved here from Ohio. You must be Evan." She extended her hand.

Evan jumped up and wiped his hands on his Levi's. As he took her hand, all he could focus on was her glossy pink nail polish.

"Hi, I'm Evan." He stood staring at her, his cheeks slightly flushed.

"I know, silly. Didn't I just say that?" Katie said and smiled. "How long are you going to be staying with your grandma, Evan?"

"Uh, probably the whole summer. All depends on what happens with my mother's new job," he replied.

"We have to drive back to Ohio tomorrow. Be there for about a week, then we'll be here to stay. Maybe you can show me around when I get back, introduce me to some of your friends," Katie said.

"Okay," Evan replied. There was silence. *What's wrong with you, lamebrain? That's the only thing you have to say?*

"Where you headed, Katie?" Beatrice interjected.

"I'm off to Woolworth's. My mother needs some hair curlers, and my dad wants a big jar of Vicks VapoRub. He goes through a jar a week. He uses it for everything. I even saw him stuff a glob up his nose one day. Gives me the willies," she said and feigned a shiver. "I hate that smell."

"Yeah, well, how'd you like to have that stuff heated up and rubbed all over your chest? When I was little, I—" Evan stopped in mid-sentence when he saw Katie clasp her hand over her mouth and begin to giggle. He glanced down, suddenly aware of the two burgeoning mounds beneath her cotton blouse. "Oh, uh, I didn't mean *your* chest. I meant muh-m-m-*my* chest," he said, patting the front of his soiled tee-shirt. "*My* chest. What I really meant was—"

"Why, you're as red as a beet, Evan. You may have gotten a little too much sun today," Beatrice said and winked at Katie.

"I'm just fine, Grandma," Evan said emphatically and snuck a glance at Katie to see if she was still giggling. She had turned her bicycle and was straddling it.

"Do you want me to pick up anything for you while I'm there, Mrs. Mason?" she said.

"No, dear, thank you," Beatrice said.

Katie looked at Evan. "See ya later, alligator," she said, then pushed off down the walk.

Evan watched as she crossed the street. She glanced back at him, smiled, and gave a little flip of her ponytail as she rounded the corner at Brackston's.

"What a pleasant girl," Beatrice said. "I understand she's a straight-A student. I had a short chat with her mother. She's a seamstress. Mr. Dobbins has a machine shop out on County Line Road. He took over the business after his brother died." She looked at Evan. "What's the matter, cat got your tongue?"

"She's nice," Evan said nonchalantly and began loading the garden tools into the wheelbarrow.

"I don't know if *nice* is quite the right word for what I'm sensing. Seems to me, Cupid may be flitting around somewhere up there," Beatrice said, scanning the treetops, "slinging arrows in this direction."

Evan rolled his eyes, grabbed the wheelbarrow and headed for the shed.

10
——

Beatrice and Evan strolled along Elm Street toward the cemetery. Beatrice carried a basket containing several bunches of flowers. It was going to be a hot day, and she had wrapped them in damp newspaper to keep them fresh.

They had just left the First Baptist Church, having attended the Sunday morning service to pay tribute to Beatrice's lifelong friend, Beulah Noland. Beulah had taught Sunday school for over thirty years and participated in almost every fundraising venture since the church was built. The congregation had honored her by presenting her with a leather-bound gold-leaf Bible. Her name had also been engraved on the Friends of the Church plaque that hung in the vestibule.

It had been a while since Beatrice had been to church. She certainly hadn't lost her faith, but now she only attended services on Easter, Christmas, and enough regular Sundays to remain in good standing with Pastor Nelson and the congregation. She wasn't sure why she had stopped attending regularly; it was simply one of many things in her life that changed after Walter died.

"I'm glad the week is over," Beatrice said as they walked along. "I'm not as young as I used to be. I'm worn to a frazzle."

They had worked in the garden every morning that past week, and Evan had spent the afternoons with Richie and Donnie, doing all the things young boys do during summer vacation, going nonstop until well after dark.

"I didn't realize gardening was such hard work," Evan said.

"Yes, and it gets harder every year. I'm glad you were here to help, dear."

They continued along Elm Street, past Barwig's drugstore and the VFW post, finally arriving at the Jamboree Café, directly across the street from the Newberry Cemetery, one of the oldest and largest cemeteries in the county.

"On the way home, we'll stop for ice cream," Beatrice said and nodded toward the café.

"It looks like it's closed," Evan said, peering through the plate-glass window.

"Needn't worry about that," Beatrice said. "I've been coming here for twenty years, and I've never known Tom Fyfe to be closed on a Sunday afternoon. He lives upstairs, so I guarantee you, if he's alive, the place is open. Probably trying to save on his electric bill. He's as tight as a doornail, but he serves up the biggest and tastiest sundaes you'll ever dip a spoon into."

They crossed the street, headed for the main gate of the cemetery.

"Watch out for snakes," Beatrice said. "They like to slither around under these headstones. They won't hurt you. They're just garter snakes, but you don't want to step on one and have it crawl up your pant leg."

"They do that?" Evan said, scanning the area around him.

"They will if you step on one. They're hard to see in this tall grass. Not an enjoyable experience," Beatrice said. "It happened to your father once. He almost jumped out of his shoes."

They laughed.

"Looks like everyone in the family is buried here," Evan said, moving slowly along the row of headstones.

"Not everyone, but a good number of them," Beatrice said. "Your dear father is here." She pointed. "And your granddad is there in the second row, the white stone."

"How come Granddad has that type of marker?" Evan said.

"That's a military headstone. He told me that was what he wanted. The government provides those for people who served in the armed forces," Beatrice said.

Evan looked out across the rows of headstones and said, "Kind of sad. All those people were alive once, and now all that's left is a big hunk of rock."

"Come on," she said and took Evan's hand.

They walked along the access road toward the oldest section of the cemetery. There was a newly opened grave at the edge of the road, and a robin was fluttering about atop the mound of earth, tugging at a worm that had been unearthed by the backhoe.

Along the back fence, they came upon a row of weathered stones, some broken and indecipherable. There were two headstones beside a cluster of lilac bushes; one was fully inscribed, the other had only a name and date of birth.

"Mary was my mother, your great-grandmother. She was a strong woman, smart and hard working. She held you on her lap many times, always made a fuss over you," Beatrice said.

"I don't remember her," Evan said, apparently trying to retrieve a snippet of memory that might be lingering somewhere in the archives of his mind.

"You were just a baby, too young to remember," Beatrice said and gestured toward the second headstone. "John was your great-grandfather."

"I don't remember him, either," Evan said.

"You wouldn't. No one knows much about *him*. Mother was living in a tiny little town in Indiana called Merom when they met. He showed up at a fourth of July celebration in 1889. The story is that he came in with a crew of men from somewhere in Ohio to work on the construction of a bridge. Within two months they were married. That we know for sure. I've got a copy of their marriage certificate. Unfortunately, that's pretty much all we know of him. He's not even buried here. We had the headstone put in shortly after Mother passed away."

"Didn't anyone ever ask her about him, what happened to him?" Evan said.

"Everyone did. I asked her myself, many times, but she would simply say that he had died and change the subject. She never wanted to speak of it. I guess people finally grew tired of asking."

Evan stood for a few seconds looking at the headstone and said, "It's like he never even existed."

"Yes, but we know he did." Beatrice put her arm around Evan. "You and I are proof of that." She placed her hand over her heart. "His spirit is here in both of us." She looked at Evan and smiled. "Help me with these flowers, then we'll go have our sundaes."

11
——

Evan sat on the front porch swing. He had spent the better part of the morning with the Hohner, practicing scales and exercises. He knew Grandma Bea could hear him as she went about her morning chores in the kitchen. She seemed pleased to see him back in touch with his music, even if it was just a "Mississippi saxophone."

Now he was practicing the blues licks Sergeant Gus had taught him during the last leg of the bus ride.

"Hey, Evan. I'm back," Katie said as she hopped off her bike and headed up the walk.

There it was again, he thought, *the tingling that now seemed to be linked, not only to the sight of her but the mere sound of her voice.* He stood to greet her. "Are you all moved in?" Evan said.

"Yeah, pretty much. My dad has a few things to take care of back in Akron, but it looks like the Dobbins family is here to stay. I learned one thing from all this. Moving isn't much fun."

"I know what you mean. I'm not sure where home is anymore," Evan said as he opened the case to stow the harmonica. "Sometimes it's tough not knowing—"

"Oh, don't stop. I like hearing you play," Katie said, sitting down on the edge of the porch.

"I've only been at this a couple of months. I'm really not very good at it," Evan replied, then, determined to change the subject, followed with, "How 'bout you, Katie, you play an instrument?"

"No, I sing a little. That's the only way I can make music . . . unless you count the record player. I'm *very* good at that, and I like to dance." She snapped her fingers and did a little shoulder shimmy. "Learned all my moves watching *American Bandstand*."

"I saw the Crickets when they were on," Evan said.

"Yeah, I saw that show too. I like Buddy Holly, even more than Elvis," Katie replied.

"Elvis has a new song coming out. It's supposed to be—"

"Alright, Evan, enough stalling," Katie said and widened her eyes. "Play something for me."

"I don't have much of a song list."

"Just play what you were playing before. What was it? Jazz or something?" Katie asked.

"Blues . . . just some stuff I'm working on," Evan said and shrugged.

"C'mon," she said and patted the spot beside her.

Evan sat down. "Okay, but you have to promise not to laugh if I screw it up . . . and I will. You promise?"

Katie crossed her heart with her index finger and leaned back against the porch railing. For the next ten minutes, Evan played, surprising himself with a nearly flawless rendition of "Sixteen Tons" and an abbreviated, though impressive, version of Sergeant Gus's "Folsom Prison Blues."

"That was spectacular, Evan. You're good," Katie said.

One thing for sure, Evan thought, *adoration can do wonders for a man's confidence.*

As they turned the corner onto Gable Street, Katie spotted the park. There were two large maple trees toward the back of the grounds, several flowering crabs, and a single row of lilac bushes bordering three sides of the playground. Either by chance or masterful planning, the Dairy Queen was located directly across the street.

"Are you sure they'll be okay with a girl hanging around?" Katie said.

"It'll be fine. You'll be one of the guys in no time," Evan said.

"I'm not quite sure how *that's* going to work," Katie said.

"What I'm saying is, no one will mind as long as you don't complain and start talking about *girly* stuff," Evan said.

"You don't have to worry about that," she said, placing her hand on her cheek, cocking her head, and batting her long eyelashes playfully. "I'm a *lot* tougher than I look."

They rolled the front wheel of their bikes into a slot in the metal rack near the entrance to the park and headed for the three boys who had commandeered one of the picnic tables staggered throughout the grounds.

"Hey, guys, this is Katie Dobbins, my new neighbor," Evan said as they approached. "She's from Ohio. Going to be starting school here in the fall." He turned to Katie, put his hand on Richie's shoulder and said, "This guy here is Richard Parker."

Richie hopped up and bowed from the waist, yanking his baseball cap off and sweeping it across his chest in a chivalrous, knightly sort of gesture. "Pleased to make your acquaintance, milady," Richie said, his voice sounding unnaturally deep.

Katie smiled, curtsied, and said, "Sir Richard."

"Call me Richie. My mom's the only one who calls me Richard, and that's usually when she's pissed at me."

"And over there," Evan said and nodded, "somewhere behind that giant bubble is Donnie Jones."

As though on cue, the bubble burst, collapsing over Donnie's mouth, nose, and most of one cheek. He gathered it, and with several quick pokes stuffed the three wads of Bazooka back into his mouth. "Hi," Donnie said, chomping away. "My cousin lives in Davenport. You from anywhere near there?"

Richie jumped in. "Davenport's in Iowa, dipshit." He looked skyward, threw his arms into the air, and shook his head.

"So, shoot me. I made a mistake," Donnie said. "I was never very good in geology," he mumbled, almost unintelligibly; he had started working on another bubble.

"You'll have to forgive our friend, here, Katie. We're pretty sure he was dropped on his head when he was a baby," Richie said.

"It's okay, Donnie. *Geology* isn't my best subject, either," Katie said, smiled, and winked at Evan.

"And last, but not least," Evan said, "I'd like to introduce Eugene Madigan, otherwise known as *Beans* Madigan. I'm not going to tell you why he got stuck with that name because you'll find out soon enough."

Beans looked at Katie, gave a thumbs-up and grinned, apparently undaunted by the implications of the introduction.

Evan dipped into his jeans pocket, retrieved a handful of change, and began thumbing through it. "Okay, follow me," he said and headed across the street.

Who would have known, when the first serving of that curly-topped concoction came oozing from the nozzle back in 1938, it would become one of the comfort foods for the ages, something to soothe the pain, lift the spirits, and lighten the burdens of every man, woman, and child whose lips it touched. Thank heaven for Dairy Queen.

They ate their ice cream and talked about a number of important things that afternoon: rock and roll, the first day of school, the last day of school, Jerry Lee Lewis, a girl named Myra, and whether or not it was okay to marry your cousin.

They discussed movies and their favorite television shows. Most of *that* discussion had to do with which one of the Mouseketeers was the cutest, and who had the biggest boobs? Annette won hands down.

What a splendid time they had. Even Beans, who had planned to spend most of the morning bushwhacking the good citizens of "ratville," seemed to be enjoying the proceedings.

It had been the perfect day, and would have remained so if Richie hadn't spotted the poster in the window of the Dairy Queen and said, "So, do you think Connie Winters is dead?"

The poster was plastered everywhere throughout the valley. When the girl disappeared, her father, though struggling to keep his head above water, managed to scrape together two hundred dollars to post as a reward for information concerning her whereabouts.

The family had lived in Camden, a small town about six miles south of Laurenville, and Connie had been a sophomore at Wabash Valley High; the school was located in Laurenville proper, but it accommodated Camden and several other nearby towns, those too small to warrant their own high school.

On the first day of spring vacation, Connie had left home in the early morning hours before the family had awakened.

She had taken the babysitting money she'd saved for several months, a small suitcase crammed with clothes and some personal items, walked the three blocks to the highway, and stuck out her thumb.

Mrs. Winters later would tell the police that their daughter had left a note stating she had gone off to meet her boyfriend who had "lit out" two weeks earlier to look for a job somewhere in Florida.

They were all huddled together beside the building, looking at the poster taped to the plate glass window.

"Do any of you know her?" Katie said.

"My sister does," Richie replied. "Well, she doesn't really know her. They were in the same homeroom at Wabash Valley. She said she was real smart. Good looking too. I saw her picture in the yearbook." He gave a wolf-whistle and rolled his eyes. "Looks like Mary Hartline."

"I have dreams about her," Beans added. "Mary Hartline, I mean."

"Well, please don't give us any of the details. I don't want to barf up my Dilly Bar," Richie said, laughed, and nudged Evan a couple of times with his elbow.

"So, you're saying she just took off one day and hasn't been heard from since?" Evan said.

"That's what it said in the paper . . . and the same story my sister heard around school," Richie said.

"Still doesn't mean she's dead," Donnie said, stuffed the last dripping bite of his cone into his mouth and licked the back of his hand. "I heard they got a pet monkey a while back. Maybe she ran off with it and joined the circus."

Everyone glared at Donnie. No one laughed.

"Donnie's right, though," Richie said. "Just because they haven't located her doesn't mean she's dead. Maybe she had a good reason for leaving . . . and a good reason for not coming back."

"She'll probably show up any day now," Evan said.

They all looked at one another and nodded. It was evident from their expressions; none of them truly believed that would happen any time soon.

12
——

It was Saturday morning, and Grandma Bea had given Evan a list of errands. He had picked up a package at the post office, made a stop at Barwig's drugstore, and dropped off a get-well card for his Grandma's good friend Effie Carrol who was recovering from a bout of bronchitis.

The route home had taken him past Wabash Valley High School. When he made the turn onto Chestnut Street, he could see the football field and the adjacent parking lot. There was only one car in the lot—a light-colored convertible. It appeared to be the same vehicle he'd seen that night at the Phillips house. As he approached, he saw a man sitting alone, high up in the bleachers, the man the woman had called O'Malley that night. Evan got off his bike and stood for a few minutes, studying a second man busy painting the equipment shed at the far end of the field.

"Excuse me, Mr. O'Malley, sir," Evan called and began climbing the steps toward the top of the bleachers.

"Do I know you, young man?" O'Malley said, squinting through his wire-frame glasses as Evan approached.

"No, sir," Evan replied. "I live on East Prairie, just a few houses down from the Phillips house. I saw you that night, the night of the storm."

"Oh, I see. You're a bit curious about that evening, two men arriving under the cloak of darkness. You probably thought we were Russian spies or maybe aliens from another galaxy, something along those lines, huh?" O'Malley said, making both hands into claws and giving Evan his best Bella Lugosi stare. "I bet you're also wondering why someone would climb all the way up here to watch a guy paint a shed? Truth is, it's simply a force of habit. I always sit up top, so I don't miss anything happening on the field of play." O'Malley extended his hand. "My name is Arthur P. O'Malley. I'm a sports writer for the Tribune, nearly forty years now."

Evan shook O'Malley's hand. "Evan Ma . . ." *Keep your radar up, Evan.* "I'm Evan."

"So, Evan, what's on your mind?"

"Maybe I shouldn't be asking, Mr. O'Malley, but I was just wondering about him," Evan said and pointed." It's really none of my business. I only thought—"

"Now, hold on, son," O'Malley interrupted. "Don't get yourself all worked up over this. I don't know what you saw that night that sparked your curiosity, but you're not doing anything wrong by inquiring about my friend there," O'Malley said and nodded toward the half-painted equipment shed. "Believe me, it wouldn't be the first time Riley has raised an eyebrow." O'Malley unzipped the insulated bag at his feet and pulled out a sandwich and a couple of root beers. He opened the bottles and handed one to Evan along with half a sandwich. "Hope you like bologna and cheese. It's my favorite."

"Mine, too," Evan said. "Thanks." He took a bite and chased it with a swig of pop.

"You're welcome. I figure we'd better have a little lunch if I'm going to tell you the story of Riley Winslow," O'Malley said. He wiped a smudge of mustard off his chin with a napkin. "That something you might be interested in?"

Evan nodded and gave a thumbs-up, not wanting to speak with a mouthful of sandwich.

"It was a beautiful sunny Saturday morning, April of nineteen thirty-nine," O'Malley said. "I had gotten to the ballpark early, spent an hour or so polishing an article for Sunday's paper, and was listening to Jimmy Dykes, the manager of the White Sox, plead his case to Mr. Comiskey. Nothing he was saying was of any surprise. After all, I was the one who had given Dykes the scoop on the kid.

There was the sharp crack of a bat, and Jimmy Dykes said, "You hear that, Mr. Comiskey? That's the sweetest sound in baseball. I've only heard it a few times in my life, Ruth, Hornsby, Cobb, and I'm telling you, this kid's got it." Dykes was talking to the owner of the team, J. Louis Comiskey. They were sitting six rows up, behind home plate, watching the young man slam one ball after another into the stands. "Yes, sir, this kid is the real deal. The only problem we might have is figuring out where to play him. He's got a great arm, and for a guy his size, a lot of mobility. Hell, look at him. He looks like a damn oak tree at the plate, and he may not be done growing."

"How did you find him, Jimmy?" Comiskey said.

"O'Malley," Dykes said and winked at O'Malley over Comiskey's shoulder. "He brought him to my attention. He covered a game last week when he was pitching against the Monarchs. The kid gave up three hits and slammed two home runs himself. Struck out Willard Brown twice. Willie barely got wood on the ball. Right, Artie?" O'Malley gave an affirmative nod.

"Where does he hail from?" Comiskey said.

"Out near Joliet, a few miles east of there. The family's struggling a bit. They've got a little apartment above a butcher shop on Route 30. The good part of that is, the kid wants to stay as close to home as possible. His father has some health problems, and Mrs. Winslow needs to have her son nearby," Dykes said.

"So, what are you thinking, Jimmy?" Comiskey said.

"I say we try to get him signed immediately, if not sooner. Hornsby's been chasing the kid since he graduated high school. We all know the Browns need pitching. Hornsby is going to be relentless. The Rajah is like a bulldog when he picks up a scent."

The kid belted another ball over the center field fence.

"Hey, ease up a little. That was my best curveball," Ted Lyons shouted from the mound, "You don't want to make me look *too* bad, now, do you, kid? I haven't got many years left."

"Sorry, Mr. Lyons, I wasn't—"

"I'm just messin' with you, kid." Lyons winked, then spit a huge glob of tobacco onto the ground.

Dykes took a few steps toward home plate and threw an arm into the air, beckoning to the young man. "Hey, son!" Dykes shouted. "Get over here. I want to introduce you to Mr. J. Louis Comiskey, the owner of the Sox."

The kid leaned the bat against the backstop, took off his cap, wiped sweat from his brow with the back of his shirtsleeve, and jogged toward the stands. Riley Winslow stood six-feet-three and weighed one-ninety-five.

"The only other thing we may have to deal with is the kid's nature. He may be *too* nice a guy. I may have to work on toughening him up a bit," Dykes said to Comiskey as Riley approached.

"Good to meet you, sir," Riley said. They shook hands.

"Impressive performance, young man," Comiskey said. "Manager Dykes has told me some good things about your work. What do you think about the prospect of playing in the big leagues?"

"I'm ready, sir. I can't sleep lately, thinking about it," Riley said, the eagerness and excitement clearly visible in his voice.

"What do you enjoy most, hitting or pitching?" Comiskey said.

"It doesn't matter, sir. I just want to play the game," Riley said.

"Well, that, my boy, is the most refreshing thing I've heard in years." Comiskey looked at Dykes. "Jimmy, we need to find a place for this young man." He turned back to Riley. "The White Sox could use an injection of vim and vigor right now. I'd like to meet your mother and father, talk to them about a vision I have for your future."

"They're right up there, sir," Riley said and pointed toward the man and woman sitting thirty rows up in the stands.

"It sounds like you and Mr. Dykes had everything all planned out," Evan said.

"Right down to the last detail. I had gotten to know the family pretty well. I knew exactly what Mr. Carl Winslow deemed important in this life, and money was only a small part of it. Keeping the family together for as long as possible was the thing he wanted most in the world. Dykes knew that Riley signing with the White Sox would make everyone happy. Well, everyone but Hornsby," O'Malley said and chuckled a bit. "One thing for sure. There was no way Riley and his folks were going to walk away that day without making some kind of a commitment to the Sox, not if Jimmy Dykes had anything to say about it."

The office was richly decorated, but not ostentatious. There was a large painting of Charles Albert Comiskey on the wall. The picture was flanked by several photographs of White Sox Park at various stages of construction and a walnut plaque with a copper inlay, an image of the ballpark's façade etched into the metal. The inscription read: The Baseball Palace of the World – 1912.

Carl Winslow and Riley sat on one side of a massive mahogany table, Mr. Comiskey and Manager Dykes on the other.

"We're not fancy people, Mr. Comiskey. We just want the best for our son," Carl said.

"As do we, Mr. Winslow. You mark my words, sir, someday your boy's picture is going to be plastered across this newspaper," Mr. Comiskey said, waving a folded copy of the *Chicago Tribune* as he spoke, "and every other paper across the country. No doubt in my mind. There are big things ahead for this young man." He looked at Riley and nodded affirmatively. "He's going to make you proud someday."

"We're already proud," Carl said, smiling, leaning forward and patting his son on the back. Carl winced slightly as he settled back in his chair. The sudden sharp pain in his back traveled down his leg to his right knee like a jolt of electricity. He shifted his weight, invoking an equally painful response in his left hip. Carl Winslow had been suffering from a congenital form of arthritis that had become almost debilitating. Of course, crawling around inside boilers for twenty-five years certainly hadn't helped his condition.

"Manager Dykes has taken the liberty of drawing up a preliminary agreement for Riley to sign," Comiskey said, looking directly at Carl Winslow. He turned his attention to Riley. "This contract spells out all the details directly, son, with none of that legal mumbo-jumbo. It will give you some immediate financial security, insurance, that sort of thing. We want you to play for the White Sox, son. We'll take good care of you. You have my word on that. I think you should all sit down and talk about it for a while. You can use my office."

Evan had been listening intently, hanging on every word of O'Malley's story.

"So, Riley signed the contract, right?" Evan said.

"Hold your horses, son, I'm getting to that," O'Malley said. "Now, all the while the family was in there deliberating, Dykes was pacing back and forth, puffing on his cigar like an expectant father. He was desperate! After all, the White Sox had finished the prior season thirty-two games behind the New York Yankees who had gone on to sweep the Cubs in the World Series. Dykes needed help and he knew Riley Winslow would be a major force in turning things around. Finally, after a little over an hour, Riley opened the door, handed Dykes the signed contract and said, 'I want to play baseball for the White Sox, Mr. Dykes.' Of course, Dykes was elated. He had been cautiously optimistic about the whole thing. He even had a photographer standing by to take a picture of Riley in a White Sox uniform. He wanted to flaunt it to Hornsby the next time he saw him. By half-past one that day, everything was wrapped up. Dykes and I were hoisting a shot of Kentucky rye in his office and the Winslows were on their way home."

Carl Winslow waited as the seemingly endless funeral procession inched along 63rd Street toward the lake.

"It has to be either a politician or a gangster," Carl said.

"I didn't know there were this many Cadillacs in the entire city of Chicago," Riley said.

Finally, the cop directing traffic spotted a gap in the stream of vehicles and waved them through the intersection. The '34 Plymouth's front suspension, held together by baling wire, creaked and chattered as they traversed the stretch of cobblestone roadway. The automobile had originally belonged to Carl's landlord, Ed Hadley. The Winslows occupied the drafty three-room apartment above Hadley's Butcher Shop, and Hadley had given the Plymouth to Carl as compensation for repairs he had done on the coal-fired boiler in the basement of the building.

"Well, what do you think, son? Did you walk away with a good feeling about what transpired today?" Carl said. He took a puff on the stubby cigar clenched between his teeth and shifted into second gear.

Riley was sitting in the front seat, his mother behind him in the back. She was leaning forward, her ear perked, apparently trying to hear the conversation over the road noise and clatter of the car's engine.

"It wasn't exactly what I expected," Riley said. "I thought the process would have drawn on a bit longer. They don't beat around the bush, do they? I hope we did the right thing, signing that contract on the spot."

"They did their homework," Carl said. "Manager Dykes told me Mr. O'Malley saw you pitch that one-hitter against the House of David last year. He called you the beardless wonder. Dykes has a lot of respect for O'Malley when it comes to scouting players. As far as the contract goes, you've got thirty days to change your mind. I'll ask our company attorney to review the fine print. Mr. Padgett does legal work for a lot of the men. He's a damn sharp lawyer, and it won't cost us an arm and a leg."

"I liked Mr. Dykes," Maggie said. "He seems like a nice man. He reminds me of my Uncle George."

"Well, let's hope he's a tad smarter. I think George came up a little short when the good Lord was dishing out helpings of gray matter," Carl said and chuckled.

"Please, dear, don't talk badly about George. He had to leave school when he was just a boy. He took care of his entire family. If it weren't for him, who knows what tragedy would have befallen them," Maggie said.

"Now, Margaret, don't get your bloomers all twisted, you know I jest. I like George. He's the one guy who's there when you need him. Besides, Georgie has something that a lot of folks don't, common sense. That'll take you a long way in life. Am I right, son?" He glanced at Riley and winked.

"Well, I just know that when Uncle George was—" Maggie started, but Carl interrupted with a song.

"Take me out to the ballgame, take me out to the crowd. Buy me some peanuts and . . ." Carl was singing at the top of his lungs. "Come on, now this is one glorious day. Let's not get all bogged down in that kind of malarkey," Carl said. "Let's hear it from the cheap seats! *I don't care . . ."*

Riley joined in, *"If I never get back . . ."* He turned and looked at his mother, waving his arms like he was leading an orchestra. She placed her hand gently on his cheek, smiled, and began to sing.

They traveled south on Halsted Street. The sun was shining. The air was cool and fresh. There wasn't a dark cloud in the sky.

The three were still singing as they rolled across a section of double railroad tracks just south of 95th Street.

"Hold it! Listen up," Carl said. "I've got a few bucks stashed away. I'm going to take you out to dinner and a movie tonight. There's a doozy of a western playing over at the Orpheum. We'll have dinner and—"

Riley shouted, "Look out, Pop!" There was a frantic tone to his voice.

Carl Winslow whipped his head to his left and saw the locomotive bearing down on them. He stomped the gas pedal. The car backfired and a cloud of black smoke belched from the exhaust pipe. The car bucked and shook as the engine stuttered slightly, nearly dying, then lunged forward.

The speeding train ripped into the Plymouth's left rear quarter, the front coupler snagging the fender well. Sparks flew from beneath the locomotive, and pieces of metal and shards of glass tumbled along the track bed as the train dragged the Plymouth toward a concrete abutment. The train traveled a hundred yards before it came to a screeching stop. The car flipped end over end into the steep ravine.

It wasn't the singing nor the clatter of the car's engine that had prevented Carl Winslow from hearing a warning bell at the crossing that day; in fact, no bell had sounded, no lights had flashed. Perhaps the culprit was a faulty solenoid, a loose wire, or simply an anomaly originating from the violent thunderstorms that had moved through Chicago the previous night.

It was ten minutes before the fire truck arrived, followed moments later by two ambulances.

In the meantime, an off-duty policeman and a telephone lineman had witnessed the incident and rushed to assist. The burly lineman's legs were braced against the bridge railing and he was straining against a length of rope, lowering the officer toward the pile of twisted metal that lay at the base of the ravine. The second his feet touched the ground the officer slipped the strap of the fire-extinguisher he had slung over his shoulder, twisted the wheel valve, and began dousing the flames that had burst forth from under the hood of the Plymouth.

"I hear sounds from inside that car . . . a voice!" the officer shouted. "Get those men down here with that equipment, *now!*"

"We were still in Dykes' office when we got the news," O'Malley said. "Here, no more than an hour earlier, we had been with the family, and now Mr. Winslow was dead and Riley and his mother were fighting for their lives in Cook County Hospital."

"Riley's father was killed?" Evan said.

"Yes. He never had a chance. Someone later told me it took them three hours to extricate . . . *remove* his body from the car. It was a tragic scene. I met Mr. Comiskey and Jimmy Dykes at the hospital a short time later. Riley and his mother were in bad shape. She had a dislocated shoulder and contusions all over her body."

"Contusions? Does that mean cuts?" Evan said.

"No, more like deep bruises, but she had a good number of cuts and gashes as well. I don't want to give you all the gory details. You'd be having nightmares for a month. Let's just say, she was a mess," O'Malley said. "Both of Riley's legs were broken in several places. The doctors didn't think he would ever walk again."

"That's why Riley limps like that?"

O'Malley nodded and said, "It was almost six months before he could even stand without assistance. He had all kinds of internal damage, but the worst thing was the head injury. The swelling created a lot of pressure on Riley's brain."

"Did he ever play baseball again?" Evan said.

"No, that was lost forever. He can still hit a baseball a country mile. For some reason that appears to be ingrained in him, but because of the legs he couldn't run or throw. Early on, everyone thought there might be hope. Dykes gave it a try. Took him to spring training to assess his abilities. He hit a rocket to center field, then just stood there at home plate, waving his hat and singing *Take Me Out to the Ball Game*. Sometimes he's just in his own little world."

"That's sad," Evan said, watching as Riley put the last few strokes of paint on the front of the shed.

O'Malley stood and waved. "Riley!" There was no reply. *"Riley!"*

"I'm painting, Mr. O!" Riley shouted from the top of the ladder, waving the paint-laden brush.

"I can see that," O'Malley shouted, "but it's time for lunch. It's okay to stop for a while." O'Malley gave him a come-hither wave.

Riley stuck his brush into the bucket of turpentine, put the lid on the paint can, and walked quickly toward the bleachers, his limp even more prominent at the faster gait. O'Malley and Evan descended to meet him.

"Riley, this is Evan. He's your neighbor. He lives across the street from you," O'Malley said.

"Hi, Evan," Riley said and gave a quick wave.

"Good to meet you, Riley," Evan said.

Riley took a bite from the sandwich O'Malley had handed him and said, "I like your bicycle, Evan." He inspected the Phantom, front to back. "Nice seat." He patted the tan leather saddle. "I'm getting a new bike on Monday. Mr. O is loaning me the money, but I'm going to pay him back when I get my check. Right, Mr. O?"

"That's right," O'Malley replied. "I know you're good for it, Riley."

"I'm good for it," Riley said, plopping down beside Evan.

The three sat quietly while Riley finished his lunch. Finally, Riley stood and said, "I have to paint now."

Evan watched Riley limp back across the field, then said, "You looked after him over years, Mr. O'Malley?"

"I helped as much as I could," O'Malley replied. "He was a special kid. Not only was he the best young prospect I'd ever seen, but he was one of the best human beings I ever ran across. Like the old saying goes, they don't make 'em like that anymore."

"Is that the way he is all the time?" Evan said.

"Pretty much. At least when he's Riley Winslow. It doesn't take much to change things up. Every now and then he'll pick up on something happening around him, then, presto, change-o, there's a whole new persona on the loose. But that doesn't happen often, not anymore. Most of the time he just stays in his shell."

"Is painting going to be his regular job? Doesn't he have any money?" Evan said.

"Oh, he's okay financially. He's receiving a survivor's benefit from the Boilermakers union along with some insurance money. The White Sox helped out as well, but he needs something to keep him busy. Working helps him deal with his problem. Gives him a sense of purpose, something we all need in life." O'Malley removed his glasses, exhaled a breath on each lens, and wiped them with his handkerchief. "The baseball coach here at the high school is a good friend of mine, known him for years. I helped place a few of his boys. Let's just say, Coach Grimm is repaying a favor. He'll keep Riley busy two or three days a week through the fall. In the meantime, I'm working on turning it into a year-round job."

"So, is Riley related to the woman he lives with?" Evan asked.

"Yep. Wilma is Riley's aunt, his mother's sister. She promised to take care of Riley if it ever came to that. Don't try to figure it all out, son. It's like when some guy tells you he's your third cousin, once removed. I always feel like asking, removed from what? And if he was removed, who let him back in?" O'Malley laughed, and with a more serious tone said, "There *is* a favor I'd like to ask of you." He reached into his jacket pocket and pulled out a small notepad and a ballpoint pen. He scribbled something and handed the sheet to Evan. "My telephone number. Wilma isn't in the best of health herself, and since you're close by, I'd appreciate it if you keep an eye on things. Call me if anything goes awry. Would you do that?"

Evan nodded, folded the paper, and stuffed it into his

pocket. "I'd better get moving, Mr. O'Malley. My grandmother will be wondering where I am."

"Okay, Evan," O'Malley said.

Evan jumped onto his bike and pushed off down the sidewalk. "Oh, and thanks for the sandwich."

"What did you say your last name was?" O'Malley said.

"Mason!" Evan called over his shoulder as he rode away. "Evan Mason!"

13

——

Katie swerved onto the shoulder and plowed through a stretch of loose pulverized gravel. She slammed down hard on the pedal, stopping in a cloud of dust.

Z. AIKEN was stenciled on the mailbox in bold white letters and a few inches below, in red paint, were the words, Wapek Wanka.

"This is it," Katie said as Evan rolled to a stop beside her. "I hope he likes surprises."

"He told me to stop by anytime," Evan replied.

They stood for a few minutes, craning their necks to see what was at the top of the steep gravel driveway.

Suddenly they heard a booming voice. "You coming up, or you just going to sit there eating dust all day?" Against the clear blue sky, Zachary appeared ten feet tall. His hair was tied back in a ponytail, and he was puffing on his meerschaum pipe.

As they climbed the hill, they could see a barn at the back edge of the property. The roof was badly in need of repair, and the crimson paint on the cedar side-planks had nearly vanished. They propped their bikes against a short section of three-rail fence at the edge of the yard, and Zachary led them along the cinder path toward the white frame house. It, too, was in dire need of paint.

"Sit yourselves down anywhere," Zachary said, easing into an old rocking chair on the expansive front porch. "What are you up to this fine morning, Evan, my boy? And who's this lovely young lady in your company?"

"This is Katie. She moved here from Ohio. She lives around the corner from me. We just wanted to stop and say hello. You did invite me, didn't you, Mr. Aiken?"

"That I did, and you are both most welcome. It's a pleasure meeting you, Katie."

"Nice to meet you, sir," Katie said.

"Oh, almost forgot," Evan said. He ran back to his bike, returning seconds later with two jars of preserves. "My grandmother wanted you to have these," Evan said as he placed them on the table next to Zachary.

"Well, now, you be sure and thank your grandma for me," he said, picking up one of the jars and examining its contents. "This fine nectar can't be found on a shelf at the A&P, nothing even close." Zachary stood, picked up the jars, and disappeared into the house.

A few minutes later he returned. Three tall glasses of lemonade were balanced precariously on the tray he was carrying, and there was a towel draped over his arm. He placed the tray on the top step, wiped the bottom of one of the sweating glasses with the towel and handed it to Katie.

"Thank you, Mr. Aiken," Katie said. "You have a pretty steady hand."

"Not so steady of late," he said. He held his hand out in front of him, palm down. It was shaking slightly. "Reminds me of a time when I wasn't much older than you kids," Zachary said, handed Evan a glass, and sat back down. He took a long drink from his own glass, pulled a red paisley bandanna from his hip pocket and wiped his forehead. "I was working for Lyle MacDougal down at the Orchard Tavern on the north bend of the Wabash. Times were tough, and if I wanted money in my pocket, I had to work. I was about fifteen. Can't remember exactly. Wasn't old enough to drink, that I know."

"That place is still there, isn't it?" Evan said.

"Yes, but now Lyle's son runs the joint. Anyway, Lyle had me doing a little of everything, cleaning privies, juicing apples, filling ice-tubs, and waiting on customers. You name it. I was on it. On those hot summer days, those river rats would tie up long enough for me to run down to the levee with some refreshments. I got pretty damn good at navigating that riverbank with a tray full of Lyle's specially brewed, ice-cold apple cider. Only had one mishap the two summers I was there, but let me tell you, it was a doozy. It was about ninety degrees in the shade, and I'd been running back and forth all day, so I decided to take a tiny sip from each mug before I made the run, figuring nobody would miss a smidgen off the top."

"That doesn't sound like a good idea, Mr. Aiken," Evan said.

Zachary chuckled. "You're exactly right, son. It was a terrible idea. By mid-afternoon, I had probably consumed two or three mugs of that orchard brew. Believe me, it was some potent stuff. I'm flying down that slippery slope with a full tray, hit a patch of fish guts and go head over heels into the Wabash. Everything ended up at the bottom of the river. Old man MacDougal was ready to skin me alive. Probably would've fired me on the spot if those men hadn't chipped in and paid for everything. They got their money's worth, though. I still hear some of the old-timers laughing while they're telling that story." He struck a kitchen match on the arm of the chair and relit his pipe. He took a puff and gestured toward Evan's bicycle. "That's quite a ride you have there. What I would call traveling in style. To what good fortune do you owe that fine piece of machinery?"

"I guess, to the good fortune of having Mrs. Beatrice Mason as my grandmother. She bought it for me," Evan said.

"That makes perfect sense. Like I told you the other day, I knew your grandfather. He was an honest, hard-working man. We need more like him. I didn't know your grandmother personally, but I saw her several times over the years, most often at the train depot. She would arrive all decked out in a fine dress, a fancy hat, and an umbrella in hand. I can see her now." He paused, eyes closed. "Rain or shine, she would have that umbrella. I remember one day, I was sitting on a bench waiting for a train when she came strolling up. It was a scorcher of a day. When your grandpa stepped off the train in that heavy wool conductor's uniform, sweat was pouring off him. He looked like he was gonna keel over right there on the platform. She reached up, yanked his hat off, pulled out a damp cloth and began blotting his forehead to cool him down. Finally, she gave him a big hug and a kiss, popped that umbrella open, handed it to Walter, and the two of them strolled off together hand-in-hand down Main Street. Needless to say, that bumbershoot came in pretty handy on rainy days as well." For a few seconds, Zachary appeared to be in a faraway place, then, almost inaudibly, he said, "I always hoped that someday I'd find a woman like that. I'd have given anything to—"

Max came running up the driveway, barking profusely. He darted back and forth a few times, circled Katie and Evan. He sniffed Evan's extended hand, then curled up beside Zachary on the porch.

The man trailing up the driveway was Dr. Randall Lerner. He stopped halfway. "Hey, Zach! Thought I'd drop Max off so you wouldn't have to make the trip. Good thing, too. I can see you're a *very* busy man today," he said and laughed.

"You better believe it. This rocking is hard work." Zachary smiled and rocked a couple of times to accentuate his point. "If my guess is right, you might be headed for a little R and R yourself."

"You're an incredibly perceptive man, Chief," Doc said.

"How *is* the fishing on the Wabash these days?" Zachary said.

"Caught a dozen smallmouth and a channel cat the length of my arm last Friday. Snagged that monster under Spencer Bridge in less than an hour. It was one glorious day on the river." Doc then proceeded to give a blow-by-blow description of the event, expounding for the next several minutes with the enthusiasm of a ten-year-old boy who had just reeled in his first fish. Finally, he said, "The important thing is, your dog is fine, Zach. No infection and the bite is healing well."

"I gathered as much when I saw him tearing up the drive. I thank you, Doc. You are the best," Zachary said.

"That hound has got to learn not to mess with those nasty little critters. Raccoons are about the worst when it comes to vermin and disease," Doc said.

"What do I owe you?" Zachary stood, reached into his pocket, and pulled out a clip of bills.

"Don't you worry about that, my friend. That fly rod you gave me is worth its weight in gold. I'll let you know when I feel we're square," Doc said. He gave a wave over his shoulder as he headed back down the hill toward his car.

Max was now nuzzling Evan, his front paws stretched across his lap. Evan was petting him. "Glad he's okay," Evan said.

"He'll be fine. I just have to find a way to keep him out of trouble," Zachary said and took a long puff on his pipe.

"What's that name on your mailbox, Mr. Aiken?" Katie asked.

"Oh, you're referring to Wapek Wanka? That's a Sauk Indian name given to my second great-grandfather. It means white fox in the Algonquian language. As far as I know, the old boy was the last of my ancestors who had a hefty amount of Indian blood flowing through his veins. I found a reference to it in a bunch of old letters passed down over the years. I'm not sure I got the spelling exactly right, but it had a good sound to it. I thought it might add a little flair to the merchandise I'm peddling." He nodded toward the house. "C'mon, I'll show you my workshop."

The room off the kitchen was about ten by twelve; three windows were looking out onto a small clearing with four apple trees and a dense stretch of woodland beyond.

Evan and Katie looked around the room, wide-eyed. One wall was completely covered with a variety of beaded necklaces, bracelets, pendants, and breastplates.

Three stacks of eight-by-ten photographs sat on a secretary in the corner of the room. Most were of Zachary decked out in his buckskins in various poses against a woodland backdrop.

There was a workbench in the center of the room with an unusual looking little vice and a rack of tools, scissors, tweezers, and a few other odd utensils. At one end of the bench was a row of spindles holding spools of multi-colored thread and fine wire, copper and silver. There was also a wooden box containing feathers and small patches of fur.

"Pull up a seat," Zachary said and gestured toward several stools lined up along one wall.

Evan and Katie dragged a stool across the hardwood floor to the workbench and sat down. Zachary pulled a flat, hinged wooden box from under the bench, opened it, and placed it in front of them.

"Wow! You've got a little bit of everything in here, Mr. Aiken," Katie said.

"This is my travel case," Zachary said. "I take it to all the markets." He pointed to a section of the box containing beads, arrowheads, and bear claws. "These are all genuine. I collected them from all over the country, but most are from around here and the Dakotas." He removed the top tray, exposing another layer of compartments. "These are samples of some of the flies I've tied over the years. Each one is on the menu in some river or stream I've fished. Nothing more satisfying than tying a big juicy bug and having a three or four-pound rainbow chomp down on it."

"Would you show us?" Evan said.

"Be glad to. Slide over a touch. We'll tie us up a pretty little Caddisfly," Zachary said. He clamped a bare number six hook in the jaws of the vice and began winding brown thread around the shank. For the next hour, Zachary demonstrated the fine art of fly tying. While he worked, he told stories of his Sauk heritage and the places he'd fished over the years.

Katie picked up one of the necklaces and studied it under the canopy light. "Do you believe in those stories, Mr. Aiken? I mean, do you think there's magic in a string of beads, or feathers, stuff like that?" she said.

"I don't necessarily think it's magic, but I do believe it served a purpose for those native people, and when you get right down to it, that's all that really counts, isn't it? They believed that every living creature has an energy, a spirit, that after death becomes even stronger because it melds with every other being that came before. The beads are just *symbols*. These days, people carry a rabbit's foot or a lucky penny. Another person might wear a cross or a locket, something to give him strength. It doesn't really matter what it is, as long as the person believes in it."

"They all have different markings on them," Katie said, looking at one of the beads with a magnifying glass.

"Each of those symbols has a specific meaning," Zachary said. He cut a length of black braided twine, knotted the end, and selected a small wooden bead from the box. "Some were used to ward off evil spirits." He pinched the bead between his thumb and forefinger and pointed to the symbol etched into the hardwood, two crossed arrows. "Friendship." He threaded it onto the twine, then pulled another bead, a hawk. "Power and vision," he said as he threaded it. "Last, but not least, the morning star to provide hope and guidance." He slid it onto the twine, secured the beads, and added a clasp. "Turn around." Zachary fastened the string of beads around Katie's neck.

"Thank you, Mr. Aiken, I love it," Katie said.

"There's one thing I want you to do for me," Zachary said, "both of you. Are you listening?" They nodded and looked directly at Zachary, giving him their full attention. "You be mindful when you venture into these woods around here. Make sure you travel in groups. Don't go off alone. Some strange characters are traipsing around in that north section. I've been hearing of some unusual goings-on the last few months. Moe Grayson, one of my neighbors just south of here, found the remains of one of his cows smack-dab in the middle of his cornfield about a week back. Someone butchered it right there on the spot. And when I say butchered, I don't mean sliced up real neat and wrapped in paper and string. I'm referring to someone chopping it up, running off with a big slab of meat, and leaving the rest to rot. Who knows what kind of derelicts might be sneaking back in there? You get my point?"

"We got it, Mr. Aiken," Evan said and looked at Katie. They nodded in unison.

"Then, there's this thing concerning the Winters girl. I assume you've heard the news on that?" More nodding. "There's a dark cloud lingering over the Wabash Valley right now, and we all need to be vigilant. You'll hear all this talk about the Winters girl being a bit strange and running off to join up with some cult group, but that's nonsense, just a way for people to ease their own fears. There's nothing that unusual about her. She is just like any other teenager you might meet."

"You know her, Mr. Aiken?" Katie said.

"I met her at the fairgrounds. It was about a month before she disappeared. She and another girl were looking at my merchandise. We talked for a while, and she told me about her boyfriend and the plans they had. Evidently, this boyfriend of hers is an ace mechanic, especially when it comes to motorcycles and the like. They were planning to take the money they saved and ship out for the Caribbean. They wanted to open one of those scooter rental places for the tourists in St. Thomas, or *one* of those islands down there. It sounded like a hair-brained scheme, but who am I to judge?" Zachary said and gestured toward the shelves of merchandise around the room. "Anyway, she took a liking to one of my necklaces."

"Like mine?" Katie said, clutching the string of beads around her neck.

"Pretty close," Zachary replied. "She was short on cash, so being the kind-hearted soul that I am, I dropped the price a tad. She pulled out a high school class ring and slipped it onto the string before she put it around her neck. Her boyfriend's, I assume. It was the first thing I thought of when I heard she had gone missing. Let's hope the spirits are looking after her." He took a polished turquoise stone from the box. "Here, take this," Zachary said. He placed the stone in Evan's outstretched palm. He shifted his gaze between Evan and Katie. "The stone and the necklace are to remind you of the things we talked about."

14

———

Evan was on the screened-in back porch rummaging through the drawers in the old wooden cabinet where his grandfather had stored all his odds and ends. There were screws, nuts, bolts, and washers in two of the drawers. Four others were crammed full of fishing paraphernalia, hooks bobbers, leaders, and several spools of line. The remaining six were filled to the top with everything imaginable. Evan had already found four Indian-head pennies, a Grand Army of the Republic medal from 1861, and a pearl-handled pocket knife. That was before he had done any serious digging.

He was raking through an assortment of lead weights in one of the smaller compartments with a pencil, searching for a couple of split-shot sinkers. He had promised Katie he would take her fishing at Harmon's pond later that morning, nothing fancy, just two cane poles with ten feet of braided line, bobber, weight, and hook.

He had awakened at dawn that morning and spent a half hour behind the shed digging for red worms. The prior summer, he and Donnie had caught a couple of dozen crappie using the wriggly little critters. Donnie Jones wasn't the sharpest tool in the shed, but when it came to fishing, he was an Einstein. Heyward Jones, Donnie's grandfather, had the reputation of being the best fisherman to have ever cast a line into the Wabash. People said he was so adept he could forecast the day's catch by simply observing the barometric pressure and the direction the wind was blowing. Before he expired at the seasoned age of eighty-seven he had taught Donnie everything he knew about angling.

Beatrice poked her head around the corner. "You have a visitor."

Evan went out the back door and around to the front of the house.

Riley was freshly shaven. A small piece of blood-stained toilet tissue clung to his chin, and the strong scent of aftershave filled the air. He was dressed in khaki trousers, khaki shirt, and a navy blue baseball cap. There was a bicycle parked beside him on the walkway.

"Hello, Evan," Riley said and gave a little wave. "I'm on my way to my job. Not painting . . . I'm doing another job today. How do you like my new bike?" He pulled a terrycloth rag from his hip pocket, rubbed at a couple of spots on the rear fender, then leaned in and inspected his work.

"Uh, hi, Riley. I really like it," Evan said.

"I can't pedal fast right now, on account of this one being shorter," Riley said and patted his right leg. "But Mr. Carver raised the seat all the way up for me and he's making a special gadget for the pedal. He said I'll get the hang of it in no time."

"Maybe you and I can go riding one of these days," Evan said.

"Okay, but I don't know how I'll do with you sitting on the handlebars. I'm a little wobbly right now."

"I didn't mean on your bike. I'll ride my own bike," Evan said.

"I'll have to ask Aunt Wilma, but I think it's okay."

"Are you working tomorrow?" Evan said.

"Yep," Riley replied. "Anytime I'm there, I have to be working, otherwise, I won't get my check. It's okay to stop for lunch, though . . . oh, and breaks."

Evan smiled. "So, what time do you finish tomorrow?"

"One o'clock. I'm done at one."

"Why don't you stop by after work?" Evan said.

"Okay," Riley said and took off on his bike, fishing for the pedals as he zigged and zagged down the walk. "Goodbye, Evan!" Riley yelled as he crossed the street.

Beatrice came to the door. "Looks like you've made a new friend," she said. They watched as the lanky thirty-eight-year-old man rode off down East Prairie. "I'm anxious to hear all about it."

She drank a cup of tea while Evan told her the saga of Riley Winslow.

15

———

Evan had attached the two cane poles to the frame of his bike with short lengths of electrical wire cut from a spool he had found in one of the catch-all drawers. He had discovered two tackle boxes tucked away in the eaves of the garage. The smaller one was strapped to the carrier of his bike. The can of red worms was wrapped in tin foil and stashed in the seat pouch.

It was a brisk morning as Evan rode his bike up the gently sloped driveway and parked it under the carport. The Dobbins' yellow frame house was in the middle of the block on Juniper Street, just around the corner from Grandma Bea's.

He stepped onto the porch and rang the doorbell. There was the sound of footsteps, then a woman appeared at the door. Her blonde hair was partially covered by a bandanna and she wore a flowered cotton blouse, magenta Capri pants, and sandals. At that moment the only thing Evan could think of was the Carl Perkins song, *the girl boppin' down the street in her Pink Pedal Pushers, all the guys hootin' and hollerin' as she strolled by.*

She gave Evan a stern up-and-down gaze. "I already get *Vogue* and *The Saturday Evening Post*. Don't need any more subscriptions, thank you," she said as she closed the door.

"Mother! That's not funny," he heard Katie say as the door swung open again.

"Oh, don't be such a wet rag, Katie. I was just kidding. Please come in, Evan, before Katie has a conniption fit. As you may have already guessed, I'm Vera Dobbins, Katie's cold, insensitive, warped-minded mother," Vera said as she ushered Evan into the kitchen.

There was a strong likeness between Katie and her mother, even their voices. Vera's, of course, was a bit deeper, raspier. Evan looked around and spotted a pack of cigarettes lying on the windowsill and one smoldering in the ashtray beside it. Just about every adult he knew smoked. Smoking seemed to be one of the essentials of life, like eating and breathing.

"It'll take a while for you to get used to my mother's sense of humor. Although, some people *never* do," Katie said and scowled momentarily at her mother. "I'm almost ready, Evan. Give me just a minute or two." She scooted up the stairs.

"You might as well sit down, Evan. A *minute* can be a long time in Katie's world. How about something to drink?" Vera said.

He sat at the kitchen table, and before he could tell her he had just eaten one of his grandmother's mammoth breakfasts, there was a tall glass of orange juice in front of him.

"Uh, thanks, Mrs. Dobbins," he said, took a small sip, and studied the scene around him. Everything was extremely tidy, nothing out of place.

The room off the kitchen, probably once a bedroom, was now a sewing room. There were several dress mannequins lined up along the far wall, and bolts of fabric were stacked on a sofa in the corner. A Singer sewing machine sat in the center of the room, a panel of green satin stretched across the bed of the machine.

"Katie says you're quite the musician, Evan. I understand you play a mean harmonica," Vera said.

"I'm working on it," Evan replied.

"That's not what I hear. I bumped into Loretta Coplin at McCormick's the other day and your name came up. She said you are one of the most promising students she has ever taught," Vera said.

"I like Miss Coplin. She's a great teacher. I think she was pretty disappointed when she found out I quit the lessons."

"I can imagine. That's quite a compliment she gave you," Vera said.

Katie came bounding down the stairs wearing denim shorts and a light cotton pullover. Her hair was tied back in the usual ponytail.

"Well, someone's got a lot of energy," Vera said, opened the refrigerator and pulled out a brown paper bag. She took a quick puff on her cigarette, then placed it into the ashtray on the windowsill. "I packed some sandwiches for you two. Hope you like egg-salad, Evan."

"Thank you, Mrs. Dobbins. That'll be fine."

She stuffed the sandwiches, a thermos of ice water, two apples, and a couple of napkins into an insulated vinyl bag and handed it to Katie.

"Be careful at Gordon Junction. There'll be a lot of trucks rolling through there today," Vera called after them as they sped away.

She had a good reason for the warning and concern about the trucks. The oil refinery was being expanded. Cement and dump trucks were running almost around the clock. There had been an editorial in the *Trenton Gazette* just a week earlier lambasting Prairie Construction for not reigning in the drivers who seemed to be ignoring the speed limit along the curvy stretch of Route 33 where it intersected with Cumberland Road.

Yes, Vera Dobbins had a genuine concern about those trucks, but that wasn't her biggest worry.

The thing that kept her awake at night was the poster, the one with Connie Winters' smiling face looming on it. She had first seen it at the village hall the day she stopped to pay the deposit for their utilities.

Later that same day, she had overheard a conversation while shopping; two young mothers were looking at the same poster in a store window and reflecting on the fears they had of their children being out of their sight, even for short periods of play in the backyard. At that time, Connie Winters had been missing a little more than a month. There was no evidence to suggest the girl had been harmed in any way, yet the stark placard loomed like a distress signal—jimmy-marks on a door, an abandoned car on the side of the road, a phone call in the middle of the night. Its mere presence had elicited the worst of all fears.

Vera stood with a cup of coffee and a cigarette, looking through the screened kitchen window at the swing dangling from the limb in the backyard. As she opened the window a few more inches to allow the cigarette smoke to flee into the cool morning air, the swing began to move to and fro. Vera took one last deep drag on her cigarette, then snuffed it in the ashtray.

Like the two women in the store, I have a right to worry, she thought. *After all, it isn't Connie Winters' face on that ominous poster . . . it's every child.*

16

"Thank you for taking me," Katie said as they rode along. "I'm not much of a fisherman, uh, fisher-girl, but I'm willing to learn. My grandpa took me fishing when I was little. As I recall, I didn't do very well with the casting part of it."

"You won't have to worry about that. We're going to do some good old-fashioned bobber fishing today, put a worm on the hook and let *him* do all the work."

They didn't see any trucks as they crossed Route 33, but there was a fresh deer carcass in the roadside ditch, an indication that the trucks had been rolling through the night.

They rode another mile, then turned onto a narrow path leading to a section of dense woodland.

Evan stopped a short distance from the point where the path entered the woods and said, "Okay, here's where the fun begins. How do you feel about roller coasters?"

They traveled only a few feet before the path took a dive, then immediately made a sharp left. The path was slightly banked, and Katie was close on Evan's tail when they rounded the first turn. She glided smoothly into a series of moguls, the second of which would have probably sent her airborne if she hadn't followed Evan's instruction to the letter and braked slightly on the ascent. She was trying her best to trace Evan's route precisely. He was zigging and zagging to avoid the low overhanging branches that threatened to sweep them off their bikes into the thick bramble constricting the path.

Finally, they hit the clearing, an open, gently sloped straightaway that provided a brief respite before the final steep plunge into a gauntlet of box elders and overgrown ivy that would swallow them up and spit them out between two tall willows at the south end of Harmon's Pond.

"Wow!" Katie said as she braked to a skidding stop just seconds behind Evan. "That was cool! A bit scary, but *very* cool."

"I thought you'd be taking it slow," Evan said, "but you surprised me. You're quite the daredevil."

"And you thought this girl was nothing more than a cute, blue-eyed honor student from Akron," she said, and with the back of her hands, fluffed imaginary locks off her shoulders. They both laughed.

Evan and Katie sat side-by-side on a huge oak tree that extended halfway across the narrow south end of the pond. The fallen tree had been planted by a family who had migrated from Tennessee just before the beginning of the Civil War. William Jasper Harmon, his wife, and three children had loaded all their worldly possessions onto a single covered wagon and struck out through the Cumberland Gap for Illinois. They had farmed the land adjacent to the pond for over fifty years. The tree had been struck by a bolt of lightning in the spring of 1954, tumbling into the water just three years short of the century mark.

Most of the pond's surface at this end was covered by lily pads and shaded by the two tall willows. Pale yellow blossoms rose from the water on slender stems, and in places where the sun shone through, the droplets on the petals made them glow like street lamps on a village green.

Katie had removed her sneakers and socks and was dangling her toes in the water, watching the dragonflies skitter back and forth across the pond.

"Please tell me I don't have to do that," she said as she watched Evan thread a red worm onto the hook. She reached into the can and pulled out one of the squiggly critters. "I don't mind handling them," she said as she examined the worm, "I just don't like the idea of impaling them." She cringed. "I can almost hear *that one* screaming."

"Here, I'll do it," Evan said. "Any girl brave enough to take the plunge down Harmon's Hill deserves a little mercy. That took a lot of courage. Maybe I'll write a song about you."

"Oh, I see, now you're a songwriter." Katie smiled and elbowed him playfully.

Evan gave her a wink and handed her the pole. "Okay, all you have to do is swing that little weight toward that open spot over there. Try to land it in the center so it doesn't get hung up on the lily pads. It's about four feet deep there, so I got your bobber set to put that worm about a foot off the bottom."

Katie stood, grabbed one of the upright branches for balance, flipped the line out, and gingerly sat back down. The bobber immediately began to dance across the surface of the water, moving in small circles.

"I think I got one!" She nudged Evan, who was busy baiting the other pole.

"Nope, only minnows playing with it, taking little bites. They'll clean that hook eventually, but it'll take them some time. You'll know when one of those big bluegills shows up at the dinner table, and when he does, you'd better be holding onto that pole or it'll be in the drink."

Katie laid the pole across her lap, clutching it firmly in her left hand. "How did you know about this place?"

"My dad brought me here when I was little. He wasn't really that into fishing, but he liked being outdoors. I don't remember ever catching many fish. Most of the time I just sat and listened while he talked. He always seemed to have something to say."

"About what?" Katie said.

"Mostly about doing something with your life. He said

most people just stumble along waiting for something good to happen. Then, before they know it, they're out of time, kind of like a balloon that shoots around the room in every direction until it runs out of air. Then it just lays there."

"Maybe he was trying to teach you stuff, things that were important to him, things that *he* had learned," Katie said.

"Actually, there were times when I felt like he wasn't talking to me at all. More like he was talking to himself and I just happened to be there."

"Do you think he was happy?" Katie said.

"I guess so. He was rarely in a bad mood, and he didn't complain much. We were having dinner at a restaurant one night, and the waiter came to the table and whispered something to him. The next thing I know, he was on the stage singing. I remember how proud I was, seeing my dad up there, everyone standing and applauding. I didn't even know he could sing like that. When he came back to the table, I knew he was happy. I could tell by the look on his face."

"My grandma said that when you think of someone who's passed, it's because they're with you, trying to lift your spirits, protecting you," Katie said, leaned close, and whispered into his ear, "I think he's sitting right there next to you." She kissed him lightly on the cheek.

Evan put his arm around her and pressed his forehead gently against hers, looked directly into her eyes and said, "What would you say if I asked you to be my girl, Katie *blue eyes?*"

She smiled sweetly. "I'd say you just made your first catch of the day."

"Quick, give it a tug," Evan said as they watched the bobber disappear under a lily pad.

Katie grabbed the pole and jerked it skyward. The bluegill shot into the air, did a double backflip and landed in Evan's lap.

"I have to say, that wasn't the smoothest landing, but it got the job done," he said, pulled the hook from the fish's mouth, and held it at arm's length. "Nice fish. A few more like this and Grandma Bea will be heating up the frying pan."

"You got one on *your* line, Evan," Katie said as they watched the entire shaft of the bobber disappear. A few seconds later, it popped up and shot across the water like the mast of a tiny sailboat.

"*You* pull it in . . . gently this time," Evan said. "I'll bait the other line."

From that point on, they caught gobs of fish, Katie deftly handling the pole, Evan baiting the hook. In just under an hour, with a short break for egg-salad, they caught twenty-one bluegills.

Katie watched as Evan dropped the stringer of fish into the water-soaked burlap sack, wrapped it in a small tarp and tied it to the carrier of his bike.

"Onward!" Evan said as he climbed onto his bike.

It was that utterance that brought her back to the now and the realization that, despite the challenge it had presented on the way down, Harmon's Hill might now be an even more formidable obstacle. She pointed her bike toward the grove of box elders, threw her leg over the seat, her eyes tracing the steep path, bottom to top, and pushed off.

"Where are you going?" Evan said.

She stopped and looked over her shoulder. Evan's bike was pointed in the opposite direction. She looked at him quizzically. "That would be *my* question," Katie replied.

"I don't know about you, but after a hard day of fishing I'm not up for a climb like that," Evan said and nodded toward Harmon's Hill. "How about we go that way?" He pointed toward a tree line about a hundred yards from where they stood. "There's an old tractor road just beyond those trees that'll take us straight over to Route 1."

"You're telling me there's another way in and out of here?" she said.

"If I had brought you in *that way*, you would have missed out on all the fun," Evan said and made a rollercoaster-motion with his hand and forearm.

She stood there straddling her bike, put a hand on her hip, and said in a scolding tone, "It looks like I'm going to have to stay on my toes around you, Evan Mason."

While they rode along, Evan told Katie about Riley Winslow, the same story he had told his grandmother, only this time it took a lot longer to tell. Grandma Bea had listened quietly, while Katie interrupted numerous times with questions, the same questions that had come to Evan's mind when Mr. O'Malley had told him the story.

"That's terrible," Katie said. "Maybe he'll get better."

"I don't think that's likely. Mr. O'Malley said he's been that way for almost twenty years. Nothing's changed much," Evan said.

"It must be hard having all that ability and knowing that you'll never be able to use it. What a waste. Like being a bird in a cage," Katie said.

"Except I don't think Riley *knows* he can fly. It's like, 'what you don't know can't hurt you' or 'you don't miss what you never had,' that sort of thing."

"Yeah, or someone who's really good at something and gives it up for the wrong reasons," Katie said, looked at Evan with raised eyebrows.

"I get it . . . and I'm thinking about it, Katie Blue," Evan said and glanced at her. "I *am* thinking about it."

17

Evan gave a hand signal to Katie, veered into the alley, made a quick right turn through the Dairy Queen parking lot, then darted across Gable Street to the park.

Donnie Jones and two younger boys were sitting on the merry-go-round watching a teenage girl twirl a hula-hoop around her waist while she belted out the lyrics to "Rock Around the Clock."

"Hey!" Donnie shouted when he saw Evan and Katie. He trotted over to meet them. "Where you guys been?"

"Harmon's Pond," Evan replied.

"How'd you do?" Donnie said, snooping around Evan's bike.

"Caught a stringer-full of bluegills and a couple of small bass," Evan said.

"Did you use red worms, like I told you?" Donnie said.

"Yep. You know your stuff, Donnie," Evan said and patted him on the back.

"And, guess who took the plunge today?" Katie said and smiled broadly.

"Harmon's hill?" Donnie said, mouth agape.

"Yep, and at full throttle, too," Evan said.

"No way! It took Beans three shots before he made it to the bottom," Donnie said. "The first time, he ended up in a patch of poison ivy and was itching for a week. I can't wait to razz him. Beat by a girl."

"You want to arm wrestle?" Katie said and flexed a bicep.

"You'd better not, Donnie," Evan said. "She'll probably take you," They all laughed. "Who are they?" Evan said and pointed to the two boys sitting on the merry-go-round.

"Oh, Mutt and Jeff? They're my cousins. Got stuck babysitting. I tried to sneak out the back door, but my mom nailed me before I made it halfway across the yard. I got a half a buck in my pocket, but believe me, takin' care of two second-graders, it ain't worth it." He looked back at Evan. "You gonna hang around for a while? Richie said he was coming by later. He got in big trouble at church last Sunday."

"What happened?" Evan said.

"He slipped a whoopee-cushion under the pillow on Mrs. Shauff's organ bench. He said when she plopped that giant keester down, the fart sound was so loud Pastor Nelson nearly jumped through the roof. Now, his dad's got him painting the garage."

They had a good laugh.

"We can't hang around today," Evan said. "Got to get those fish home before they go south. I've got them wrapped in—"

There was a scream. Everyone turned and saw two boys engaged in some sort of fracas with the Hula-hoop girl. One of them was Gary Ritter, a sophomore at Wabash Valley High, at least he had been until he was expelled midway through the second semester.

The other kid, Ritter's companion for the day, was scrawny and his sandy-colored hair was cut so close that in the sunlight he looked utterly bald. Evan didn't know his real name, but he had heard kids call him "Froggy." Not a hard one to figure, as he had protruding eyes accentuated by thick horn-rimmed glasses. Froggy was a sixth-grader at Jefferson Elementary.

"Now, don't get all frisky on me, honey buns," Ritter said. He had a tight grip on the orange plastic hoop, and whenever the girl tried to duck under and escape, he would give a sharp tug, sending her reeling like one of the cars on the tilt-o-whirl. "Gimme a little smooch, honey buns." He puckered his lips and made a smacking sound, pecking at her like a chicken would an ear of corn. She was straining against the plastic hoop, arching her back to stay as far away from him as she could, struggling to keep her balance.

Gary Ritter wasn't a big kid. He was actually short for fifteen. It was probably the reason he hung around with younger kids. It empowered him, boosted his ego. Ritter was wearing faded Levi's over a pair of black leather engineer boots. The square-toed "shit-kickers" were the in-thing with all the would-be hoods. Apparently, they thought it bolstered their tough-guy façade. Of course, in Ritter's case, they served a dual purpose, the thick heels boosting his height by a good two inches. The short sleeves of the white tee-shirt he wore were rolled up several turns, and a wide fold on the left sleeve created a pouch for his cigarettes. With his pasty white, pimpled face and slicked-back hair, he looked like a character one might see darting around the screen during the Bijou's Saturday afternoon cartoon marathon.

Ritter had already been arrested several times, one of which resulted in a period of incarceration; a state trooper caught him in the act of scattering a keg of roofing nails across a heavily traveled stretch of Route 33. He had pulled the same stunt a week earlier, rendering tragic results. A family of five traveling cross-country pulling their brand-new trailer had rolled through the minefield of nails at sixty miles-per-hour, blew a front tire on the car and another on the trailer almost simultaneously. The entire family was injured, with the youngest child sustaining head trauma and barely surviving.

When Gary Ritter stood before the presiding judge and told him that he had done the dastardly deed because he was bored, the judge said, "Son, I think I can help you with that problem," and forthwith sentenced him to sixty days in Fairfax County Reformatory for Boys. Upon his release, a group of parents had petitioned the school board to bar him from returning to WVHS.

"Come on, Ritter, let her go. You're scaring her," Evan said in a firm, yet pleading tone.

Ritter shot a glance at Evan, then turned back to the girl. "You ain't scared, are you, honey buns?" The girl looked terrified. "Still waiting for that kiss," he said and smacked his lips at her a couple of more times.

Froggy smiled and applauded, glancing at Evan gloatingly.

Let her go, pilgrim, you've had your fun. Evan had no idea why that particular phrase popped into his head. Maybe it was a line retrieved from some remote ammo dump in his brain, a bank of dialogue, *perhaps from one of those old westerns on the late-night movie show.*

Surprisingly, the words he had loaded into the breech weren't the words subsequently discharged from the muzzle. What he shouted was, "Let her go, *ass-wipe,* you've had your fun!" *Not the smartest thing I could have said,* Evan thought, but it had certainly elicited the desired response.

Ritter released the Hula-hoop, sending the girl flying across the lawn into a bed of petunias. She righted herself and sat there for a few seconds, then jumped to her feet and tore down the street, arms flailing, tears streaming down her cheeks. Everyone watched as she turned the corner and disappeared from view—everyone but Ritter. He stood motionless, staring at the ground. Suddenly, like a coiled snake that had been poked with a stick, he whipped his head around and glared. "What did you say?" he said and tromped toward Evan.

"Oh shit, we're in trouble now," Donnie muttered and sidled toward Katie.

"You got a death wish?" Ritter said, his voice at least an octave higher than before. Ritter jammed the heels of his palms into Evan's chest, driving him backward. Evan tried to hold his ground, but Ritter continued to advance. Ritter was several inches taller than Evan, and the thick paunch around his midsection gave him considerably more bulk. With the third shove, Evan tumbled over a border of hedges and landed on his back in a pile of woodchips.

Ritter took a couple of steps toward Evan, then stopped in midstride, sniffing the air like a fox in the barnyard.

"Am I smelling fish?" he said. He sniffed his way over to Evan's bike and began tugging at the ropes around the tarp. "Well, lookie here." He dangled the stringer at arm's length. "Nice mess." He looked at Evan. "You catch these?"

"We both did," Katie interjected, seemingly trying to divert Ritter's attention away from Evan.

"Well . . ." Ritter said, eying Katie from head to toe, "I'll bet you didn't even have to drop a line into the water, pretty as you are. Those fish probably jumped right into your lap. I know *I* wouldn't mind jumping into your lap," he said and gave Froggy a long, exaggerated wink. "You know what kind of fish these are?" he said, directing his question to Katie.

"Bluegill," Katie said.

"Wrong! These are flyin' fish." He whipped the stringer overhead several times bolas style and flung it into one of the crab trees. "I don't know about you, Froggy, but I never seen the likes of that before. I seen a horsefly, but I ain't never seen a fish fly." He laughed wildly.

"You're disgusting!" Katie shouted.

"I'm sorry. That wasn't a very gentlemanly thing for me to do," Ritter said, wiping his hands on his jeans.

Evan was on his feet now, glaring at Ritter.

"Tell you what," Ritter said and stepped toward Katie. "I'm going to show you I'm not the cold-hearted jerk you think I am." He grabbed Katie's wrist, wrapped an arm around her waist, and dragged her toward the crab tree. "I'm gonna boost your sweet little ass up that tree so you can get your fish."

Evan flew through the air like he'd been shot from a cannon. His arms were locked around Ritter's waist as they went down. Ritter landed on top, and before Evan could scramble free, Ritter drew his legs up under him, pinning Evan's shoulders to the ground. At that moment, Evan felt as though someone had dumped a load of cement onto his chest.

"What you gonna do now, dickhead?" Ritter said. He slapped Evan, one side of his face, then the other.

Froggy was standing just a few feet away, simply watching the scene unfold. Donnie was attending to Katie. She'd been knocked off balance by the force of Evan's tackle and had ended up on her back.

"Free slaps for everyone," Ritter shouted to a couple of young boys passing by. "Hey, get your free slaps!" Both boys gave nervous glances, then hustled on down the sidewalk. "Okay, Froggy, looks like nobody else wants to get in on the fun. Get over here and get your whacks in," Ritter said in a commanding tone.

Froggy hesitated momentarily, then moved warily toward the two.

Evan's face, already peppered with reddish splotches from Ritter's slaps, turned totally crimson when he saw the scrawny kid approaching. At that moment, an irrepressible fury washed over him. He could hear Sergeant Gus's words echoing in his brain—*a strong gust of wind, and they're in tatters*. With a sudden arching of his legs and back, he threw Ritter off and was on him, pummeling him. There was a discernible crunch as Evan's fist slammed into Ritter's nose. Blood immediately began to gush from both nostrils. Instinctively, Ritter threw his hands in front of his face as a flurry of punches came from every angle.

Evan was relentless.

"Froggy! Help! Fro—" Ritter shouted, but his plea was interrupted by a solid punch that caught him square on the jaw.

Donnie looked around and spotted Froggy hightailing it across the A&P parking lot about a block south. It seemed quite unlikely he would be joining the one-sided fracas anytime soon.

Katie grabbed Evan's arm just as he was cocking it to deliver another blow. "That's enough, Evan. Enough," she said, tugging on his arm. Evan stood over Ritter, both fists still clenched.

Ritter lay there for several seconds, then rose to one knee, coughed a couple of times, and wiped his mouth with the back of his hand. There was blood dripping from his nose and the corner of his mouth as he stood and staggered toward the sidewalk. He looked back over his shoulder. "You're not—"

"Don't say another word, Ritter," Evan said, his jaw tightening, his fists clenched.

Ritter turned and walked off. He didn't look back.

Katie had gotten a cup of ice from the Dairy Queen, wrapped several cubes in a cloth, and was holding it against Evan's face. There was a bruise above his left eyebrow and a scratch on the bridge of his nose.

"Look out below," Donnie said, dangling briefly from the lower limb, then dropping to the ground with the stringer. He rewrapped the fish and tied them to the carrier of the Phantom.

"Thanks, Donnie. I never saw anybody climb a tree like that. You sure you're not part squirrel?" Evan said.

"I didn't know you could fight like that. You sure *you're* not part tiger? That Froggy punk looked like he was going to wet his pants when you tore into Ritter. I don't think we'll be seeing either of them around for a while," Donnie said.

"You come over tomorrow. I'll ask Grandma Bea to fry those fish up for lunch," Evan said.

"Sounds good to me," Donnie said. "Let's go, you two." Mutt and Jeff came running over. Donnie took them by the hand and they headed down Gable Street. As they walked,

Donnie said something to one of the boys, who looked back at Evan and shouted, "See you later, tiger!"

"You *were* pretty amazing, Mr. Mason," Katie said as she climbed onto her bike. "A man of many talents. What's next? I find out you have x-ray vision and can leap tall buildings in a single bound?"

When Evan arrived home, Grandma Bea greeted him at the door. He was sure she would quiz him immediately on the bruise and scratches, but when she saw the stringer of fish, the conversation kicked off in a different direction.

By the time he told her about the deer, Katie's conquest of Harmon's Hill, and Richie's whoopee-cushion stunt, she was cleaning the fish and only half listening to his abridged account of the Ritter incident. That was exactly what he had hoped for. *She didn't need anything more to worry about,* he thought.

Evan had filled the deep claw-foot bathtub to the top with water as hot as he could tolerate and lay submerged to his chin. Now and then he would duck his head completely under water and hold his breath. The steaming water felt good. He had several bruises, one on his lower back and a couple on his right shoulder.

Probably when ass-wipe landed on me, he thought.

He toweled off, put on his pajamas, and dabbed his face with Clearasil to hide the marks. He was reasonably sure

Grandma Bea wouldn't notice them, but he didn't want to risk resurrecting the subject.

As he descended the stairs he could see the flickering light from the television. The living room windows were wide open and when he reached the lower landing he could feel a cool breeze filtering through the screens.

Grandma Bea placed his dinner on a TV tray, and he ate while they watched their shows.

It wasn't long before Grandma Bea began dozing off. Evan woke her with a gentle nudge, and of course, each time he did, she would tell him she was "just resting her eyes."

Finally, when she was jolted awake by the volley of gunfire in the *Colt .45* introduction, she decided it was time to retire for the evening.

He loved those evenings with Grandma Bea.

It was good just knowing she was there.

18

——

At noon the next day, Evan sat at the kitchen table watching as his grandmother dipped the fillets in milk and coated them with flour and cornmeal seasoned with herbs and spices fresh from her garden. He listened while she told one of her stories. This recollection was of Walter, during the "lean years," as she referred to them.

"We had ordered a gas burning stove through the mail-order catalog," Beatrice said. "Most folks were still cooking on wood-burners at the time, so I couldn't have been more excited when it finally arrived. There was only one problem. It wouldn't fit through the door. As you might imagine, your grandfather wasn't too happy about that. He had put in extra hours to pay for it and now he would be spending his only day off tearing down a wall to get it into the kitchen. He started right after breakfast, and by the time he finished, it was almost midnight. I didn't think he would ever forgive me for that little escapade, but a day or two later I fried up a big platter of fish on that cast-iron beauty, the same recipe I'm making for you today, and by the time he finished that meal, all was forgiven. Of course, I never told him that I had known all along that stove wasn't going to fit through that door." Beatrice chuckled and gave Evan a little wink.

His grandmother had a knack for storytelling, and ordinarily, the tale would have spawned a dozen questions, but at that moment Evan had something else on his mind.

He looked into the living room, at the piano parked against the far wall, the one his father had played as a child. The piano was sixty years old, but it was in pristine condition. Beatrice had taken good care of it, having it tuned regularly.

The most recent tuning had been done two days before Evan arrived. He knew that because he had seen the bill from Hilltop Melody Mart atop a stack of sheet music Grandma Bea had retrieved from a box in the hall closet and placed conspicuously on the table beside the piano; they were some of her favorite pieces. *Her way of guiding me back to my music,* he thought.

"Grandma."

"Yes, dear?" Beatrice said, lifting the lid from the pan of potatoes cooking on the back burner. There was the sound of sizzling grease, and the smell of bacon and onions filled the kitchen. She gave the mixture a couple of quick stirs, replaced the lid, and went back to battering the fish.

Evan opened his mouth, seemingly poised to speak, but instead gave a long sigh.

Beatrice paused and looked at him. "Go ahead, Evan, spit it out. I'm a woman of many talents, but mind-reading isn't one of them."

"I probably shouldn't even be asking this, especially after you bought me the new bike and everything, but I, uh . . ."

"I know there's something important rattling around in that head of yours. I just hope I find out what it is before the good Lord calls me home."

"Well, I know money is tight right now, but I was thinking, maybe I'd like to start taking piano lessons again. I don't know what Miss Coplin charges these days, and whether she'd even take me back, but I was hoping—"

"First of all, what makes you think your grandma's hurting for money? You may not be aware of it, but this old lady always has a little extra squirreled away. I'll give Miss Coplin a call this very afternoon."

"I just didn't want to—"

Beatrice interrupted again. "In Beatrice Mason's world, there's always money for the important things in life, and your music falls into that category. You concentrate on the piano. I'll handle the finances in this operation." She walked over and planted a kiss on Evan's forehead. "Now, not another word about it."

"Thanks, Grandma."

Beatrice ladled several scoops of Crisco into a large cast-iron frying pan and said, "I hope your friends are on time. Don't want to have to reheat anything."

"That was great, Mrs. Mason, you're a really good cook," Donnie said.

There was one hefty piece of bluegill remaining on the platter.

"Why don't you have that last piece, Donnie," Beatrice said.

"I'm stuffed. I can't eat another bite," Donnie said.

"Go ahead, Donnie," Evan said. "You earned it. If you hadn't shinnied up that tree, that stringer would still be hanging there."

"It *would* be a shame to let it go to waste," Donnie said and speared it with his fork.

Beatrice grabbed a potholder and opened the oven door. The smell of persimmon pudding enveloped the kitchen. "We'll let this cool for a minute while I whip up a little topping." She began pulling things from the fridge. "What time does your show start?"

"Two o'clock, but we want to be there by one-thirty to get some good seats," Katie said.

There was a knock.

Evan went to the door. "Riley, come on in," Evan said and swung the screen door open. "This is Riley Winslow, everybody."

Riley hesitated briefly, smiled, and stepped into the kitchen. He was wearing gray trousers and a crisply pressed light-blue cotton shirt. His dark wavy hair was parted on the side and neatly combed. There was the robust fragrance of Old Spice aftershave.

"Glad to meet you, Mr. Winslow. I'm Evan's grandmother, Beatrice. You're just in time for dessert."

"Everyone calls me Riley, Mrs. Mason."

"Alright, Riley. Please, sit down there at the table. Don't be bashful now. There's plenty to go around," Beatrice said.

"I'm Katie. I live just around the corner," Katie said and offered her hand.

"Pleased to meet you, Katie. I'm Riley." When he shook her hand it completely disappeared.

"Donnie Jones," Donnie said. Riley made *his* hand disappear as well.

"Evan tells me you used to play baseball, Riley," Beatrice said as she plated a slice of pudding and piled on a mountain of whipped cream.

Riley nodded. "That was a long time ago. I was younger then. Would you like to see a picture?" Riley pulled a wallet from his hip pocket, flipped it open, and handed it to Beatrice.

Beatrice studied the photograph thoughtfully. The yellowed and worn photo showed Riley wearing a baseball uniform. He was flanked by a man and woman and there was a crowd in the background.

"That's my mother and father with me. They're in heaven now," Riley said.

"They were a handsome couple," Beatrice said and passed the photo to Katie, who shared it with Evan and Donnie, then handed it back to Riley.

He looked at the picture briefly, folded the wallet and

tucked it away. "I don't remember much about that time. It hurts when I try."

Everyone sat quietly until Beatrice broke the silence. "Okay, grab a spoon." She placed a tray in the center of the table. "I know you're stuffed, Donnie, but try to make room."

"Maybe just a small piece," Donnie said and scooped up the largest serving on the tray.

"I think Riley should come to the show with us today," Katie said.

"Good idea. You like movies, Riley?" Evan said.

"I used to go to the movies, but not so much anymore," Riley said and devoured a spoonful of pudding.

"This one's about a guy who flies an airplane across the Atlantic Ocean all by himself, way back in 1927," Evan said.

"You remember that, Riley?" Donnie asked.

Riley thought for a few seconds and said, "No, but I like stories about airplanes."

19

———

As it was most Saturday afternoons, the Bijou was packed. They had arrived early enough to grab seats in the middle section, about halfway back. Riley had the aisle seat, Evan beside him, then Katie. Donnie reluctantly agreed to sit with Richie, who had finally finished painting the garage and arrived five minutes before the show started; they were stuck in the last row.

The first movie was about a man who was smacked in the face by a cloud of radioactive dust and began slowly shrinking to the size of a gnat. *A bit far-fetched,* Evan thought, *but exciting, nonetheless.*

Tucked between movies were three cartoons and a newsreel on how to prepare for a nuclear attack. Russia's testing of an atomic bomb a few years earlier had touched off an arms race and cast a blanket of fear over the entire world. The first half of the film instructed people on the fundamentals of constructing a sturdy, well-stocked bomb shelter. The second half featured a cartoon turtle named Bert who lectured kids on the duck-and-cover, an ill-conceived maneuver to ensure that students were crouched under their desks with their hands clasped around their heads when the nuclear blast reduced them to ash.

The film also provided details on where a citizen could go to sign up to be a Civil Defense warden. People who volunteered received a plastic helmet, an armband and a page of instructions outlining their duties should Russia one day decide to drop the "big one." It was a well-intended strip of celluloid, but, unwittingly, it probably scared the bejesus out of most of the kids in the audience, and a good number of the adults as well.

The second movie, *The Spirit of St. Louis*, told the story of Charles A. Lindbergh, the first man to fly solo across the Atlantic. The movie had several lively scenes presented in the form of flashbacks, but for the most part, it was a dramatic portrayal of Lindbergh's agonizing ocean crossing with a lot of soliloquy and not much action.

There was still twenty-minutes-of-film left on the reel when Evan looked around and saw that the Bijou had emptied out considerably. Most of the adults were still in their seats, but a good number of the kids, including Donnie and Richie, had bailed early.

Evan found the story compelling. He looked at Katie, who also appeared to be watching intently. He leaned in and whispered, "What do you think, Katie Blue?"

"Good movie," she said softly, "and I think someone else likes it, too." She pointed a thumb at Riley, who appeared mesmerized, his eyes riveted to the screen. Now and then, without altering his gaze, he would cram a handful of popcorn into his mouth.

Later, as the Spirit of St. Louis settled on the runway at Le Bourget, Evan felt Katie's soft kiss on his cheek.

"I'll love you 'til the day I die, Evan Mason," she whispered and gently squeezed his hand.

20

——

The following Monday Evan had gone to Will's Barbershop for a haircut. There were four men waiting when Evan sat down in one of the two remaining chairs.

"Well, what's the verdict, Will?" the man in the barber chair said. "Does she have a bun in the oven or not?"

Will Johnson was looking through the bottoms of his glasses, trimming the man's thick gray mustache with a small electric clipper. "Damn it, Clyde!" Will said. "Can't you quit talking for two minutes? I just took a chunk out of the left side of this muff-duster of yours and now I'm going to have to make another pass to even it out. This is like whacking my way through sagebrush. Now, shut your pie hole and sit still, or from now on you'll have to break out the hedge clippers and have the little woman do you."

Evan watched as Clyde struck a rigid pose and Will plowed through the man's whiskers, the clippers sounding as though they were on the verge of overheating and crapping out any second.

"There," Will said, "now that wasn't so hard, was it? I knew you had it in you." Clyde stepped out of the chair, adjusting one of the straps on the bib overalls he was wearing, while Will grabbed a broom and began collecting the pile of wiry gray hair at his feet. "I'd say you got your money's worth today, Clyde."

"So, what do you think, is Ginger gonna have some explaining to do when the old man gets back to the homestead?" Clyde said, picking up the conversation where he'd left off.

"Word is, she's been taking a lot of sick days of late and appears to be getting a little thick in the engine room," Will said.

"Well, all I can say is, if that Stinson boy is responsible, he'd better join the Army himself, because when Corporal P. R. Oakley comes back from that jungle to find his little Ginger with a baby hanging on one of those exquisite boobs of hers, there's gonna be hell to pay," Clyde said, as he moved to the second barber chair and sat down.

The man sitting beside Evan said, "C'mon, Clyde." He nodded toward Evan. "Let's clean the conversation up a bit. What do you say?"

"Sorry, son. Didn't see you there," Clyde said, then leaned toward Will and muttered, "I'm bettin' he's heard worse."

Will rolled his eyes and said, "How 'bout those Cubs?

The way they're playing right now, they'll be lucky to finish fifteen games back."

"*Fifteen?*" Clyde said. "My money says it's closer to *twenty*. The young fella I feel sorry for is Ernie Banks. The kid's playin' his ass off every game and he can't get any help . . ."

The men talked baseball for the next half hour.

Will had just lathered Evan's neck and was strapping the razor when a man streaked by the shop on a bicycle. He was wearing a beat-up brown leather jacket, khaki trousers, and an old pair of amber-lensed goggles. A five-feet-long span of cardboard covered with tin-foil was attached with twists of wire, like a wing, to the bicycle's handlebars. A similarly fashioned tail adorned the rear fender. A playing card was clamped onto the rear fender strut with a clothespin.

Everyone in the shop watched as the man circled the town square, finally stopping at the drinking fountain on the corner across the street. He bent over and took a drink.

"Who the hell is that?" Clyde said, peering out between the two stuffed pheasants suspended by lengths of cord in the plate glass window.

"That, my friend, is your proverbial village idiot, Riley Winslow. He came in for a haircut about a week ago," Will said, "and the minute he opened his mouth, I knew there was something not quite right with the man. I'm trying to talk a little baseball with him, who was going to be in the World Series this year, that sort of thing, and he immediately begins spouting off about how he used to play the game himself.

Needless to say, I was a bit skeptical, but I decided to play along. I ask him what position he played, and he says, 'all of them.'"

One of the patrons said, "Maybe he was just pulling your leg."

"That's what I was pressing to find out, so I decided to give the man the benefit of the doubt, thinking maybe he's talking high school ball or something along those lines," Will said. "I asked him what was the biggest game he ever played in, and what do you think he said?"

"What?" Clyde said, wide-eyed.

"'When I hit a game-winning homer off Hilton Smith,'" Will said.

"Wasn't Smith a right-hander in the Negro League?" Clyde asked.

"Kansas City Monarchs, I believe. Played with Satchel Paige," another man interjected.

"Of course, when I start pressing him on the details, he said it was a long time ago and he can't remember much," Will said. "Evidently, Mr. Winslow lives with his aunt up at the old Phillips house. George Phillips was the woman's uncle. When George croaked back in June, he left the property to her." Will chuckled and nodded toward Riley, who was flying back and forth in front of the shop. "Babe Ruth, there, was living somewhere near Chicago before he moved in with her."

"So, you're thinking he's lost all his marbles?" Clyde said.

"Let's just say, after seeing him in action today, I got a

strong feeling there aren't many aggies left in the bag," Will said.

Will unfastened the paper band around Evan's neck and, with his trusty duster, engulfed him in a cloud of talcum powder. Evan hopped down from the chair coughing, trying to keep from choking.

"Hold it, son." Will splashed a little Jeris tonic into his palm and rubbed it into Evan's hair, massaging it vigorously into his scalp. He ran a stiff-bristled brush through the sculpted hair, closed one eye, and sighted across the flattop like a sniper with a rifle. He grabbed his scissors, snipped a small tuft that had evaded his clippers, gave Evan a pat on the back of his head, and said, "*Now* you're good to go, son. Nobody walks out of Will Johnson's barbershop without a peek and a tweak."

Evan dug into his pocket for the fifty-cent piece and handed the coin to Will.

"Riley's not crazy, Mr. Johnson," Evan said. "I know him. He was in a bad accident."

"Well, I just tell it as I see it, my boy . . . as I see it," Will said.

Evan stepped toward the screen door. As he pushed it open, Riley zipped toward the shop on his bicycle, snapping a crisp salute to the edge of his goggles.

"I shall not stop until my mission is complete!" Riley shouted over the ratcheting wail of his playing-card engine.

He veered off and sped away, the silver wings of his fabricated plane flapping in the breeze.

The patrons had all collected at the window to witness the spectacle.

Evan glanced at Will, who shrugged and said, "I rest my case." He gave the chair a quick three-hundred-sixty-degree spin. "Next victim, please."

21

———

Agent Michael Traxler shoveled the last bite of ham steak into his mouth along with a smidgen of toast covered with over-easy egg yolk. He pushed his plate away and stared at the small yellowed sign taped to the back-counter wall that read: HENWAYS – $1.00.

I'm supposed to ask, what's a Henway? he thought. *The waitress will say something like . . . about three pounds, fully dressed, then smile and wink at me. Not falling for that old gag.*

"Got a fresh pot brewing, honey. Be there in a flash," the waitress with the big orange hair shouted, in a voice so shrill Traxler expected every glass in the joint to shatter.

A half-hour ago the diner had been full. Now, except for the old gentleman working a crossword puzzle at a table near the window, Traxler was the only patron remaining.

Finally, the waitress descended upon him with a steaming pot of coffee and began dumping it into the cup on the counter in front of him. There were several chips in the white porcelain, and a brown-stained crack ran from the handle to the brim, pretty much the same cup he had found in every truck stop since he left Chicago.

He looked at the nameplate pinned to her uniform and said, "You been working here long, Abby?"

"Since I was sixteen. Gone through four owners, two remodelings, and three boyfriends in that time." Abby was slender, well proportioned, and despite the orange hair, a reasonably attractive woman in her forties.

"So, about ten years, huh?" Traxler said.

"You keep up that kind of talk, sweetie, and you could be number four," she said and winked.

Traxler was thirty-five years old. He had blue eyes, sandy-colored hair, and stood six-one, the kind of guy most women swooned over. He smiled at Abby and said, "Before we move on to that, I'm wondering if you could help me out with some information?"

"Are you a detective of some sort?" Abby said.

"Agent Michael Traxler, FBI." He showed her his I.D.

"Abby Garner," she said. "The second I saw you, I had a feeling you were a lawman. You have that look . . . like your mind is working overtime. You know what I mean?"

He nodded. "I'm looking for a young woman by the name of Irene Sanford. Sometimes goes by the name Rena." He took an envelope from the breast pocket of his jacket, removed three photographs and handed them to Abby.

"Is she a runaway?"

"Just a teenager wanting to visit a friend and not willing to take no for an answer," Traxler said. "We're not sure how she would have been dressed. These photos were taken over a span of about eighteen months." He pointed to one of the photographs. "This one is the most recent. She's sixteen here."

Abby studied the photograph. "I *do* remember her." She pondered awhile and said, "She came in around two-thirty, looking for a ride. The place was empty at the time, just a couple of kids sitting in the corner booth having ice cream." Abby glanced at the calendar on the wall. "It'll be four weeks ago tomorrow."

"You're positive about the day?" Traxler said.

"I know it was a Wednesday. It's the day Mrs. Olivia Kelly takes that fancy car of hers in for a wax job, then drives south to visit her sister. She comes by every month, rain or shine. Always orders a cup of tea, then heads to Andy's Auto Salon just down the road a bit," Abby said and nodded. "She sits there and drinks her tea while they clean and polish that big Cadillac of hers. When they're done, she gives it the old white glove test. You know what I mean. If you ask me, that's why her old man left her. He realized that car was more important to her than he was. Anyway, before Olivia left for Andy's, she offered to give the girl a ride. The girl sat down on that bench out front to wait and—"

"I think I get it, Miss Garner," Traxler said, growing noticeably agitated with the breadth of the conversation. "Mrs. Kelly gave the girl a ride. Is that what you're trying to—"

Abby threw a finger into the air. "That's not quite the way things unfolded. As it turned out, the service wasn't to Olivia's liking, so the whole thing was taking forever. I could tell the girl was getting a bit antsy. Next thing I know, she pokes her head in and tells me to thank Mrs. Kelly for her, but she had decided to accept another ride."

"You saw her leave?" Traxler said.

"Not exactly. The phone rang a second later, and I got a bit distracted. It was a dark-colored pickup truck. That's about all I can tell you. I caught a glimpse of it as it pulled away. Couldn't see who was in it, but I'm assuming she was in that truck."

"Any other thoughts on the pickup?" Traxler said.

She shook her head. "There are a lot like that around here." Abby had been stuffing flimsy white paper napkins into the stainless-steel holders that lined the counter. She paused, appearing to be deep in thought. "The girl isn't related to those folks up in Chicago, is she? The *bigwig* politician. Whatshisname?" Abby said.

"Joseph Sanford, the alderman," Traxler said. "He's her father."

"You suspect something bad has happened to her?" Abby said.

"We don't know. Let's just say, the FBI wouldn't even be involved at this point if she wasn't Sanford's daughter," Traxler said.

"This isn't going to help the situation around these parts, you know that, don't you?" Abby said. She pointed to the poster on the wall adjacent to the door. It was the Connie Winters poster. "People are already on pins and needles, especially those folks with kids."

"That's why I'm asking you to keep this conversation to yourself. I know it's asking a lot, but I think at this point it would be best. Think of it as an act of community service," Traxler said and patted her arm. "You think you can do that for me?"

Abby nodded. "I'm not like those busy-bodies around here. I know when to keep my trap shut."

Traxler had his doubts about that.

Later that same day, Traxler sat in the lobby of the Dixmoore Hotel on the Laurenville town square, scribbling on a notepad, the phone receiver pressed against his ear.

"I have your party on the line, Mr. Traxler. Go ahead," the operator said.

"Sophie, you there?" Traxler said.

"Yes, Trax, I'm here," Sophie Denton replied. Sophie had been with the FBI's Chicago office for a little less than two years, her first job fresh from college. She had received two promotions in that short time and was making a name for herself as one of the Bureau's top criminologists. "Are you making any progress?"

"It's slow going. Still nothing material as of yet," Traxler said. "Sophie, I need you to focus on that stretch of Route 1 we mapped out, same east and west boundaries, but let's constrict the northern and southern perimeters, say a total of sixty miles," Traxler said.

"Hold on a second, let me grab the map . . . okay, that would put the bottom perimeter about a mile north of Evansville. Is that what you want?" she said.

"That should work. The Jansen girl was traveling north, and the Sanford girl was headed south. Both were last sighted in that corridor," Traxler said.

"I think we should solicit *all* missing person reports. We don't have any idea what we're dealing with at this point," Sophie said. "If we restrict it to adolescent females, we may miss something. It's a rural area. I think the numbers will be manageable. If I see it's getting out of hand, I'll make some adjustments."

"Feed them to me as you get them, Sophie. One of them may point me in the right direction," Traxler said. "How's Mrs. Sanford holding up? The last time I saw her, she was a mess."

"She finally pulled herself together. Mr. Sanford is the one who's out of control. They say the Bureau Chief was receiving a phone call an hour. The mayor had to intervene to rein the man in," Sophie said.

"I can't blame him. If it were my daughter, I'd likely react the same way," Traxler said.

"Sounds like your optimism is waning on this one, Trax."

"I'm starting to get that feeling. It's working its way up from my gut. Not a good sign."

"Let's hope it's just indigestion from the road chow," Sophie said.

22

———

Evan stood on the porch of the two-story brick house looking at his reflection in the pane of the parlor window, checking his shirt to be sure it was tucked in before he rang the doorbell. He was careful to push the button only once. Miss Loretta Coplin didn't like it when someone leaned on the doorbell. She had a fastidious nature about her.

"Well, who is this young gentleman standing before me?" Loretta said as she swung the door open. She was wearing a long pale yellow skirt, white silk blouse and a string of large pearls. Her hair was dyed strawberry blonde, swept back on the sides and piled high on top with curls. Her tortoise-shell glasses hung on a braided cord around her neck, the frames adorned with a single row of rhinestones above each lens.

"Hello, Miss Coplin," Evan said as he stepped into the foyer.

"It's good to have you back, Evan," Loretta said as she led him past the wide center staircase toward the parlor.

The room was just as Evan remembered it. On the long outer wall was a fireplace flanked on either side by shelves crammed full of framed photographs and memorabilia. On the adjacent wall was a bay window with several hanging plants and a large terrarium.

Most of the hardwood floor was covered by an ornate oriental rug. In the center stood a mahogany Steinway baby grand that had been given to Loretta back in 1933 by a wealthy Hollywood movie producer who had hired Loretta to consult on one of his movies. Over two decades a relationship developed between the two that would likely have culminated in wedding bells had the man not died unexpectedly. That was the closest Loretta Coplin would ever come to marriage.

"My, my, how we've grown," Loretta said. "I remember a time when you could barely reach the latch on the gate. Sit down and tell me what you've been doing."

Evan sat on the edge of the piano bench and Loretta in the armchair beside him. While they talked, she began thumbing through a stack of sheet music, selecting several pieces and placing them on the table beside her. They discussed his mother's new job, school, his grandmother's garden, and of course, the most pressing issue.

"So, tell me, dear boy, why the change of heart? What made you decide you wanted to resume your lessons?"

"I got a harmonica for my birthday and when I play it, all I think about is how much I miss the piano," Evan said.

"I'm glad you came to that realization sooner rather than later. How are you doing with the harmonica?"

"It took me a while to get the hang of it, but I'm making a lot of progress lately. My tone is getting better and the single notes are cleaner," Evan replied.

"People often assume the mouth organ is an easy instrument to play, but they soon find out it's a bit more challenging than they thought, especially if one aspires to play it well. I hope you realize, it's your experience with the piano that made it possible for you to pick it up so quickly. That leads me to another question. Why did you abandon the piano in the first place? I know how much you missed your father, but you were making such wonderful progress. It doesn't seem like your nature to give up, Evan," she said and widened her eyes.

"When I went back to Chicago Pointe, it was hard. You weren't around and I—"

Loretta interrupted. "I find it hard to believe there aren't some talented teachers around Chicago. Not as talented as I, of course," Loretta said and smiled. "Are you sure there weren't other factors involved?"

Evan looked surprised. "What do you mean, Miss Coplin?" he said.

"Does your grandmother know your mother sold the piano she bought for you?" Loretta said.

"I, uh . . . how did you know about that, Miss Coplin?"

"I received a telephone call from a gentleman in Chicago. He had identified yours truly as the original owner of a spinet he was looking to buy and called to validate the history of the instrument. Of course, I was disappointed to hear that your mother was selling it, especially at such a bargain price, but even more distraught knowing it likely meant you were without a piano."

"My mother felt bad about having to sell it after Grandma went to all that trouble and expense to get it for me. She told me she didn't want Grandma Bea to know how tight money was."

"Well, one thing is indisputable. It's difficult to learn to play if one has no piano. Nonetheless, we have all summer to solve that problem. Now, young man, let's see what those long, somewhat bruised fingers can do on the ivories." She edged her chair a few inches closer and placed a piece of music on the rack. "And no more fisticuffs. A budding virtuoso must be protective of his hands."

Evan gave her another bewildered look.

"There isn't much going on in this town that Loretta Coplin doesn't know about, young man. I can assure you of that. Now . . . play."

For a solid thirty minutes, Evan played. Loretta would place a piece of music in front of him, then sit back in her chair, eyes closed, arms folded across her chest, and listen. Sometimes she would have him play the entire piece, other times nothing more than a passage or a few bars.

"Well, monsieur Evan, I'm tremendously impressed. Taking into consideration you haven't played for quite some time, you did well. Your rhythm sense is impeccable and your ear will be an asset to you forever. Now, with that said, don't let it go to your head. We have a lot of catching up to do, but with hard work, you can be back on track in no time."

Evan nodded and began gathering the music she had given him.

"Leave that, it's much too easy for you," she said and began searching through her stack again. She pulled three selections, placed them into a folder and handed it to him. "These will provide a challenge for you. You can't learn anything by playing something you've already mastered."

"Thank you, Miss Coplin. For taking me back, I mean," Evan said as they walked toward the door.

"All I ask is that you work hard, Evan. A talent such as yours is not to be wasted."

23

———

Shortly after noon on Friday, Evan was returning from the Parker house. It was the first time since his piano lesson he'd done much of anything but practice. Katie had gone back to Ohio to visit her grandmother, so it had seemed like the perfect time to concentrate on his music. He had been practicing several hours a day that entire week.

His mother would be arriving toward evening. She and Aunt Gladys were driving down from Chicago Pointe. This would be his mother's first visit, and Evan was looking forward to seeing her. He was sure she would be pleased with the progress he had made with his music.

Suddenly, the burning sensation under his ear began to intensify. Mrs. Parker had smeared the throbbing welts with a pasty concoction made with baking soda and a dash of camphor oil. It had taken away the itching, but not the pain.

Evan had spent the morning helping Richie in a feeble

effort to smoke out a nest of yellow jackets that had taken up residence in a hollow space above the Parker's front door. The plan was to shoot smoke into the void, then suck the little critters up with a vacuum cleaner as they exited.

Richie had assured his mother that he and Evan could handle the job. "It can't be that hard," Richie had told her. "They're just bugs."

Richie had been stung four times and Evan three before Mrs. Parker decided it was time to call the exterminator.

As he turned the corner, he spotted Gladys's car parked in front of the house.

They're early, he thought.

The pain of the wasp stings seemed to dissipate. A more pressing matter had crept into his brain, something he'd been thinking about since the last phone conversation with his mother.

He didn't want to go back to Chicago Pointe in the fall. He was tired of bouncing around. He wanted to stay with Grandma Bea, go to school in Laurenville, where his good friends were, his music teacher—a girl named Katie. The hard part would be talking to his mother about it. He didn't want to hurt her feelings.

Hopefully, he thought, *when the time was right, the words would come.*

When Evan came through the back door, Grandma Bea was

in a flowered apron, flitting around the kitchen, a spoon in one hand, a potholder in the other.

There was a bouquet of daisies in a crystal vase in the center of the white linen tablecloth that covered the dining room table. Four places were set with powder blue linen napkins and Grandma Bea's *best* dinnerware.

Lila was sitting in one of the two Victorian spoon back chairs in the parlor. Upon seeing Evan, she stood and said, "Here's the brave knight, back from his battle with the venomous little yellow dragons."

The comment caught him by surprise. His mother was an intuitive person, but as far as he knew, she didn't have any sort of telepathic skills.

"Mrs. Parker just called and gave us the rundown," Beatrice said. "She wanted to know how you were doing."

"How *are* you doing?" Lila said. "Do you need to visit a doctor?"

"No, Mother. I'm fine, just a little sore at this point," Evan said, rubbing his neck, trying to preempt any commiseration that might be headed his way. He walked over and hugged her.

"I missed you, Evan," she said. She placed her hand gently on his cheek.

"Missed you, too, Mother. I didn't expect you to be here until tonight," Evan said.

"I put in a lot of hours this week, so my boss gave me the day off," Lila said. "It worked out well. Gladys had the car gassed up last night and we were on the road at daybreak. She was elated when she realized she wouldn't have to drive after dark."

"Where *is* Aunt Gladys?" Evan said, looking around.

"Bathroom. She was feeling a bit frazzled after the trip. She needed a quick touchup," Lila said and smiled.

"I need to clean up a little myself," Evan said. He bounded up the stairs.

"There's a fresh shirt hanging on your bedroom door," Beatrice called after him.

Evan washed his hands and face, splashed on a little bay rum, *probably a bottle that Grandad had used*, he thought. *He must have bought the stuff by the case.* Evidently, Beatrice couldn't bring herself to get rid of it. There were bottles in just about every cabinet in the house.

He dabbed a smidgen of calamine lotion on the welts, put on the new plaid button-down collar shirt Grandma Bea had ordered through the Sears catalog and headed back downstairs.

Gladys was sitting in the parlor with her back to him.

"Hi, Aunt Gladys," Evan said, flanking her and firing a peck to her cheek before she had a chance to gather herself and unleash a full-frontal assault.

She turned, gave him one of her lopsided smiles, and said, "I hadn't noticed before, Evan, but you are the spitting image of your father when he was your age."

Evan wasn't sure if that was good or bad, but he took it as a compliment. He'd seen lots of early pictures of his father, and he appeared to be a fairly normal-looking kid.

"Okay, everything's ready," Beatrice said, placing the platter of pork chops on the table. "Dig right in."

During lunch, Lila talked about her trip to New York, the training she had received, people she had met, and as she put it, "the sheer grandeur of the Big Apple."

Not to be outdone, Gladys decided to provide an excruciatingly detailed description of her disastrous dinner date with Alvin Greenberg, the guy who owned the Rexall Drugstore in Chicago Pointe. By her account, not only were the oysters Rockefeller cold and her steak overcooked, but midway through dessert, Alvin developed a "dreadful headache" and was forced to cut the evening short.

Mr. Greenberg must have lost Aunt Gladys's number because, to her dismay, he hadn't called her since that first date.

Later that afternoon they sat in the parlor and looked at some of Grandma Bea's old photo albums and other memorabilia. Among them, Evan found several early tintypes. They were in a small cedar box, wrapped individually in sheets of tissue paper. One was a photograph of Grandma Bea's grandparents, taken in May of 1865 somewhere near Lebanon, Indiana. The couple had traveled by wagon for six hours simply to watch a train roll by. It was no ordinary train, however. It was the funeral train carrying Abraham Lincoln's body to its final resting place in Springfield, Illinois. At some point during the day, they had solicited the services of a local photographer who had been hawking the event. They paid ten cents for the tintype.

As Evan wrapped the thin metal plates and put them back into the box he noticed they were only slightly faded and showed few signs of wear.

Grandma Bea had taken good care of them over the years. Not surprising, he thought, *Grandma Bea took good care of everything she valued.*

It had been a long, eventful day for everyone, and by nine-thirty Beatrice and Gladys had retired. The house was dark, and Evan and his mother sat together on the front porch swing. It was a warm, clear night. There was the ever-present chirping of crickets, and a blanket of lightning bugs dotted the lawn like sprinkles on an ice cream sundae.

"So, what have you been doing besides being stung by bees?" Lila asked. "Are you having any fun?"

"I always have fun when I'm here. I've been hanging around with Richie and Donnie. I've made some new friends, and I've started back with Miss Coplin. I had my first lesson already."

"Grandma Bea and I talked about that this morning, before you got home, Evan. That's wonderful. I'm so happy for you. I'm dying to hear you play," Lila said.

"Mother, there's something I wanted to talk to you about. I haven't mentioned it to Grandma yet, but I—"

"If it's about the piano, you needn't worry. I already told Grandma Bea about having to sell it, so it's no longer a secret. She understood. I have a plan to replace it when the time is right. In the meantime, I think there's something more important for us to talk about." She put her arm around him. "Evan, how would you feel about staying with Grandma Bea a while longer, starting school here in the fall? Your grandmother and I have already discussed it, and she would love to have you. It would give me a bit more time to get myself established in my new job."

"I guess I wouldn't mind," he said, trying not to show his elation over the proposition. "Grandma has a lot to do around here. She said the porch needs to be painted before winter. If I were here, I could help her."

"That's thoughtful of you, dear," Lila said. "I was hoping and praying the idea wouldn't be upsetting to you. I brought the rest of your clothes with me, and we'll go uptown and buy you some new things as well. I know you need a new winter coat. Then, before Gladys and I head back on Monday, we'll go to the school and get you registered. I'll call you every week and—"

Evan interrupted. "Don't worry, Mother, everything will work out. It'll all be fine," he said.

"Thank you for being so understanding, Evan," Lila said and hugged him.

24

The construction crew had started work at dawn and by mid-morning, the mercury had hit eighty-five degrees. More than forty drain tiles were in place at the north edge of the marsh, and water was already draining in a steady flow toward Sand Bottom Creek. The man at the controls of the six-ton backhoe had made two passes on the south edge and was now making the final cut to accommodate the last row of tiles. Water was rushing into the trough, working its way toward the creek sixty yards below, when suddenly, over the growl of the diesel engine, one of the crew shouted, "Hold it, Luke . . . there's something here!" The man waded into the murky water. "Oh, my God . . . it's a body!"

An entire arm and shoulder were protruding from the wall of the trough, like an exposed tree root, the girl's fingers dangling in the water.

"Grab a tarp and a couple of shovels," the Crew Chief shouted, "and get dispatch up on the radio."

Several county vehicles were parked bumper-to-bumper on either side of the highway and a contingent of townspeople had arrived; they were milling about. The local press was onsite, and a Chicago crew from WGN television had arrived.

Deputy Sheriff Roland Kincaid had spent the last half hour answering questions. It was the typical interview. The reporter would ask the same question a dozen different ways, Kincaid would give a bullshit answer, followed with the official phrase, "It's too early in the investigation to say."

Now, he was trying to bring order to the scene, regain control so the investigation could proceed unobstructed.

"Move those damn barricades out to the edge of the highway," Kincaid shouted.

"Where do you want people to park?" one of the men said. "We've got four more—"

"Damn it, Murdock, I don't want any lip," Kincaid said. "They can park in town and walk, as far as I'm concerned. Now, get it done!"

Kincaid had paused briefly for a cup of coffee and a cigarette. He took one last drag, dropped the cigarette and mashed it into the dirt. When he looked up, he spotted a man walking toward him. "And where the hell do you think you're going?" Kincaid yelled.

"Agent Michael Traxler, FBI," Traxler said and flashed his I.D.

"Sorry, Agent," Kincaid said. "I was told you were on your way, just didn't expect you so soon. I thought you were one of those reporters. What did you do, fly in on a rocket?"

"I was just down the road, soaking up the hospitality at the Dixmoore Hotel," Traxler said as they shook hands.

"I understand you're investigating the disappearance of the Sanford girl," Kincaid said.

Traxler nodded. "For about two weeks now."

"Well, your search may be over. There's a damn good chance she's the primary victim," Kincaid said.

"There were multiple bodies uncovered?" Traxler said.

"Skeletal remains. Two additional victims so far," Kincaid said. "The dogs found them almost immediately, forty feet from the spot where the body was uncovered. We're still searching." He glanced at Traxler. "You don't seem that surprised."

"We've been investigating the Sanford case in conjunction with several other missing persons, young women," Traxler said.

"What's the connection?" Kincaid said.

"Proximity, for the most part," Traxler replied. "There's a forensic team en route from Chicago, some good talent. This is going to be high-profile. No offense, but I have to say I'm surprised the sheriff isn't handling the case personally."

"Maybe you haven't heard. The old boy's not in the best of health. The legwork in a case like this might be a little too much for him."

"He must have a lot of confidence in your abilities, Deputy," Traxler said.

"Known the man for a long time. I think I've earned his trust," Kincaid said.

"What do you say we dispense with the formal bullshit? Some people call me Mike, but most tend to call me Trax. Either is fine," Traxler said.

Kincaid nodded. "Some call me asshole, most call me Rollie. I prefer the latter."

Traxler nodded and laughed.

Traxler had completed his examination of the body and talked with the construction crew. Now he was walking the meandering road back toward the highway. It wasn't much of a road, nothing more than two shallow ruts in the hard clay, separated by spotty patches of crushed gravel, bramble closing in on both sides. *Maybe an old hunting road?* Traxler thought as he walked along. *Whatever the original purpose, it serves none now.* The road led nowhere.

"Agent Traxler!" one of the uniformed men shouted, running to catch up to him. "Here." The man handed Traxler a four-feet-long tree branch, one end whittled to a sharp point. "I suggest you refrain from poking around in that shit with your foot. I just ran across a moccasin about twenty yards back and he didn't look happy. I'll make myself another one," the man said as he hustled away.

"Thanks," Traxler called to the man, "I owe you one."

"What are you doing there, Trax, giggin' frogs?" Kincaid said when he spotted Traxler on the path, poking around in the weeds.

"What do you make of this?" Traxler said, not looking up. He outlined a patch of ground with the point of his new staff.

Kincaid leaned in for a closer look. "That would be corn mash," he said, staring down at the grain embedded in the exposed red clay.

"There's another patch about thirty yards back. I'm thinking someone was driving back in here with a load of this shit, hit a couple of these craters," Traxler said and gestured with his pointer, "and lost some of it. Isn't this the stuff they use to make whiskey?"

"You're damn right it is," the man said as he approached. Agent Traxler and Kincaid both turned at the same time to see a middle-aged man walking toward them. The man was tall and at least twenty pounds overweight. He was dressed in khaki pants and a long-sleeved green shirt under a tan vest. Trickles of sweat ran down his cheeks from the band of the red cap he was wearing. A badge was pinned to his vest, and there was a .32 revolver in the holster belted around his waist. "Good thing you spotted it when you did." He gestured toward the crows circling overhead. "Between those nasty buzzards and the squirrels, it wouldn't have been there much longer."

The man reached to shake hands with Traxler and said, "Game Warden Stanley Conrad at your service."

"How you been, Stan?" Kincaid said as he shook Conrad's hand. "Haven't seen you since that day at the county fair."

"Been on the road a lot the last few months. Hopefully, they'll be putting some additional men on the payroll. Don't have the vinegar I once had," Conrad said, looking around the area as he spoke. "Looks like you got your work cut out for you."

"You know the situation here?" Kincaid said.

"Yeah, I got a briefing when I arrived on the scene," Conrad replied. "I've been chasing a shiner around these woods for about two years now. I busted up three of his campsites. About a week ago I tore down a still near Jonesville Junction, a half mile from Spencer Bridge. Didn't catch the man. This guy seems to have the uncanny ability to skedaddle just before I show up."

Traxler had traded his stick for a pen and was scribbling in a small notebook. "What makes you think those sites were all the work of the same man?" Traxler said.

"I've been doing this job for a long time," Conrad said. "It's like picking up a copy of the *Saturday Evening Post*. You don't have to look at the artist's signature to know it's a Norman Rockwell on the cover. These jackrabbits all have their own style, especially the seasoned ones. The way they stack the furnace, pack the mud between the rocks, the material they use. They might as well stamp their name on it."

"What happens to the stuff you confiscate?" Traxler said, continuing to write in his notebook.

"I turn it over to the state police. They lock it up. Not sure how long they hold on to it, but that's the way it's always done," Conrad said.

"I'd like a copy of the report you filed with the evidence, and if you can provide any details that would help us identify the man, I'd appreciate it. I've got a talented sketch artist in Chicago, probably sitting there twiddling his thumbs. Might as well give him a workout," Traxler said.

"I don't think I can help you there. The closest I ever got to the man was a hundred yards, and he was haulin' ass at the time," Conrad said, "but I'll keep my eyes and ears open."

25

Evan had the phone clamped to his ear, listening as it rang for the fifth time. He was ready to hang up when he heard a click.

"*Tribune*, O'Malley here."

"Hello, Mr. O'Malley. It's Evan."

"Evan, how are you?"

"I'm fine. I just wanted to talk to you about Riley. Do you have time, Sir?" Evan said.

"I certainly do. What is it?"

"Riley is acting a little strange . . ." O'Malley listened while Evan recounted the incident at the barbershop.

"I thought about the whole thing for a few days before I decided to call," Evan said.

"You did the right thing, son. I understand why you would be concerned," O'Malley said. "Believe me, that wasn't the first time Riley has acted out like that. Tell you what, I'm going to be in Laurenville on Saturday. I'm meeting with Coach Grimm at the high school. He wants me to take a look at one of his players, some hotshot he thinks might be ready for the majors. I'll be checking in on Riley and Wilma while I'm there. Are you interested in coming along? It might be fun, and it would give us a chance to talk."

"I'd like to, Mr. O'Malley. Thanks," Evan said.

"No, Evan, thank *you* for watching out for Riley. He needs people in his corner. I'll see you on Saturday morning, around eight."

26

———

Evan was sitting on the porch step when O'Malley pulled up in his '56 Sunliner. The top was down and the car was gleaming in the sunlight like a newly minted silver dollar. O'Malley hit the horn a couple of times as he rolled to a stop.

"Top of the morning to you, Evan my boy," O'Malley said.

"Hi, Mr. O'Malley," Evan said, springing up and heading toward the curb. "Wow, the car looks great!"

"If you're ready, jump in. I'll take you for a little spin," O'Malley said.

"It looks a lot different with the top down, all washed and polished," Evan said as he plopped down on the seat and surveyed the interior. "It's the first convertible I've ever been in."

"I wanted a ragtop all my life," O'Malley said, "but I kept putting it off. A couple of years ago I decided to spend a few of my hard-earned bucks before I was too old to climb behind the wheel and enjoy it."

O'Malley made a U-turn and drove the four blocks down Prairie Street to Route 1, then headed north. Evan put his head back on the seat and looked up at the sky, the cool morning air rushing all around him. For the next few miles, neither of them spoke.

Finally, as O'Malley slowed to make the turn onto Gable Street, he said, "So, it sounds like Riley Winslow is getting a little negative press around here."

"Yeah, I don't know why people have to be that way," Evan said.

"They observe peculiar behavior and they don't know how to react. Sometimes, it even scares them," O'Malley said. "Do you know anything about the human brain? Did they teach you anything about it in school?"

"We learned a little in biology . . . you know, all the basic parts," Evan said.

"Well, after the accident, I talked to a lot of doctors and did a ton of research on the subject. I wanted to find out what the boy was up against. You ever heard of amnesia?" O'Malley said.

"That's when you can't remember things," Evan replied.

"You're exactly right, only it's a bit more complicated because there are several different types of amnesia. The best way to describe it is, if you were to roll an apple off the top of a flight of stairs, by the time it gets to the bottom, it's going to have bruises in several different spots, some deeper than others. That's the way it is with Riley's brain. Some of the damage affected his recollection, and in other places, it changed his perception of the things going on around him. Remember when I told you how he can go off into his own little world?"

Evan nodded. "Is that what was going on that day at the barbershop?" Evan said.

"Exactly. He sees something on the television or in a movie, maybe just a picture in a magazine, and he begins to fixate on it. Sometimes he creates his own little fantasy world and begins to act it out. It sounds a bit strange, but that's the way it was explained to me. The brain is an incredibly intricate thing."

"Isn't there anything they can do for him? Medicine, an operation, or something?" Evan said.

"They've been giving him medication for years now," O'Malley said, "and it seems to help. This recent incident was the first in quite a long time, at least as far as I know."

"How long does it last, before he's himself, I mean?" Evan said.

"Usually, not long. He's like an actor in a play," O'Malley said. "I've seen him rattle off dialogue from an entire movie scene. One minute he's the character, the next, he's back to reality, whatever that is for him."

"Sometimes he seems more like a kid than a grownup," Evan said.

"That all has to do with the way this thing affects his

thinking. He's forgotten a lot of what he's learned. It comes back in flashes."

"Maybe the reason people are scared is that he's so big," Evan said.

"He's an imposing figure," O'Malley said, "but the truth is, he's as gentle as they come. There's not a mean bone in the man's body. In fact, the one concern we all had about him when he was playing ball was that he was *too* nice a guy and might not have the mental toughness to compete with some of the ruthless characters in the big leagues. Unfortunately, we never got to find out."

"Maybe it's just easier for him to be someone else than to be himself," Evan said.

"I think you may be on to something, son," O'Malley said.

There were a dozen vehicles in the Wabash Valley High School parking lot when O'Malley pulled in. One of them was a station wagon with the University of Notre Dame logo painted across the side. Another was a VW bus with a placard in the side window that read Northern Illinois University Baseball. Several men were milling around the entrance to the locker room, and another group was sitting in a section of bleachers along the third base line watching a dozen high school players work out.

As O'Malley and Evan walked toward the bleachers, they were greeted by Coach Louis Grimm. "Good to see you, Artie," Grimm said and reached to shake O'Malley's hand. "Thanks for making the trip."

O'Malley introduced Evan to the coach and followed with, "You know I'm always eager to discover new talent. Besides, I had to check up on my boy. How's he doing?" O'Malley said, looking around for Riley.

"He's doing fine. We have a little problem communicating, here and there," Grimm said and chuckled, "but he's a hard worker and as honest as the day is long. He should be back any minute. I sent him over to the supply building. The school board finally loosened up the purse strings a bit and bought us some new equipment. Lord knows we needed it."

"Who's the kid you wanted me to look at?" O'Malley said, surveying the players on the field.

"Ken Tidwell, the one loosening up along the first base line. Big strong kid. Throws hard. Has a decent curveball and great control," Grimm said.

"Well, let me get up there on my perch and take a look at him," O'Malley said. "Come on, Evan, let's see if we can figure out what this kid's got to offer." He put an arm around Evan's shoulder and they headed for the bleachers.

The Tidwell kid had moved to the mound and pitched to five batters, a couple of high schoolers from the area, a local college player, and two minor league players who had been brought in by the Notre Dame contingent. They were all good hitters who had been invited that day primarily to test Ken Tidwell's arm, but also to allow them to put their own skills on display. Of the batters Tidwell faced, only two were able to get wood on the ball— weak ground balls and popups. Tidwell had made easy work of them.

O'Malley and Evan watched as Coach Grimm shuttled players on and off the field. In addition to Tidwell, they had seen a promising young man from Lincoln College take a couple of dozen balls at shortstop and second base. Now and then, O'Malley would make an entry in a small notebook he carried, and during the lulls, he told Evan stories about some of the unique characters he'd encountered during his years on the job. A man couldn't cover the likes of Lou Gehrig, Joe DiMaggio, and Jackie Robinson without accumulating a few stories.

The sun was now high in the sky, and the northerly breeze that had been there in the early hours of the morning had now vanished. It was going to be one of those stifling hot days in the Wabash Valley.

O'Malley pulled a handkerchief from his pocket and mopped his brow. "Hey, Coach!" O'Malley shouted. Coach Grimm looked up at him from his position behind the backstop. O'Malley gave him a look of desperation, fanned himself a couple of times with his notebook, and feigned passing out.

Grimm smiled, nodded and said, "Okay, men, let's take a break. There are some soft drinks in the cooler over there. Take fifteen, then we'll get back at it."

"Well, Evan my boy, I think I've seen just about everything worth seeing from this vantage point. How about we wander down and grab one of those sodas?" O'Malley said. "I've got to get out of this sun for a while. I think my thermostat's on the fritz."

27

———

O'Malley poked around in the cooler for a while, finally pulling out a bottle of orange soda pop. "This work for you?" he said, holding the bottle up with one hand while he continued to fish around in the icy water with the other.

"That'll be fine," Evan replied.

"You sure? Be happy to keep on searching. It's a rather refreshing experience." Finally, he grabbed another soda for himself, and they sat on a bench in a shady spot beside the gymnasium.

A moment later, Riley came around the corner of the building wearing his khaki outfit and the blue baseball cap. He was carrying a large cardboard box. He placed it on the ground beside several others, then went to the fountain, leaned over and took a drink.

"Riley!" O'Malley yelled.

"Hey, Mr. O!" Riley looked like a man in a three-legged

race as he limp-trotted toward O'Malley. "What are *you* doing here?"

"Coach Grimm invited me, and I came to see *you*, Riley. How are you?" O'Malley said.

"I'm good. Coach says I'm one of his best workers."

"Hi, Riley," Evan said.

"Evan! I didn't know you were here, too," Riley said. "I'm through working for the day. Maybe we can ride home together." Riley looked around. "Where's your bike?"

"I didn't ride my bike today. I came with Mr. O'Malley."

"How do you like Mr. O's convertible? Pretty sharp, huh?" Riley said.

"*Very* sharp," Evan said.

"Mr. O let me drive it once," Riley said. "I, uh . . ." He glanced at O'Malley, then back to Evan. "I only drove in the parking lot, though, and Mr. O was in the car with me. I . . ." His gaze shifted back to O'Malley. "Sorry, Mr. O. I know I wasn't supposed to tell anyone, but—"

"It's okay, Riley. Calm down. Evan can keep a secret. You won't tell, will you, Evan?" O'Malley said.

"Not a soul," Evan said, smiled, and did the zip-lip gesture.

"Thanks, Evan, because I'm not supposed to be driving," Riley said.

O'Malley had relinquished his position at the top of the bleachers, trading his bird's eye view for a partially shaded spot along the first base line. He watched two more young men display their talents in the outfield and made a few more entries in his notebook. He was about to wrap things up when Mr. Ralph Tidwell approached, his son trailing closely. Mr. Tidwell didn't look happy.

"Ralph Tidwell, Mr. O'Malley. I wonder if I might have a word with you?" he said.

"Why, sure, Mr. Tidwell, what's on your mind?" O'Malley said.

"Coach Grimm told me you weren't that impressed with Kenny's pitching. Is that true?" Tidwell said.

Coach Grimm overheard the comment and came rushing over. "Hold on, Mr. Tidwell, that's not what I said. What I said was—"

"It's okay, Coach," O'Malley said, "I can understand Mr. Tidwell's concern." He looked back at Ralph Tidwell. "I think your boy is extremely talented. He throws hard and he has good control. I do believe he needs more movement on his pitches, especially his slider. A couple years under a good college coach, a little work in a farm system, and I think he'll be ready."

"He's ready now!" Tidwell said. "I don't know what you were looking at. The Notre Dame coach told me he'd love to have my boy on his roster."

"Take it easy, Mr. Tidwell, please. I'm sure you're disappointed, your boy, too. Coach Johnson is one hundred percent correct. Your son would be an asset to any big-time college program, but in my opinion, he's just not ready for the jump to the majors. Now, I don't profess to be the last word on this matter. As a matter of fact, all I can do is pass on my findings. I'd be happy to—"

"Forget it, O'Malley. I don't need some over-the-hill sportswriter screwin' with my son's future. We'll look for someone who knows what the hell he's talking about," Tidwell said and stormed off.

"Hold it, Mr. Tidwell," O'Malley called after him, then turned to the young Tidwell and said, "You feel like throwing a few more pitches, son?"

The kid shrugged.

"What's this all about, O'Malley?" Ralph Tidwell said, turning to Grimm and throwing his arms up in disgust. "Everyone's seen my boy throw."

"You've got nothing to lose," O'Malley said, "and who knows, you might even learn something."

Ralph Tidwell glared at O'Malley for a few seconds, then turned to his son, nodded toward the field and said, "Go ahead, Kenny."

O'Malley was standing in the home team dugout, watching as the kid warmed up.

"You ready, son?" O'Malley said. The Tidwell kid nodded. O'Malley walked to where Evan and Riley were sitting, leaned over, put his hand on Riley's shoulder and said, "Okay, Riley, get on out there and take a few cuts."

"I don't know, Mr. O," Riley said. "I'm not a baseball player anymore." He looked at Evan. "I can't run. I hurt my leg in an accident."

"Everything is okay, Riley. I already told you, you won't have to run. Just go out there and have a little fun. Swing the bat a few times. The pitcher wants to try out some new pitches and he needs *your* help." O'Malley picked up a helmet and handed it to Riley. "Here, put this on and grab a bat."

Riley took a couple of warm-up swings, then limped toward the plate.

"What's going on here?" Ralph Tidwell yelled. He rushed toward Coach Grimm. "What are you running here, Coach, a circus, some kind of sideshow?"

"Just throw a few pitches!" O'Malley said to the Tidwell kid.

"Go ahead, Kenny, this oughta be a riot," the young man doing the catching shouted. "Just don't throw anything too tight. I don't think he'll be able to get out of the way." He laughed and set up for the pitch. Tidwell smiled and stepped brashly onto the rubber.

Riley edged into the batter's box and cocked the bat. Tidwell wound up and threw a low fastball over the center of the plate. Riley pounded it into centerfield.

The second pitch was another fastball, down and away. Riley hit a rope into right field. "That was better," Riley shouted to Tidwell. "I had to reach for that one."

The next pitch looked like it would be outside, but dipped in at the last second and caught a piece of the plate. Riley watched it go by.

"Good pitch!" Riley said. "Try to keep it down just a little. You'll get more grounders that way."

"He can't hit that pitch, Kenny!" the catcher shouted, crouched, and flashed a sign.

Tidwell threw the same pitch with slightly more velocity.

Riley slammed it down the first baseline.

At this point, everyone had dropped what they were doing and were gathered around the backstop to watch the proceedings on the field.

They watched as Riley pounded pitch after pitch, one of them a monster drive over the left field fence that seemed to be in the air forever.

"Hold it!" Ralph Tidwell yelled, marched onto the field, making a B-line for the mound. "What in the hell are you doing? Quit fooling around and dust this clown! You're turning us into a joke."

"Us? I'm the one pitching here, Pop. Believe me, I'm trying. I've never seen a guy track the ball the way he does."

"Well, do *something*, damn it! Your chances of playing big-time baseball are going right down the shitter!" Ralph Tidwell shouted, stomped off the field and planted himself behind the backstop.

The catcher pulled off his mask and trotted out to the mound. "What the hell was that all about?" he said.

"My old man . . . he doesn't get it," Tidwell said.

"Look, forget about what he thinks. This guy can flat out hit. What do you want to do?" There was no reply. "You're not going to get this guy with heat. We can try some more breaking stuff inside. I don't think he can get to it with that bum leg." Tidwell nodded.

The catcher trotted back and set up.

Tidwell wound up and threw a curve that dove toward the inside corner of the plate. Riley swung, turning his hands over at the last second and yanking the ball down the third base line. Riley's short leg buckled. He lost his balance and stumbled backward, spinning completely around. He ended up on his knees behind the plate.

"You okay, mister?" the catcher said. He grabbed Riley's arm to help him up.

"I'm okay. That's why I'm not a baseball player," Riley said and pointed to his leg.

"Oh, you're a baseball player," the catcher said as he helped Riley to his feet. "There's no doubt about that!"

O'Malley and Evan ran to Riley. "That's enough," O'Malley said, waving his arms.

"C'mon, Riley," Evan said and took hold of Riley's arm with both hands, steadying him as they walked toward the dugout.

Tidwell raced in from the mound. "Is he alright?" he said.

"He'll be fine. It's an old injury," O'Malley said.

"Who is he, anyway?" the Tidwell kid asked.

"His name's Riley Winslow. No one you would know, just a good soul who came up a bit short," O'Malley said.

"I didn't mean for that to happen, Mr. O'Malley."

"It's okay. I can see what's going here," O'Malley said

and put a hand on Tidwell's shoulder. "You've got plenty of talent, son. Don't let *anyone* rush you."

As O'Malley walked away, the kid called to him. "Thank you, Mr. O'Malley . . . and thank Mr. Winslow for me."

O'Malley waved over his shoulder and nodded.

28

Kincaid and Traxler had departed the County building at daybreak. They wanted a first-hand look at the southernmost stretch of Route 1. They planned to question a few people along the way and at the end of the day meet with the parents of Bonnie Jansen, the seventeen-year-old from Evansville, Indiana. She had been reported missing almost three years ago.

They were now sitting in a small, stuffy office in Camden, Illinois. A wrought iron fan was oscillating on a shelf, high in the corner of the room, and there was the smell of cooked coffee from a carafe that sat on a small hotplate just outside the office door.

The twenty-five-year-old man sitting across from them was officer Brett Reynolds. He was sipping a bottle of RC Cola and flipping through the report Kincaid had handed him.

Camden's Chief of Police, James Bogart, was off attending a funeral, and on this particular day, he had put his nephew, Brett, in charge.

"Officer, I don't mean to rush you, but we need to get back on the road. We've got a lot of stops to make between here and Evansville. We've already discussed the pertinent details with you. What are your concerns?" Kincaid said.

"I don't see nothin' in the report to link Connie Winters to this here recent homicide," Reynolds said. "I don't know a thing about the girl from Evansville, but I knew the Winters girl pretty damn well. Connie had a wild hare up her ass and plenty of guys sniffing around all the time. I knew her folks, too, and let me tell you, that whole family is wacky as hell. I'm bettin' that girl is just fine. She's probably living in one of them communes that are croppin' up out west."

"Well, we don't know that for sure, now do we?" Traxler said.

"I want you to know, we did a thorough investigation at the time Connie was reported missing. We beat the bushes for three weeks, and there was nothing that pointed to any foul play," Reynolds said, "nothing at all!"

"Officer, we're not accusing you of incompetence," Traxler said. "I'm sure Chief Bogart conducted a top-notch investigation. The relevant point is, there were three separate missing person reports filed over the last three years, and all of those girls had planned to hitch their way to wherever the hell they were going. They all started out along Route 1, and now we've got a body and the remains of two unidentified females at that site."

"Hell, thousands of people go missing every year. What makes you think those are the bones of these two?" Reynolds said.

"Well, for one thing, the dates match up," Traxler said. "The girl from Evansville was the first reported. She was last spotted in a little Illinois town called Norris, thumbing her way north. Then Connie Winters disappeared. You know the details on her. We're waiting for dental records and some additional data to arrive. We'll know definitively when we get the final lab reports. In the meantime, we've got to consider every possibility."

"Where exactly is the site?" Reynolds asked.

"Two miles south of Laurenville, the marsh just west of Redmond Stables," Kincaid interjected. He seemed to be growing more impatient by the second. "It's *all* in the report."

"Look, officer, I pray you're right and both girls are alive and well," Traxler continued, "but we have a sixteen-year-old Chicago girl by the name of Irene Sanford who was molested and strangled, and the only reason her body was discovered is that a wealthy man decided to spend a chunk of money to drain the swamp behind his property because he didn't want all those mosquitos feasting on his thoroughbreds. It's also pretty damn clear, whoever dumped her there didn't expect her to be found, at least not so soon, and certainly not intact."

"That still doesn't mean the killer is local," Reynolds said.

"No, but the killer had to know that marsh was back there.

No one stumbles upon a remote spot like that by chance. Now, we're not implying the killer is right here in your backyard, but we can't rule out the possibility that there's some lunatic prowling for young women along this stretch of Route 1," Traxler said.

"Can you tell us how soon after her disappearance the Winters family moved away?" Kincaid said.

"About a month. Packed up everything they had, including five kids and a monkey and headed south," Reynolds said, a toothpick dangling from the corner of his mouth. He took another big swig of soda, reclined in his chair, put his feet up on the desk, and said, "Okay . . . what is it you want me to do?"

"As we've already told you, we don't have a lot to go on at the moment," Kincaid said. "The corn mash is the only tangible evidence we have, that and some tracks that probably match the tires on half the pickup trucks in the state. Now, you and I both know malted corn is a good indication that someone is—"

Reynolds interrupted. "Hold on now, Deputy. You ain't gonna find any *moonshiners* around here. They know better than to set up shop in *my* backyard." He gave a nod and slapped his palm on the desk to accentuate his point.

Kincaid removed his glasses and rubbed the bridge of his nose in an attempt to soothe the pain that had started behind his eyes and was now gradually working its way to the base of his skull. "Uh, once again, Officer, we're not here to contest the fine job you and your uncle are doing policing your town. We just want you to contact us if you see anything suspicious going on. Maybe someone using corn mash to cook up some whiskey, not in *your* town, of course, but perhaps in some hollow in these woods around here."

"How much mash did you find?" Reynolds asked.

"Well, as the report indicates," Kincaid said, "nearly a half bushel scattered along the back road leading to the marsh. There were traces of it on the body. The theory is, the killer might have driven back in there to dump her and lost some of his load along the way."

"The FBI lab is doing further analysis to determine if there are other elements present in the samples," Traxler said. Reynolds appeared to be in deep thought. "What's on your mind, Brett?"

"I'm Trying to come up with another reason why a man might be hauling around a load of corn mash," Reynolds said.

"Well, perhaps the killer was selling muffins on the black market," Traxler said.

Reynolds stared at the agent with a sullen, speculative expression that, after a few seconds, broke into a broad smile. He shook his finger at Traxler in a scolding sort of gesture and said, "I get it. You're funnin' with me, aren't you, Agent?"

"Yeah, Brett, I'm *funnin'* with you," Traxler said, reached into his pocket and pulled out a card. "Make sure Uncle Bogart gets this." He handed it to Reynolds. "Have him call me or Deputy Kincaid if anything new develops. The Sanford girl is the daughter of Joseph R. Sanford, one of the most influential politicians in Chicago, and Magpie Joe wants answers." Traxler leaned across the desk and looked Reynolds directly in the eye. "Keep this conversation under your hat. We don't want any more tidbits of information popping up in the newspapers. Do you understand?"

Reynolds sunk back in his chair and said, "We know what we're doing around here." There was a sudden uneasiness in his voice.

"That's good," Traxler said, "because this case is going to be a media circus, and we're going to be *center ring*. Believe me, Brett, you don't want to be the clown who fucks up the act."

The two sat in the car outside the Camden Police station, Kincaid puffing on his cigarette, Traxler sipping on a bottle of Coca-Cola.

"I think it was wise not to open up about the needle mark," Kincaid said.

"It would have been a waste of time and energy. That moron doesn't have a clue," Traxler said.

Kincaid shifted the patrol car into gear, made a U-turn, and headed for the highway.

"I've heard good things about Chief Bogart. There's a chance we can get some sensible information out of *him*," Kincaid said.

29

—

Two days after Traxler and Kincaid visited Camden, a young woman poked her head into the conference room and said, "Deputy Kincaid, line three, Chief Bogart. Has to do with the case."

"Kincaid, here."

"Hello, Deputy. Sorry I missed you the other day. An old friend of mine passed away. I had to be there to hoist a few with the boys. You know how that goes," Bogart said.

"I understand. We've got to take time out for the important things in life," Kincaid replied.

"What I'm even more sorry about is that you had to deal with that nephew of mine. I should have known better than to leave him with the keys to the castle, even for a day. That nitwit can't even take a leak without pissing all over his shoes."

"Don't worry about it, Chief. We've all got one in the family," Kincaid said.

"Well, anyway, my nephew told you there are no moonshiners working these woods around here, but as usual, he's mistaken. I know for a fact that the local game warden rounded up a shitload of paraphernalia about a week ago somewhere in Sherman's Woods, I believe. I was at the state police depot when the stuff was impounded. They unloaded a still, a couple of wooden barrels, and I don't know what the hell else."

"We've already talked with Conrad," Kincaid said. "He was at the scene. The forensics team has taken possession of all that shit. There were several bushels of corn mash and a few bags of sugar among it. We're waiting for a report on the girl. There's something that looks like a needle mark on the body," Kincaid said.

"Interesting. That would open up a whole new can of worms. I'll do some poking around and see what I can come up with. In the meantime, I got a couple of names for you," Bogart said.

"Hold on a second. Let me grab a pencil," Kincaid said, flipped the lid on his lighter, and lit the cigarette he'd been rolling between his thumb and fingertips. He took a drag and motioned to Traxler to pick up the extension. "Shoot."

"There's a ne'er-do-well by the name of Harvey Markes who's been known to do some bootlegging in this area over the years," Bogart said. "Lived most of his life in Kentucky. That's where he perfected his craft. I hauled his ass in a while back for assaulting a guy in a bar. He spent a few days in my lockup, but got off with a slap on the wrist."

"Where should we be looking for this asshole?" Kincaid said.

"At one time he had a girlfriend who worked as a bartender at one of the local gin mills. She bailed him out on the assault charge. Can't remember her name. Milly, Mindy, something like that," Bogart said. "I also heard some talk of another man. Strictly hearsay, mind you. It seems Markes was drunk one night and shooting his mouth off about some guy messin' with him. Markes was pissed because the man was trying to horn in on his business."

"So much for honor among thieves," Kincaid said and chuckled. "We appreciate your cooperation on this, Chief," Kincaid said. "We're trying to keep the press from dwelling too much on the local angle, at least for now. If folks start believing there's a stone-cold killer living among them, we might have an all-out panic on our hands."

"I get it," Bogart said, and in a more somber tone followed with, "Do me a favor, Deputy. If the news is bad and we find out those *are* the remains of the Winters girl, I'd like to be the one to track down the family. They're a strange lot, but still decent folks. Probably best if the bad news comes from me. I knew the old man pretty well."

"I'm sure no one will deny you that unpleasant task, Chief," Kincaid said.

30

___

The Hole-In-The-Wall was a little saloon on the Wabash River halfway between Bargetown and Laurenville. It was a lopsided shoebox-shaped building constructed of cinder blocks, painted white, with a corrugated rusty tin roof that sloped slightly from front to back.

Someone had made a feeble attempt to paint a western landscape across the building's facade. The image included a backdrop of red rock buttes, several cactus, and an ill-proportioned painting of a cowboy on horseback; the pinto he was riding more closely resembled a giraffe than a horse. The name Butch Cassidy was scrawled under the drawing.

There was a beer garden with several picnic tables in a grove of trees adjacent to the building. A woman who looked to be in her early forties sat at one of the tables smoking a cigarette. She was wearing jeans and a white cotton blouse. Her straight jet-black hair cascaded down her back almost to her waist. She watched as Agent Traxler and Deputy Kincaid approached.

"Good afternoon, ma'am," Kincaid said as they arrived. The woman said nothing and took a drag on her cigarette.

"I'm County Sheriff's Deputy, Kincaid." He pointed to his badge, "And this is FBI Agent Michael Traxler from the Chicago office. Is your name Missy Jyles?"

"Nope," the woman said and took another drag on the Lucky.

"Someone told us she works here. Is that true?" Kincaid said.

"Yep," she replied.

"What's your name, ma'am?" Kincaid said.

"Edith Jyles. Only my family and my drinkin' buddies call me Missy. I don't recall you and I ever having a drink together and I'm damn sure we're not related."

"Okay, *Edith,* the point is, we'd like to ask you a few questions about a man named Harvey Markes. We were told you know the man?" Kincaid said.

"I might, and I might not. If I was to know who told you that, I—"

"Cut the bullshit, *Missy!*" Kincaid said and sat on the edge of the table. "Now, I can be as polite as the next man, but we don't have time to play your little *backwoods* games. Now, I'm going to ask you again, do you know this man, Markes?"

Perspiration appeared on her forehead. "Buy me another drink?" she said. "I'm not on the clock until four."

Kincaid glanced at Traxler, who nodded. "I think we can handle that, Missy," Kincaid said.

Missy threw back the shot of cheap bourbon and chased it with a swig of Pabst Blue Ribbon.

"How well do you know the man?" Traxler said.

"I met him about four years ago, right here on this very spot. Dallas was throwin' a big shindig and—"

"Who's Dallas?" Traxler said.

"Dallas Milsap, he owns the Hole. It was a hell of a party. He roasted half a pig that night," Missy said and nodded toward the massive brick barbecue pit behind the building. "Had a band and everything. By midnight, you couldn't get near this joint. Cars were lined up all the way to the highway. The word was out that some young up-and-comer was gonna make an appearance, a kid named Waylon Jenkins, or Jennings . . . something like that. The kid was on his way to New York to make a record. Dallas was workin' for some radio station in Texas when he first met the young man, and when he heard he was headed east, he asked him to make a pit stop at the Hole." Missy stood, took one last drag and flicked the butt away. "I have to use the little girl's room. You boys think you can entertain yourselves while I'm gone?" She flipped her hair and strolled off.

"What do you think?" Kincaid said.

"She may be able to tell us something if we can just keep her focused," Traxler said.

A few minutes later, she reappeared with another can of beer. "Now, where was I," she said as she sat back down.

"We're hoping you were planning to tell us a little something about Markes," Kincaid said.

"Oh yeah, my mind has been a bit cloudy of late," she said, closed her eyes, took a deep breath and exhaled slowly. "So, the party's goin' gangbusters, and out of nowhere this handsome young lad appears, jumps up on the stage with his guitar and starts knockin' 'em dead. I'm standin' there enjoyin' the festivities and all of the sudden a guy comes up behind me and grabs me around the waist. Next thing I know, he's got both hands on my ass and we're slow dancin'. It was the first time I met him."

"Markes?" Traxler said.

"Yeah," Missy replied, "he told me he was from Kentucky. Said he was a businessman."

"He didn't happen to mention the nature of that business, did he?" Traxler said.

"He didn't say, and I didn't ask. Of course, I found out soon enough. Hell, every man and his dog knew he was a moonshiner. You can't keep something like that a secret for long . . . not if you're plannin' to make money at it."

"Did he make money?" Traxler said.

"He was never short of cash," Missy said. "I can tell you that much."

"Do you know where we can find him?" Kincaid said.

"No," she replied.

"You have no idea where he is?" Traxler said.

"I haven't seen him in a month, maybe longer. If I did know, I'm not sure I would tell *you*," she said.

"You haven't even asked us why we're looking for him. Aren't you even the least bit curious?" Traxler said.

"You're only gonna tell me what you want me to know, anyway. I've got my own opinion of the man," Missy said.

"You know him that well?" Traxler said.

"I took a few midnight tumbles in the bed of Harvey's pickup, got into his head a few times. I don't know why, but men love talkin' to me. I know the man pretty damn well," she said and flashed a saucy grin.

"Does he have a violent side?" Traxler said.

"Harvey is a lot of things, but *violent* isn't one of them," Missy said.

"What about the incident in the bar? Our information indicates that Harvey broke two of the man's ribs, put him in the hospital," Kincaid interjected.

"That man was drunk as a skunk, came at Harvey with a jagged beer bottle," Missy said.

"There can be a lot of sides to a man," Traxler said.

"Look, sonny," she said. "I've been on my own since I was fifteen years old. Spent time in the penthouse and the shithouse. I think I'd recognize Lucifer if I saw him."

"Well, then you need to help the man. If you talk to him, let him know we're looking for him. He hasn't been charged with anything. We just need to sit down with him and ask him a few questions," Traxler said.

"If I see him, I'll tell him you came callin'," she said.

"One other thing, did Harvey have a partner, an associate?" Traxler said.

"Not that I ever knew of. Harvey liked to work alone. He was fussy about the hooch he made. Didn't want anyone to know his secret recipe," Missy said, "sort of like one of them mad scientists."

Kincaid turned his head slightly toward Traxler and muttered from the side of his mouth, "It's the *mad* part I'm worried about."

"You're sure he never spoke of another man, maybe someone on the fringe of things?" Traxler said.

Missy lit another cigarette, took a long drag and exhaled what seemed to be an endless stream of smoke in Traxler's direction. Finally, she said, "There *was* a strange moment last fall. We were at my trailer. I woke up and heard his voice. It was the middle of the night, two or three in the morning. I stepped outside and found him sittin' on the porch, sippin' on a glass of whiskey, talking to himself. When I asked what was wrong, all he said was that there had been some crazy asshole rootin' around in the woods that day. When I pressed him, he told me not to worry about it. He would handle it."

"That was all he said?" Traxler replied.

"That was it. He didn't want me involved in anything to do with his business. Said the less I knew, the better. But I could tell he was worried. Even with a snootful, it wasn't like Harvey to sit and chew on something like that, and he sure as hell wasn't prone to talkin' to himself in the dark. Normally, he didn't let anything get under his skin."

"Can we buy you another drink?" Kincaid said and tapped the shot glass on the table.

"No, I've got to get in there and get my tables ready," Missy said. "My regulars will be driftin' in soon." She picked up the tray of glasses and headed for the door.

31

———

"Today's not lesson day. What brings you by, Evan?" Loretta said as she ushered him into the parlor.

"I was hoping you might have some time to help me with something, Miss Coplin," Evan said.

"I was on my way to the post office, but that can wait. What is it?"

"I'm working on a song, uh . . . writing a song, and I'm sort of stuck," he said and handed her several pages.

"Have you been studying your chords?" she said.

"Yes, Ma'am," Evan said, "every day for at least an hour. I've memorized most of them."

"That's good. You can't be a successful songwriter if you don't know your scales and chords, forward and back. The melody pulls you along the path, but the chords add the color along the way. Is this song going to have lyrics? I see only notes on these pages," Loretta said.

"Yes, I have most of them written," Evan said.

"Well, might I have a look at that version?" Loretta said.

"I thought maybe . . . uh—"

"Oh, I see," Loretta said and looked at him over the top of her glasses. "You know, this wouldn't be the first song created to woo a young lady. Many a lad has captured a young lass's heart with sonnet or song, but you must keep in mind, a song is a blend of melody, rhythm, and harmony all moving in lockstep with the lyrics. It's difficult to evaluate them independent of one another. I can be much more helpful if I see your lyrics. I promise you, I shall be discreet."

Evan pulled several pages from his folder and handed them to Loretta. His face turned a rosy pink as he watched her peruse the pages.

She sat at the piano and played the first eight bars. "How long did it take you to write this?"

"I worked on it over the last couple of days," Evan said.

She played the rest of the piece, filling in with a broken chord here and there. "Alright, now you sit down here," she said, "and give me *your* interpretation." She scooted over and Evan sat beside her.

"I'm not much of a singer," Evan said.

"Don't worry about that. Songwriters come in all shapes and sizes. Some of the best would have starved to death if they had to sing for their supper. Irving Berlin couldn't sing a note. Then, there are those who think they can sing, but can't," Loretta said.

"I'm not even sure I have it in the right key," Evan said.

"C will work for now. It's a good range for most voices," Loretta said. "We can address that later. Just give me an idea of how *you* want the piece to sound."

They worked on the song for nearly an hour.

"Okay," Loretta said, grabbed the sheets, and began marking them with a colored pencil. "I like it, Evan. A little tweak here and there and you're in business. These are just suggestions, mind you." She circled a phrase on the third line and scribbled something under it. "It's up to you to decide what you want to change and how to do it. It's your creation . . . and quite excellent, I might add."

"Thanks, Miss Coplin."

"The first thing we need to do is transcribe it onto some decent manuscript paper. It'll be a lot easier to read. Then, when you're ready, we'll take one last look at it," she said.

"I want to finish it over the weekend. Her birthday is next Thursday and—"

"Ah, a birthday present. I have an idea, a way we can spruce it up. I'm sure she'll be thrilled. Have you decided on a title?" Loretta said.

"Not yet."

"Not to worry, my dear, I'm sure you'll be inspired somewhere along the way."

32

———

Traxler sat at a table in the small conference room on the second floor of the county courthouse. There were several folders and a few papers strewn across the table. The door was partially open when Kincaid knocked.

"Come in," Traxler said, stuffing a report into a large envelope along with several other documents.

"You're exactly where I left you last night, Trax. You get any sleep?" Kincaid said.

"I got back to the hotel about eleven. Slept off and on. My mind was going in every direction. Fortunately, I don't need much sleep. Been that way all my life," Traxler said.

Kincaid had a thermos in one hand and a stack of paper cups in the other. "I hope you can drink it black."

"Works for me," Traxler said.

Kincaid poured steaming coffee into a cup, handed it to Traxler, then poured one for himself. He sat down in a chair by the window and looked around. "Not much of an office for a man of *your* stature," he said. "I'd get claustrophobic in a room like this." He shook his head and gestured toward the table. "You'd think we could have dug up a real desk."

"It's fine," Traxler said. "You should see some of the broom closets I've been stuck in over the years. At least I have a view," Traxler said and nodded toward the large latticed window overlooking the courtyard. "You making any progress?"

Kincaid took a sip of coffee and said, "We've got a team searching the woods along the river. One of those hounds seems to have a keen sense for bones."

"Isn't that what dogs do?" Traxler said.

"Yeah, I guess you're right," Kincaid said and smiled. "Let's just hope we don't uncover any more victims. Folks around here are upset enough as it is. I was having lunch at the diner across the street yesterday, sitting at the counter, when a little girl walked by holding onto her mother's hand. She tugged on my sleeve, looked up at me with that sweet little face of hers and said, 'Excuse me, mister policeman. Am I gonna get kilt?' She had tears in her eyes."

Traxler turned and looked at Kincaid, shook his head, and said, "That's what something like this does to a community. It rattles people right to their core."

Kincaid pulled out a pack of cigarettes, lit one, and said, "The last time people around here were dealing with something like this was about twelve years ago, forty-seven, I believe. They found some guy on the railroad tracks up near

Bargetown with his arm lopped off. The man had been run over by a train. A good friend of mine by the name of Bert Thatcher was the Chief of Police at the time. He's retired now, but I've talked to him a few times since the incident. Seems they identified the man but never did figure out how he got there."

"I think I remember that. It was all over the news. The guy was military . . . Navy, as I recall," Traxler said.

Kincaid nodded and said, "Point is, if you were to ask the folks around at that time, you'd probably hear the legend of the butcher of Bargetown, the story of a homicidal maniac running around with an ax chopping people into pieces. Not a shred of truth to it, but it goes to show you how something like that can grab hold of folks and spin out of control, get all twisted around." Kincaid took a drag on his cigarette. "What did you hear from your office? Any update on the toxin?"

"They think it's some type of tranquilizing agent that depresses the central nervous system," Traxler replied. "Evidently, there's a broad spectrum of substances that fall into that category. I'm told, whatever it is, the drug is dangerous, the kind that can kill a person if not administered properly."

"How would a person get ahold of a drug like that? I'm assuming you don't buy it at your local drugstore?" Kincaid said.

"It's a controlled market. We're checking privileged access, thefts, every possible distribution channel. The good thing is, those drugs are closely monitored," Traxler said.

"Do they think that's what killed the Sanford girl?" Kincaid said.

"It might have contributed, but the official finding is strangulation. I don't think the killer was looking to administer a lethal injection. He had other intentions." Traxler grabbed a report lying on the table, studied it for a short time, stood and began poking colored pin markers into the map on the wall.

"What've you got there?" Kincaid said.

"Missing persons report for the last forty-eight months, girls between the age of fifteen and twenty-five. The report lists the locations where they were last seen, all within a radius of thirty miles of the crime scene," Traxler said.

"What are the colors?" Kincaid said.

"The white pins are the sightings of two of the victims, Winters, and Jansen. The four yellow are locations where *other* missing young women were tentatively spotted."

"The red is the crime scene?" Kincaid said.

"Yeah," Traxler replied. He spiraled his finger over the circle drawn on the map. "This is a tight cluster. Odds are good the killer is local. Proximity and timeframe dictate it. It seems the killer has turned this stretch of highway into a gauntlet."

"Let's hope those four girls made it through," Kincaid said.

Traxler nodded and said, "You keeping an eye on Missy Jyles?"

"Yeah, she's not showing us anything. I think Markes flew the coop."

"You got the info out on him?" Traxler said.

"As of yesterday," Kincaid replied.

Traxler pulled a mugshot from the folder on his makeshift desk, studied it, and said, "What are your thoughts on this guy?"

"Hard to say. Everything seems to be pointing his way, but from what I'm gathering, it'll be a surprise to a lot of people if he turns out to be our man," Kincaid said.

"We have to keep an open mind in this case. It wouldn't be the first time the quiet, mild-mannered guy down the street turned out to be Jack the Ripper," Traxler said.

Kincaid removed his glasses and rubbed the bridge of his nose with his thumb and forefinger.

"You okay?" Traxler said.

"Yeah, just a bit of a head-thumper, that's all," Kincaid said, snapped open the tin of Anacin he carried, and popped three tablets into his mouth, washing them down with a swig of coffee. "Cases like this make me regret not taking over my pop's hardware business when he offered."

33
—

Katie and her mother were on their way back from their Saturday shopping excursion in Terre Haute. Katie was feeling good about the day they had spent together. They had gotten along well; there hadn't been the usual bickering over how she should spend her birthday money. She had been allowed to pick out her own school clothes, something that had never happened before.

Maybe there's magic in turning thirteen, Katie thought. *Maybe the day you become a teenager, something snaps inside your mother's brain, and from that day forward she begins to treat you like an adult.*

"When we get home, please hang up your new clothes so they don't get all wrinkled, dear. I know that new material is supposed to be wrinkle-free, but believe me, there's no such thing," Vera said, "and don't forget to spray your shoes. They'll be a lot easier to keep clean."

"Yes, Mother," Katie said. *So much for that theory,* she thought.

Vera shifted the station wagon into second gear and turned onto Juniper Street. "Your father is making cheeseburgers for your birthday dinner, American cheese, just the way you like them," Vera said.

That was no surprise. He'd been doing it for her birthday for as long as she could remember. It was the only thing her father ever cooked. *He grills a tasty cheeseburger . . . but more important, he's a good father,* Katie thought. *There's no doubt about that.*

The house was quiet when they entered.

"Dad, we're home," Katie called.

"Maybe he's out back," Vera said.

Katie put the packages on the sofa, went to the back door, and peered through the screen.

Ted Dobbins was wearing a plaid bibbed apron and standing beside a large kettle grill. He held the lid in one hand and a can of lighter fluid in the other.

"Oh, you're back!" he shouted. "Can you come out here, Katie? I think I'm going to need a hand with this grill."

Halfway across the yard, she heard a chorus of voices, "Happy birthday!"

Evan, Richie, Donnie, Beans, and Riley came around from behind the garage.

Glenda Lavin and Janet Miller, the two girls Katie had met

at the Dairy Queen, popped out from behind the shrubs at the corner of the house. Glenda was carrying a cluster of balloons.

Vera and Beatrice came out of the house with a tray of glasses and a pitcher of lemonade.

"Well, did I do a good job keeping you in the dark, dear?" Vera said.

"You sure did. That's not like you, Mother," Katie said. "Keeping secrets isn't one of your strong points."

"Just shows what you can do if you put your mind to it," Vera said and laughed.

By early evening, everyone had eaten. Ted sat in the living room watching *People Are Funny* on television while Vera and Beatrice chatted in the kitchen. There was a pot of coffee brewing as Vera put the final decorative squiggles on Katie's cake.

Katie's portable phonograph was on a folding table at the corner of the patio. Beans, the self-appointed DJ for the evening, was flipping through a stack of records while Richie and Donnie did some sort of contorted version of the bunny hop with Glenda and Janet.

"C'mon, Evan," Katie said, "anyone with your sense of rhythm has to be able to dance." She tugged on his arm, trying to pull him up off the folding chair where he'd been perched for the last ten minutes. "Look, even Richie and Donnie are dancing."

"You call that dancing?" Evan said. He thought about the

visit to the cemetery. "Donnie looks like a snake crawled up his pant leg."

Katie looked back at Donnie and smiled. "Now that you mention it, you may be right," she said, "but at least he's trying." She gave his arm another tug. "Just give it a shot. I'll take it slow."

"Okay, but if I start looking like either of those two, I'll never dance again."

Katie scurried over and pulled several records from the stack, sorted them, and handed them to Beans. "Play these next, Beans, please."

She grabbed Evan's hand and dragged him around the corner of the porch to the driveway. "No one will see us here. Now, give me your other hand. Dancing is just a few basic steps, a lot of rocking side to side, and a little tap of the toe now and then. Okay, step with your left foot, then a tap," she said, pulling him toward her, "then, rock back . . ."

Katie guided him around the dance floor to "Rockin' Robin" and "Stupid Cupid." By the time Chuck Berry began belting out "Johnny B. Goode," Evan was really getting into it, even throwing in a couple of hand-jive moves he'd seen on *American Bandstand* a few days earlier.

"What'd I tell you? You're a natural," Katie said, gave Evan's arm a tug, and did a little duck under spin move.

"You two look perfect together!" Vera said. "Like Kelly and Hayworth."

They stopped dancing and looked up at Vera, who was

peering through the kitchen window, her elbows resting on the windowsill, chin propped on the heels of her palms.

"Mother! You're not supposed to be watching. Isn't there any privacy around here?" Katie said. "I suppose you've been eavesdropping as well?" She looked up at her mother disgustedly.

"Of course not . . . music's too loud," Vera muttered and retreated from the window.

"Sorry about that, Evan," Katie said, shaking her head.

Evan shrugged and said, "Who are Kelly and Hayworth, anyway?"

"No idea. Probably a couple of my mother's friends back in Akron," Katie said.

"Don't forget to make a wish, dear," Vera said, then nudged Beatrice, and in a flat sarcastic tone followed with, "Hopefully she won't wish me out of the picture."

Katie blew out the candles and everyone cheered.

"Why don't you open your gifts while we serve the cake and ice cream," Vera said.

Katie sat on the sofa and Vera placed the gifts on the coffee table in front of her.

Glenda and Janet had chipped in on a leather-bound diary with Katie's initials embossed on the cover. "It has a lock and key so you won't have to worry about someone peeking," Janet said.

"That was thoughtful," Katie said and looked at Vera. "Don't you think so, Mother?"

Vera smiled a dry smile and continued slicing the cake.

Donnie and Beans had done *their* shopping at Western Auto. What girl wouldn't appreciate a set of fluorescent pink handlebar grips with streamers?

At his mother's suggestion, Richie had opted for a more traditional gift. "There's nothing more appropriate for a young lady than an elegant hand-mirror," she had told him. Richie had spent the entire morning shopping; he had no idea there was such a wide selection of mirrors. Finally, after exhaustive deliberation, he had settled on the one at Woolworth's, the "elegant" one with the laminated picture of Elvis on the back.

Riley handed Katie an envelope and a small white box tied with a red ribbon. Inside the envelope was a card that said, *To a special person on her birthday*. It was signed, *Your friend, Riley Winslow*. Inside the box were two tickets for admission to the Bijou, two boxes of Milk Duds, and a certificate good for two dollars in trade at Trudy's Burger Shack, the new restaurant that had opened around the corner from the Bijou.

"Now you and Evan can go on a date," Riley said.

"Thank you, Riley. That was so nice of you," Katie said.

"This one is from Aunt Sandra," Vera said and handed Katie a small brightly wrapped package.

Katie opened it and found a radio about the size of a bar of Ivory soap.

"She said it's the newest thing. It has those transistor things built right in. The clerk told her you don't even have to wait for it to warm up . . . and it comes with a tiny little ear thingamajig," Vera said.

"This is really neat! I'll phone Aunt Sandra later and thank her," Katie said, examining the radio.

"You're probably going to be the only kid in school with one of those," Beans said. "I don't think they even make them in this country."

"My science teacher said that most of them are made over in Japan," Richie added.

"Isn't Japan somewhere in India?" Donnie said.

Richie rolled his eyes and shook his head.

As everyone gathered around the table to get a closer look at the little techno-miracle, Evan leaned over and whispered into Katie's ear. "I have a gift for you, but it's going to have to wait 'til later."

She looked up at him inquisitively.

By eight-fifteen all the guests had departed except Beatrice. She and Vera were chatting as they tidied the kitchen. Ted, who had been up since the crack of dawn, had already retired for the evening.

Katie and Evan walked along Prairie Street. It was a pleasant night. The stars were shining brightly and a crescendo of Cicadas filled the night air. This was an off-year for the alien-looking little creatures. A few years earlier, after a primary emergence, the sound had been deafening. People had needed shovels to clear their foul-smelling, rotting little carcasses from their sidewalks and driveways.

"It was a nice party," Evan said.

"Yeah, I'm glad my mother decided to have it. I was feeling a little sad, thinking about my old school," Katie lamented, "some of my friends back in Ohio."

"Anyone would feel that way. It's hard when you get used to something, then all of a sudden, it's gone," Evan said. "Believe me, I know."

"You're right, Evan. I shouldn't be feeling sorry for myself. I don't know how *you* manage to deal with the change. I'd be flipping out. The first week I was here, I felt like crying all the time."

"You get used to it. I guess, after a while, change starts seeming normal," Evan said.

"Do you know what my wish was when I blew out the candles?" Katie said.

"What?"

"I wished that you wouldn't be going back, that you could stay here in Laurenville, go to school here," she said, grabbed his hand and squeezed it.

"Sometimes wishes come true," Evan said and grinned.

Katie stared at him. "What's that supposed to mean?"

"I'm going to start school here in the fall."

"Are you kidding me?" Katie said.

"Nope. My mother's going to be busy with her job, and she thought I should stay here with Grandma Bea for a while."

"That's wonderful, Evan. I'm so happy. It's the best birthday present you could have given me," Katie said.

"I'm glad you feel that way, but that's not your present," he said and laughed.

"What is it, then?" Katie said as they arrived.

"Come on," Evan said, took her hand and led her up the walk.

The table lamp in the living room was on, as was the light over the kitchen sink. The rest of the house was dark as they entered.

"People aren't going to jump out at me again, are they?" Katie said, a tinge of genuine concern in her voice.

"No, that part's over," Evan said as he escorted her to the piano in the corner of the room. He switched on the light, pulled out the bench and sat down. "Okay, sit."

Katie sat down beside him. He opened a folder, removed a sheet and placed it on the music rack.

"Katie Blue," she said and stared at the sheet for a few seconds. *"Katie Blue* . . . that's me! Evan, you wrote a song for *me?"*

"It's my first crack at songwriting, so I don't know how good it is, but yes, it's for you," he said.

"It's printed, just like the songs you see in a music store. How did you manage that?" she said.

"Only a few copies," Evan said. "Miss Coplin helped me with it. You wouldn't believe all the people she knows. I couldn't have done it without her help."

Katie hugged him, then gripped his arm and squeezed. "Well, let me hear it, boyfriend! Don't keep me in suspense."

Evan played the song for her. It was a simple melody, with plain words and basic chords, but it was a good song, a beautiful song—it came from the heart.

Katie had trouble falling asleep that night. *After all, it isn't every day that a girl became a teenager.*

She had listened to music for a while on her new radio. It was nice being able to lie there and listen without her mother chiding her to turn the volume down, but she had turned it off after a short while. *Don't want to run the battery down on the very first day,* she thought.

Now, as she lay there in bed, there was an endless stream of thoughts surging through her mind; she thought of her friends back in Akron, how they might be getting along. She thought of Riley, and how difficult it must have been to have something so devastating occur in the prime of life. She tried to imagine what her new school would be like, her teachers . . . and interspersed with all of that were remnants of her wonderful day.

Katie Blue . . . it had a nice ring to it, she thought. *It was a name like Sweet Lorraine, Suzy Q, Miss Molly, a name that set a girl apart.* She was no longer simply Katherine May Dobbins. She, too, had earned a place in the heart, if only the heart of a twelve-year-old boy with a flattop.

Her song was playing in her head as she nodded off.

34

As always, the site Markes had selected was well hidden and protected. It had been an arduous trek from the truck to the spot where he now stood. He had spent half of the previous day chopping his way through the heavy brush with his machete, and now in the early morning hours, he was nearly finished.

The site was ideal. The patches of water-weed along the edge of the ravine had led him to the spring. A good source of water wasn't easy to find. The flow wasn't as deep as he would have liked, but it was steady, and the water was as clear as any he had found in the area. Equally important was the dead oak tree not more than twenty-five yards away. Hardwood burned hot and long and didn't create a great deal of smoke.

He unslung the double-barrel 12-gauge, leaned it against a tree, and surveyed the site. The dense, thorny canopy of honey locusts would provide excellent cover and help disperse the smoke from the furnace. The thick ivy along the south edge of the stream would act as a barrier for anyone walking the river bank.

The only access would be the meandering path he had opened with his trusty blade. It was about a ten-minute walk from the spot where he had parked his truck. Most of the terrain was level, but there were some treacherous slopes at several points along the way that had been difficult to negotiate, especially when lugging a thirty-pound wooden thump keg.

Metal containers would have been lighter, but metal would give his brew a bitter taste, could even make a man sick, poison him. Markes wasn't the type to deliver an inferior product. He had a reputation to protect.

He walked to the pile of supplies, threw back the heavy canvas tarp, and began taking inventory of the things he had lugged in the prior day.

One more trip to the truck and I'll be able to start assembling, he thought.

There were plenty of boulders at the bottom of the shallow ravine, on either side of the stream. They were all sizes and types, perfect for constructing the furnace. He needed to pay particular attention to the rocks he chose. Once he packed the mud into the cracks, the heat inside the furnace would be intense. A rock with the wrong mineral content might crack or crumble. Flint could even explode.

Building the furnace would be back-breaking work, lifting

and stacking, but that came with the territory. He could have paid some derelict a paltry sum to do the heavy lifting for him, but there would have been risk involved. Most of those willing characters would betray their own mother for cigarette money. The risk wasn't worth it.

He removed the cap from the pewter flask he carried and savored the aroma for a few seconds before he took a swallow. *No wonder they like Markes's Wabash Whiskey,* he thought, wiping his mouth with the back of his hand. *That's pretty damn good hooch.*

The first thing he would do after he put his operation together would be to visit the Hole-In-The-Wall. He wasn't that keen on the joint itself, but he liked Missy Jyles. She had a good sense of humor, was a hell of a dancer, and she listened to most of what he had to say. *The kind of woman that's hard to find.* He took a big swig of whiskey. *Looks pretty damn good naked, too,* he thought.

He hadn't seen Missy for a couple of months. He had headed south to replenish his supplies. The hills of Kentucky were his home. There, he had connections; he could buy things on the cheap without a lot of questions.

In fact, the only reason he had come to Illinois in the first place was to help an old friend, Roscoe Landry, who wanted to try his own hand at moonshining. That had been almost four years ago now.

Roscoe had been a quick learner, and within a month Markes had taught him the rudiments of the business. The operation was soon at full throttle, turning out the finest brew north of Kentucky, and Markes, having honored his commitment, was packed and ready to head home.

The two men were hoisting a glass of Roscoe's Revenge, a name chosen after some serious deliberation, when suddenly Roscoe clutched his chest and fell face-down in the mud beside the still.

Perhaps the excitement had been too much for him, or maybe the unfamiliar labor of building the site had done him in. In either case, he had taken his last breath that hot July day, 1954.

Markes had tracked down Roscoe's mother and seen that the man received a proper burial. It was the least he could do for a lifelong friend and protégé.

Looking back, he wasn't sure why he had decided to stay in Illinois after Roscoe died. Perhaps it was his innate sense of adventure. *Life would be pretty damn boring if we knew what was around the corner,* he thought. He lit a cigarette, took a couple of drags, and watched the hawk circling overhead.

The serenity of the moment was interrupted by a rustling behind him. *Could someone already have found my clandestine outpost?* he thought as he turned to investigate.

"I should have known it would be you," Markes said. "I'm not going to argue about—" He paused when he spotted his 12-gauge draped over the man's arm. "Look . . . if it's money you want, you're welcome to it." He reached into his trouser pocket and pulled out a roll of bills. "Here, take it all." The man raised the shotgun and pointed it directly at Markes's chest. "There's over a hundred bucks here!" Markes began retreating in slow, steady steps, his knees nearly buckling. "There's no reason to—"

The force of the blast threw Markes ten feet. He landed on his back, the front of his jacket drenched in blood.

The forest was now still, but for the sound of the water flowing from the spring. As he lay there, he could see a splinter of sunlight piercing the treetops, and the silhouette of the red-tailed hawk circling; it settled on one of the highest branches, the frail limb straining under its weight.

It was the last image his brain would ever record.

35

—

Traxler reached for the phone. "Yeah?" he said, his head still buried in the pillow.

"Is that you, Trax?" Kincaid said.

"Yeah, Rollie, it's me," Traxler grumbled and sighed.

"Didn't sound like you. Thought I had the wrong room."

Traxler glanced at the clock on the nightstand and said, "You do realize it's four-thirty in the morning, don't you?" He yawned, threw the covers back, and sat up on the edge of the bed. "My guess is, you found another body?"

"Yeah," Kincaid said, "but it's not a girl, it's a man. A guy on his bread route spotted a truck about a quarter mile north of Spencer Bridge. He saw it there yesterday, and when it was still there today, he decided to report it. We brought the dogs in and they led us straight to the body."

"I'll call my team and get them moving. Don't let those

reporters anywhere near the scene. I'm on my way," Traxler said.

The dense stretch of woods where the body had been found was four miles northeast of Camden. It was still dark when Traxler arrived. Heavy rain had been falling for several hours, but it was now just a light mist. Kincaid and another officer met him as he exited the car. They were both wearing dark green rain slickers.

The young officer introduced himself simply as Hutch and said, "Maybe you better put this on, Agent Traxler. It looks like it's going to pour again." He handed Traxler a slicker like the one he and Kincaid were wearing. Traxler slipped it on, and they started off down the muddy, recently-carved path, Hutch leading, the beam of his flashlight illuminating pitfalls along the way.

It was a ten-minute walk to the clearing, a spot about seventy-five yards from the Wabash River. It was entirely surrounded by honey locusts, the thorny branches enveloping the clearing like barbed-wire encircling a prison camp. The outmost perimeter was roped off, and there was a deputy standing watch at the edge of the clearing.

Hutch led the two men to a spot illuminated by three lanterns and removed the tarp that covered the rapidly decaying body. "I'll be close by, sir. Give a holler if you need me," Hutch said. He walked toward another man who was busy taking an inventory of the items at the site.

Kincaid cast the beam of his flashlight on the body and said,

"It's Markes. There was a driver's license in his wallet and we got a print match right out of the chute. There was a side-by-side 12 gauge found here." Kincaid pointed to a spot marked by four wooden stakes. "The killer emptied both barrels into him at point blank range."

"Someone must have been mighty pissed off at the man," Traxler said, slowly circling the body. "Anything on his person besides the wallet?"

"A pocket knife, keys, comb, and a little change. No cash. We know the truck's registered in his name, but we were waiting for your team to arrive before we started going through it," Kincaid said. "Didn't want to crap on your lawn."

"He must have spent several days chopping his way through that brush to get to this spot. I'm thinking that would be the only way in," Traxler said and looked around. "You sure as hell couldn't come through there." He pointed to the thick bramble along the river bank.

"He must have been one determined son-of-a-bitch to walk that path carrying all this shit," Kincaid said as he threw back the tarp, exposing a copper pot and cap, several feet of coiled copper tubing, a supply of jars, corn mash, and three wooden barrels. "And he wasn't done yet. There were some things left in the truck."

"Why do you think he picked this particular spot? What made it so special?" Traxler said, scanning the surrounding woods.

"For one thing, he knew there was a source of water,"

Kincaid said. "See that patch of green over there?" Kincaid said and pointed. "That's what shiners call water-weed. Where that stuff grows, there's often a spring close by." He put his hand to his ear. "Hear it? It's at the base of that ravine, just past that boulder there." He pointed toward a rock about the size of a Volkswagen.

"Makes sense. He'd have good clean water, and he wouldn't be trudging back and forth to the river through all that thorny mess down there," Traxler said.

Kincaid pointed to the base of the ravine. "Those boulders are just the ticket for constructing a furnace. Stack those babies up, pack a bunch of mud into the cracks, and you're in business."

"How is it you know so much about moonshining, Rollie? You dabbled a bit yourself?" Traxler said and chuckled.

"No, but I had a great granddaddy who made a living at it when he was a young rogue. Later in his life, he made it solely for his own enjoyment. Had a small still in the barn."

"Did you ever sample his brew?" Traxler asked.

"No," Kincaid replied. "Oh, I contemplated taking a swig one day when he was off somewhere, but I took a whiff and decided against it. I think I was only about ten at the time. Probably made a good decision. I heard guys say that stuff would light you up like a Christmas tree. Never had the opportunity again. He had a stroke that same year."

Traxler smiled. "He sounds like quite the character."

"That he was," Kincaid said and nodded.

"So, from what you're telling me, I'm guessing there's a

damn good chance Markes was raking in some decent money in the moonshining business," Traxler said.

"Most likely," Kincaid said. "He definitely knew his craft."

"If that's true, we have to assume there were people who wanted a piece of the action, maybe enough to kill the man if he didn't cooperate." As Traxler knelt beside the body, sunlight streamed through an opening in the treetops, flooding the clearing. He leaned in, examined Markes's swollen face, and said, "We know you could cook up a fine batch of hooch and that you liked to dance, Harvey, but the bigger question is . . . were you a man inclined to pick up girls every now and then, rape them, and dump them in some deep, dark hollow of these woods?" He stood and stared at the body as though he expected Markes to rise up any second and begin pouring out his mangled heart.

"It seems he didn't hear you," Kincaid said and chuckled.

"Agent Traxler!"

Traxler turned and saw Hutch trotting toward him with a walkie-talkie.

"Just got a call from one of your team," Hutch said and took a deep breath. "They found something in the truck."

There was a long metal folding table standing about twenty yards from the pickup. The table was covered with a sheet of white butcher's paper, and there were several items strewn across it. A number was printed below each item, and a man with a flash-camera was snapping photographs. He backed away as Traxler and Kincaid approached.

"Thought you needed to see these before we sent them to the lab. They were under the seat wrapped in the towel," the man said and tapped the center of the table. There was a clear plastic pouch containing a hypodermic syringe and a twenty-milliliter vial containing a small amount of a clear liquid. There was no label nor markings on the vial. Beside them was a white terrycloth hand towel. The man gestured toward a shovel, coil of rope, and a roll of tape lying at the end of the table. "Those were bound up in a tarp in the truck bed."

Traxler examined the items briefly, then walked to the truck and peered into the bed. He stood there for a while, rubbing his brow. "Get this truck inside immediately and do a full sweep of this area from the highway to the edge of that line of trees. I want a complete summary by noon, and have someone drive that shit straight to the lab," he said and pointed to the vial.

"It seems Markes may have decided to confess after all," Kincaid said.

36

—

The killer sat in his truck smoking a cigarette and reading the newspaper. The headline plastered across the *Trenton Gazette* read:

FEARS ABATED; SUSPECT IN MURDERS DEAD

The killer felt emboldened. After all, Markes had been the primary focus of the investigation. Now he was dead, and a highly incriminating piece of evidence had been found in his truck. Suddenly, the authorities were faced with the daunting task of tracking down a phantom who, perhaps unwittingly, had disposed of their key suspect with the man's own double-barrel shotgun.

Some of my best work, the killer thought as he stared at the headline, grinning. *That should keep them busy for a while.*

His truck was parked on Chestnut Street at the end of a

row of six cars. The street bordered the Washington Junior High parking lot. School had let out an hour earlier and most of the teachers had already departed. Only a few vehicles remained in the lot.

Three girls exited one of the side doors of the gymnasium, each carrying a canvas gym bag with the image of a tiger head and the words *Washington J.H.S. Cheerleading* stenciled across one side.

He grabbed the binoculars, focusing on the girls, tracking them as they walked west toward Poplar Street.

When they reached the corner, they stopped and chatted briefly. The three hugged one another, then separated, two of the girls continuing on together, giggling and waving, the third girl turning and walking south on Poplar.

She walked another block, stopped and placed her bag on the ground. The wind had picked up and it began to drizzle. Leaves swirled around the girl's feet and droplets of rain pelted her face as she took the yellow rain slicker from the bag, slipped it on, and pulled the hood up over her head.

As she reached the end of the street, heavy dark clouds rolled in and squelched the daylight. A few seconds later, rain began to fall in torrents. The killer started the engine, switched on the wipers, and used a towel to clear the fog that had formed on the inside of the windshield.

Now, the girl was nothing but a blur, a splash of yellow behind a shroud of rain, but he remained transfixed, watching as she turned the corner and disappeared from view.

Those manipulative little bitches need to be dealt with before they have a chance to perfect their craft, turn into jezebels like that cheating wife of mine, he thought. *It's a nasty job, but somebody has to do it.* An air of excitement washed over him. It had been nearly three months since he'd quenched his voracious appetite, but he would soon remedy that.

He had found the new object of his disfavor. Soon it would be business as usual, and he had a few tricks up his sleeve.

37

Vera had spent most of the day cutting a pattern for a gown she was creating for one of the town's socialites. Initially, most of the work she had received had been rudimentary, sewing on buttons, stitching a seam, things most anyone could do if they had a little ambition. But it hadn't taken long for the residents of Laurenville to discover that Vera Dobbins was an incredibly talented seamstress. Her business had picked up considerably, and that was a blessing because it would be a while before the machine shop would be bringing in a consistent income.

The shop had been mismanaged for years, and it was going to take some time to regain the trust of the community in and around the valley. Ted had always been a hard worker, and Vera had complete confidence in his ability to get things back on track.

There were several lights on throughout the house. *A waste of electricity and hard-earned money*, she thought, but she hated being in a dark house. Gloomy days always sapped her energy and dampened her spirits. She also liked to have the radio on while she worked. It made her feel less isolated. Being around people was probably the thing she missed most about her job at the department store back in Akron.

"That was the silky-smooth voice of Mr. Nat King Cole," the radio announcer said. "I hope you enjoyed the last hour of the show. We're only halfway home, so stay tuned, because a bit later, I'll be bringing you more of the songs from that album. Now, here's our own Kyle Fredericks with the news."

"A spokesman for the White House said earlier today that U. S. troops will continue to withdraw from Lebanon in an orderly fashion and that all ground troops will be back on U.S. soil by the end of the month. President Eisenhower plans to address the American people on the subject in the next twenty-four hours. In other news, demonstrations continue in Little Rock, Arkansas as over seventy percent of ballots cast in a special school district election were in opposition to the integration of Little Rock schools. Democrat Governor Orval Faubus pledges to continue the fight against school integration despite an impending Supreme Court ruling. The decision is expected to—"

Vera snapped off the radio.

That's enough of that, Vera thought. *As if the murders aren't enough to deal with. A person's brain can focus on madness like that for just so long before it starts to go numb. What a mess the world's in. The last thing we need is—*

Her train of thought was broken by the sound of the front door opening.

"Mother, I'm home," Katie called as she stepped inside.

"I'm glad, dear. I was worried about you. Thought you might get washed away by all this rain. I laid out a towel for you."

"I found it," Katie said.

Vera stood and peeked around the corner into the foyer. "Now, aren't you glad you took your rain slicker?"

"Yes, Mother, you were right . . . as usual," Katie replied, a hint of sarcasm in her voice.

"Well, did we make the team?" Vera said and gave Katie a wide-eyed look.

"Yep, I did better than I thought I would. A lot of girls tried out, and I was a little nervous, but I guess it didn't show," Katie said, her somber expression breaking into a big smile.

"That's wonderful, Katie." Vera rushed over and hugged her. "I knew you would do it. Your father is going to be ecstatic when he hears. I'm so happy for you."

38

Evan and Katie sat on the edge of the porch. Grandma Bea had put them to work on a basket of string beans her good neighbor Mr. Garnett had left beside the front door earlier that morning. They were pinching the tops and tails off and tossing them into a large kettle.

They heard an engine backfire, looked down the street and saw an old rust-bucket sedan pulling some sort of wagon. The rig came to a clattering stop at the curb. The front passenger door opened and Zachary Aiken climbed out. His right arm was in a cast and draped across his chest in a sling.

"Mr. Aiken! What happened?" Katie said. She and Evan jumped up and ran toward him.

"Took a nasty fall down by the creek," Zachary said. He yanked off his hat and tilted his head to the side. There was a shaved spot several inches above his right ear and a lump partially covered by a gauze bandage. "Hit my head on a rock."

"Wow! That's a doozy! You must have really banged it," Evan said.

"You should see the rock. Split it clean in half," Zachary said and chuckled. "My head actually isn't that bad. The arm's the thing giving me fits. Broke it in two places. Can't use the damn thing for much of anything. Can't even drive my truck."

"Sorry to hear that, Mr. Aiken," Katie said. "I'm sure it hurts something fierce."

"I'll get by," Zachary said. "I'd like you to meet my good neighbor, Moe Grayson." Zachary gestured toward the man standing beside the car.

"Howdy," Moe said and touched the brim of his cap.

"Moe was kind enough to help me lay claim to this beauty," Zachary said and pointed to the wagon. It was about eight feet long, six and a half feet tall with a slightly rounded roof, and sat on a frame with four spoked wooden wheels. It had a broad hinged panel on one side.

"What are you going to do with it?" Katie said.

"Next Friday is Halloween, you know, and there's going to be a big shindig at the Pioneer Trading Post. They're going to have a bluegrass band, dancing, and all sorts of fun stuff. So, I'm planning to spruce this old wagon up a bit, load it with genuine Indian artifacts," Zachary said and gave a little wink, "and haul it over to the Trading Post. To top things off, they're holding some kind of an event over in Indiana.

Evidently, they're planning to do tours, shuttle people around to all the old covered bridges in the area. A couple of ladies over near Rockville came up with that idea."

"Doesn't make much sense to me," Moe interjected, "why anyone would want to ride around and eyeball covered bridges, especially if you have to lay down good money to do so, but I guarantee you, there'll be a few oddballs showin' up."

"I'm hoping there will be a steady stream of those *oddballs* passing through here over the weekend," Zachary said.

"Sounds like a good idea, Mr. Aiken," Evan said.

"What kind of wagon is this?" Katie said.

"Belonged to a guy folks called *Mr. Sharp,* a negro gentleman. He had two gray mules hitched to this thing. Traveled all over the valley sharpening knives, saws, axes, anything that needed an edge. He was also a bit of an artist. Crafted some beautiful knife handles."

"His name was Mr. Sharp?" Katie said.

"That wasn't his real name. His real name was Mayberry . . . Oscar Mayberry," Zachary said. "Been dead for twenty years. This old wagon was stashed way back in the corner of an old barn up near Bargetown." Zachary unlatched the side panel, raised it, and dropped the support strut. It formed an awning over the open side of the wagon.

"That'll keep the rain out," Katie said.

"Yep, and provide a little shade. See all those bins? Those will be perfect for my merchandise, and there's plenty of room for a counter," he said, waving his hand around in the empty space. "A nice fresh coat of paint and we're in business. Which brings me to the reason for my visit," he said and raised his eyebrows. "How would you two like to help me out? There'll be a lot to do to get this wagon ready."

"When do you need us?" Evan said.

"Halloween, for a while. I'll need some help getting the wagon stocked up," Zachary said. "You can come after school. When we're done, you can hang around for the fun stuff. Then, on Saturday and Sunday, you can help peddle the merchandise. I'll give you each a couple of bucks and a commission on anything you sell. How does that grab you?"

"Great, Mr. Aiken. I think school lets out early on Halloween, some kind of PTA meeting that day," Evan said.

"Should we wear costumes?" Katie said.

"That's a good idea. Think you can come up with a costume to compliment a one-armed Indian?" Zachary said and laughed.

"Do you need someone to help you fix the wagon, Mr. Aiken? Maybe painting? I know someone who's real good at it," Evan said.

Zachary flashed a telling smile and said, "Are we talking about your friend down the street?"

Evan nodded.

"Tell Riley he's got the job . . . if he wants it," Zachary said.

39

It was the evening before Halloween, and the ladies were gathered for their Thursday night pinochle session.

"I've got a hand like a foot," Effie said. "I just can't seem to get any cards."

"Keep the faith, Effie, we'll get on track," Beatrice said.

Effie glanced at the score pad. "We're only down sixty points," she said.

"Yes, and remember who we're playing against. Lucy and Ethel can't keep this up forever, you know," Beatrice said.

The women all giggled.

"Your feathers are ruffled because we're outplaying you, dearie, that's all," Adelle Benning said. She glanced across the table at her partner. "Right, Hazel?"

Hazel nodded and gave a muffled reply, apparently trying not to choke on the huge piece of red velvet cake she had just crammed into her mouth.

"Well, that double pinochle you drew didn't hurt any. You two better hold onto your hats because we're hot on your heels," Beatrice said as she arranged her cards.

Evan was passing through with a bowl of popcorn and two bottles of Coke.

"Do you and Katie have everything you need, Evan?" Beatrice asked.

"Yes, we're fine, Grandma," Evan replied, tugging on the sliding doors between the living room and parlor, pulling them closed.

"They seem to be having a good time," Katie said as Evan plopped down on the couch beside her.

"It's hard not to have a good time when my Grandma's around. She has a way of making people feel at home," Evan said. "She always has. I know there are times when she's feeling down, but it doesn't seem to last long."

"I think that's the key to being happy, not letting your mind wander off into those dark, dreary places," Katie said. "Sort of like that *song* from the Peter Pan movie. My dad took me to see it when I was about seven years old. After the movie I actually believed, if I thought about happy things, I'd be able to fly."

"Well, where did you flap off to? Neverland, Disneyland . . . the North Pole? I hope you took a warm coat along," Evan said.

"Please don't make fun of me, Evan."

"I'm sorry," he said. "I didn't mean to."

"All I'm saying is, I think that being happy has a lot to do with being able to control the thoughts that come into your mind," Katie said. "Your mind can take you anywhere you want to go . . . right?"

"Yeah, I guess."

"And you can't be sad while you're thinking of something good because you can only think of one thing at a time, right?" Katie continued.

Evan pondered the question for a while. "That makes sense," he said and nodded.

"Well then, that means all we have to do is ignore the bad thoughts and focus on the good," Katie said.

"That might be easier said than done."

"I guess you're right. It would definitely take some practice," Katie said.

They heard tapping on the door. Evan brushed the lace curtains aside and peeked out. "It's Riley," Evan said, opening the door.

"Sorry, it's so late. I've been painting for Mr. Aiken. I worked every day this week. I had to paint with two different colors and two different brushes. Not at the same time, though," Riley said. "The wagon's finally done. I finished a little while ago, then Aunt Wilma heated up my supper, and—"

"Don't worry, Riley, it's not that late. Come on in," Evan said. "We're getting ready to watch *Zorro* on TV."

"I've never seen that show," Riley said. He spotted Katie and gave a little wave. "Hi, Katie."

"Hello, Riley," Katie said.

"You can watch the show with us. It's a good one. You'll like it," Evan said.

"Mr. Aiken wanted me to give this to you," Riley said and handed Evan a shopping bag. "He needs some more bracelets for tomorrow. There's a note inside." Riley watched as Evan poked around in the bag. "He tried to make a couple himself, but he had to stop on account of his arm. He seemed kind of mad about that."

"Did he say anything else?" Evan said, still rummaging through the bag.

Riley hesitated, then replied, "Yeah . . . but he made me promise not to tell anyone what he said."

Evan and Katie glanced at each other; they were both grinning, clearly holding back laughter.

"Take off your jacket and sit down. I'll get you some popcorn," Katie said.

For the next half-hour, the three watched as Diego de la Vega, affable dandy by day, and Zorro, the masked avenger by night, slashed his way across southern California, dispensing with every adversary he encountered. During the action scenes, Riley flopped around in his chair like a man possessed, ducking and twisting in concert with the sword-wielding crusader's every move. At one point, Riley cheered so loudly Beatrice peeked in to make sure everything was okay.

Evan had been right. Riley liked the show a lot.

"I can work on the bracelets," Katie said, putting on her sweater.

"No," Evan said, "you still have to finish your costume. I'll get the bracelets done. I can take them over to the Trading Post right after school, and you can come over after your practice."

"Mr. Aiken said I should go to the Trading Post after I finish my job at the high school," Riley interjected.

"Do you have your costume ready, Riley?" Katie said.

"No . . . but I have an idea. Aunt Wilma's got boxes full of stuff, lots of old clothes I can use," Riley said.

"You're not going to tell us about your costume?" Katie said.

"It's a surprise," Riley replied.

"Not even a little hint?" she said.

"Nope," Riley replied, shaking his head.

"Okay, but if you need some help putting it together, you can ask my mother. She loves a project like that," Katie said. She scooted across the room, hugged Evan, then turned and grabbed Riley's arm. "Come on, Riley, you can walk me home."

40

Katie sat in the Washington Junior High School locker room. She pulled her bag from the locker, placed it on the bench, and tucked a three-ring binder and a paperback edition of *The Old Curiosity Shop* into the bottom of the bag. Most of her teachers had been merciful in assigning homework. They knew much of the student body would be out trick-or-treating that night and headed for a busy weekend. Katie had completed most of her homework during study hall. The only thing left was to write a book report on the Dickens classic. Ordinarily, it would have been an assignment she enjoyed, but this book had some dark scenes. The death of the character, Nell, had been particularly disconcerting for Katie. She would be glad to be finished with it.

The practice that day had been short, nothing more than a brief run-through of their routines. The main reason Miss

Rocklan had called the session was to present them with their new uniforms. She wanted the team to have them for the next day, the first basketball game of the season against their rival, Bargetown Junior High.

Traditionally, the "big game" was played on the first Saturday of November. There was always a big turnout by the community. After the game, the women would host their annual bake sale, while the men drifted over to MacDougal's Orchard Tavern for a meeting of the Tiger Booster Club.

Most of that meeting would be spent playing pool and shuffleboard while consuming vast quantities of Lyle's special cider. At the conclusion of the session, the chairman would pass the hat and set the date for the next meeting. It wasn't the most functional of organizations, but it raised a tidy sum for the athletic fund, the members exhibiting tremendous spirit and enthusiasm during the boosting process.

Katie pulled the sweater off the hanger and held it up, admiring it. It was white, and there was a large royal blue **W** appliqued across the front. She folded it and placed it on top of the blue and white pleated skirt on the bench beside her.

"You trick-or-treating later, Katie? It's supposed to be real nice weather tonight," Glenda said as she looked into the mirror and adjusted the blonde wig she was wearing. Katie's friend Glenda was one of the five other girls on the cheerleading squad.

"No," Katie said, "I volunteered to help a friend later today."

"Who's the friend? Anyone I know?" Glenda said, continuing to fuss with the wig.

"Mr. Aiken. He lives out on Cumberland Road. Sells Indian jewelry and stuff like that. He had an accident, broke his arm. He asked us if we would help him out at the Pioneer Trading Post."

"Who's *we?*" Glenda said.

"Evan Mason and I," Katie replied.

"Evan Mason, huh? He's cute. Every girl in school thinks so. He really likes you," Glenda said. "Richard Parker told me *you* are all he talks about."

Katie blushed slightly and said, "I like him, too, but I didn't realize it was such *common knowledge.*" Intent on changing the subject, Katie followed with, "I like your costume, Glenda. Did you make it yourself?"

"I helped," Glenda said. "My mother did most of the work. I wanted to be Marilyn Monroe, but my mother said, 'You can just get that idea out of your head this very second, young lady'." Glenda was doing her best impression of her mother. "'No good Christian would allow her daughter to parade around dressed as a woman with such questionable moral principles. Besides, there isn't enough cotton in the entire county to pad your boobs out to that size.'"

The girls giggled.

"Your mother seems pretty cool. At least you got to wear the blonde wig," Katie said, sizing up Glenda's costume. "Cinderella?"

"No, *Alice* . . . you know, the girl who falls into the rabbit hole," Glenda said and shrugged, "but in my mind, I'm still Marilyn." She looked Katie up and down, watching as Katie placed her gym shoes and uniform into her bag and pulled on a pair of rawhide boots. "Your cowgirl costume is pretty cool as well. Too bad you won't have a chance to show it off."

"I'll be wearing it while I work for Mr. Aiken, so at least the people who stop will get to see it," Katie said, stood, and adjusted her faux rawhide skirt.

Two of the other girls on the squad came around the bank of lockers, chanting, *"We're the Tigers and couldn't be prouder, and if you can't hear us, we'll yell a little louder."* The girls paused, and one of them said, "See ya, Glenda."

"See you at the game, Katie," the other girl said. "Say hello to Evan for me." Both girls giggled and waltzed on through the locker room arm in arm, picking up their chant again as they exited.

Katie looked at Glenda and rolled her eyes.

"That's the price you young lovers have to pay," Glenda said.

"Pleeeeze," Katie said.

A car horn sounded in the parking lot. "That would be my mother," Glenda said and picked up her gym bag. "You need a ride somewhere?"

"No. I rode my bike today. Thanks, though," Katie said.

"Okay, see you tomorrow." Glenda gave a little wave and breezed out the door.

41

———

Vera pulled the length of cord through the casing and tacked it in two places. She draped the cape over one of the dress forms and tied the drawstring.

Vera had made the garment by joining three separate panels of satin, remnants from a bolt she had used to create a dinner jacket a few years back. Despite the contouring and double stitching, it had taken her just a little more than an hour and a half to complete. She stepped back to inspect her work. *Not bad for a short notice patchwork project,* she thought.

She went to the kitchen, lit a cigarette, took a puff, and twisted the volume knob on the radio.

"Now, here she is to sing a little tune to get you into the spirit of things. Ladies and gentlemen, Miss Jo Stafford performing *That Old Devil Moon,*" the announcer said.

The little goblins will be showing up any minute now, Vera thought. She spotted the empty basket on the dining room table. *Candy! That's what I forgot. How can you forget the most important thing?*

She began rummaging through the cabinets for anything that might pass for a *treat.*

When the search was over, she had discovered half a bag of saltwater taffy, four Twinkies, and a pack of Juicy Fruit gum. She took one last peek into the pantry. *May have to start handing out cans of lima beans,* she thought.

There was a knock at the front door.

"Hi, Mrs. Dobbins," Riley said.

"Hello, Riley. Come in, please."

He stepped in and said, "Aunt Wilma wanted you to have these." He handed her a shirt box loosely bound with an orange ribbon.

Vera opened the box. Inside were several rows of shortbread cookies decorated with jack-o'-lanterns and ghosts. "That's so kind of her." *Aunt Wilma may have just saved the day,* Vera thought.

"She baked them special for Halloween. There are two missing. Sorry, I ate them on the way," Riley said.

"That's okay, Riley, there are plenty here. You be sure and thank your aunt for me. Have you eaten? I have a pot roast in the oven. I'd be happy to fix you a plate," Vera said.

"No, thanks. I already had something to eat. Besides, I can't stay too long. I have to run an errand, then I'm going over to the Trading Post. Mr. Aiken is expecting me. He's got a broken arm, and I've been helping him."

"I know, Riley. Katie and Evan are probably already there.

Ted is picking them up on his way home from the shop tonight. I think it would be a good idea if you rode along as well. You shouldn't be on that bicycle late at night, especially with those trucks zipping around the area. He'll pick up all the bikes tomorrow morning."

"Yes, ma'am," Riley said, looking around, craning his neck to see into the next room.

Vera smiled and said, "I have a feeling you're eager to see your costume."

Riley nodded.

"Okay, close your eyes. Don't peek," she said, taking him by the arm and guiding him into the sewing room. "Okay, you can look now."

"Wow! It's spectacular, Mrs. Dobbins. Thank you for making it for me," he said. He ran his fingers along the edge of the fabric, excited as a kid on Christmas morning.

"Go ahead, try it on," Vera said. She picked up a box from the floor, placed it on the table, and removed the lid. "I picked up a few accessories for you at the dime store. It should all work perfectly with the shirt and trousers you're wearing."

He hurriedly put everything on, threw his shoulders back and gazed at himself for a few seconds in the full-length mirror. He turned and looked at Vera, his clear bright eyes shining through the slits in the mask. "How do I look, Mrs. Dobbins?"

"Like you just stepped off the silver screen," she said.

42

———

Katie stepped out onto the landing, the gymnasium door closing behind her with a heavy thud.

It was one of those rare Indian summer days, a mild breeze blowing out of the south, the temperature close to seventy degrees. She slipped the canvas bag off her shoulder and plopped it at her feet, closed her eyes, and tilted her head back to let the warm sunlight wash over her face. It was quiet but for the sound of birds singing and the flag flapping on the pole in the courtyard.

She heard voices, looked toward the parking lot and saw Miss Rocklan and another teacher walking toward the two cars that remained in the lot.

"Goodbye, Miss Rocklan!" Katie called and waved.

The two women both turned. "Goodbye, Katie," Miss Rocklan replied. Katie watched until the women got into their cars and drove away, then headed for the bike rack.

Much too warm for this sweater, she thought. She removed it, folded it, and stuffed it into the basket beside her gym bag. She turned the sleeves of her blouse up a couple of folds to the elbow, unbuttoned the bottom two buttons of her vest, and climbed onto her bike, hiking her skirt a bit as she took off.

She pedaled along the path that ran parallel to the high school until she reached River Road, then headed north. The roadway had recently received a topping of crushed bluestone, and Katie was careful not to hit one of the shallow pools of recycled motor oil that had percolated up through the compacted stone in several places. The road had little traffic. It dead-ended three miles south at a point where the Wabash made a sharp bend west. For the most part, the only folks who used it were those who had camps along that stretch of the river.

She could hear the small fragments of oil-soaked stone pelting the inside of the fenders as she labored up Sycamore Hill. It was stand-up-pumping all the way, but she knew when she reached the top and crossed Spencer Bridge, the last leg of the trip on Cumberland Road would be a breeze.

Halfway up, she stopped to catch her breath. She could see the highest point of the bridge rising above the treetops. Against the sky, with the sunlight streaming through the lattice bents, the structure resembled the spire of a cathedral. *The only thing missing is the cross,* she thought.

She heard sounds and glanced toward the riverbank below. Starlings were collecting in a willow tree at the edge of the river. As Katie watched, their number grew, as did the intensity of their raucous chatter. It had reached a fever pitch when suddenly the flock took to the sky, soaring over the top of the bridge with such mass it briefly eclipsed the sunlight. Katie watched the spectacle in amazement, mesmerized by the majesty of the aerial ballet. The birds moved across the sky like a single giant wing, changing shape and direction in the blink of an eye, twisting and turning before descending in a spiraling plume toward the bridge, settling on it like a dark shroud.

She resumed her ascent, and after a short time she glanced up and saw the starlings had departed. By the time she reached the bridge, the birds had settled back into the willow, their incessant chatter even louder and more irritating than before.

Fascinating, how something can so suddenly . . . and completely change form, Katie thought, as she shifted her weight backward and pulled up on the handlebars, helping the front wheel up onto the apron of the bridge.

It wasn't until she heard the muffled clunk of the rear rim contacting the concrete that she knew something was wrong.

43

"If you had let me know you were stopping by today, I would have had that file all ready for you," Doctor Silas Felson called in a muted voice. He was in the back storage room rummaging through a stack of boxes. "I know it's here somewhere."

Doc Felson had been practicing veterinary medicine for over forty years, the last thirty in his current location, a rural patch of Henry County between Greensboro and Newcastle, about forty miles east of Indianapolis.

"Take your time, Doc," Traxler shouted. He and Kincaid sat in a small office just down the hall. He looked at Kincaid and said, "That's why I'm afraid of growing old, Rollie. I talked to the man just yesterday and told him we would be here today."

"You know, when I was a kid, my father and a few of his buddies were sitting around the table drinking beer,"

Kincaid said, "talking baseball, trying to remember the name of some player who played for the St. Louis Browns. They were all racking their brains. Then, my pop looked up and said something that for some reason stuck with me. He said, 'You may not realize it, boys, but I know a helluva lot . . . if I could just think of it.' I didn't have any idea what he was talking about at the time, but it makes perfect sense now."

Traxler looked at him, smiled, gave a little nod, and said, "Yeah, I guess it's something we all have to face sooner or later."

"We just have to pray it's later," Kincaid said. "I hope you don't mind me tagging along, Trax. I don't plan to make a habit of showing up uninvited, but I had to get out of that office. There's a ton of paperwork associated with this case, and you know where the boss dumps it, don't you?" Kincaid pointed a thumb at himself.

"I'm glad you're here, Rollie. I tend to receive a better reception when you're along," Traxler said. "Besides, I hate driving. Thanks for volunteering."

"Sorry about the wait. My filing system went to hell after my wife passed," Doc Felson said, sitting down at the table. He opened the box and rummaged through it for a while, finally removing a manila folder. "Ah, here we are," he said. He handed it to Traxler.

"We already have this first document. Our contact at Lyon Pharmaceutical sent it to us," Traxler said. "That's how we found you." He flipped through the pages until he came to the police report. "They didn't have a copy of this," Traxler said, tapping the report with his fingertips. He studied it briefly. "You notified the *local* police, not the county?"

"Had to," Doc replied. "This building sits on a parcel of land that was annexed back in fifty-three. Some big developer out of Chicago had a grandiose plan for a retirement community, but the company went belly-up before the project got underway."

"Tell me about the break-in," Traxler said and pulled a pen and notebook from his pocket.

"Someone had brought in a border collie that day. It had been hit by a car over on Highway 36. I was out in the barn, and when I came back inside, I found the glass in the supply cabinet broken."

"So, this didn't happen in the middle of the night. It was while the clinic was open?" Traxler said, scribbling in his notebook.

"Around three in the afternoon. I was only in the barn for about thirty minutes. It had to have happened in that timeframe," Doc said.

"The drug, the acepromazine, that was the only thing missing, is that correct?" Traxler said.

"That and the carton of syringes," Doc said. "It took a while to sort everything out. Broken glass and supplies were scattered across the floor. The place was a mess. At first, it looked like the cabinet had been ransacked, but after I was able to do a thorough inventory, I realized nothing else was missing."

"What can you tell me about this drug, Doc?" Traxler said, settling back in his chair.

"It's an effective tranquilizer that was originally developed for human applications six or seven years ago, but there were some serious side effects associated with the drug. It was linked to seizures, and in one instance, cardiac arrest," Doc said.

"So, they pushed it off onto man's best friend," Kincaid interjected.

"That's not unusual. You'd be surprised how many of the drugs I'm using have gone down that path. At this point, I use it mainly for a fractious animal that needs immediate attention. It takes effect quickly, and if administered properly, is basically sound. Thus far, I haven't seen any adverse effects. Only time will tell on that point," Doc said.

"Have you ever heard of a man by the name of Harvey Markes?" Traxler said, pulling several photographs from his pocket.

"Not until I read his name in the newspapers," Doc said.

"So, you are aware of the investigation?" Traxler said.

"Of course," Doc said. "There aren't many people around here who aren't. That's all folks were talking about over the summer. From what I read, it seemed the case was pretty well wrapped up."

"There are some loose ends, a few unanswered questions," Traxler said. "Ever seen this man?" He handed Doc the photos.

Doc studied them. "No, not that I recall. Should I have?"

"That's Markes. He had a quantity of ACP in his possession when he was killed, and we need to know how he got his hands on it. We're fairly confident he didn't have a prescription for it," Traxler said.

Doc looked down and shook his head. "He used acepromazine on those girls? There was no mention of that in the papers." He glanced at Kincaid. "What kind of a man would do something like that?"

"That's one of the questions we're trying to answer," Kincaid said.

"Is there anything else you can remember about the incident?" Traxler said.

Doc thought for a while. "I do recall, at the time, there was some speculation that the break-in might have been the work of some college students. The *Cincinnati Enquirer* had published an article on the use of amphetamines and barbiturates on the university campus, as a recreational drug, I mean. A couple of those beatnik characters had broken into a drugstore about an hour east of here and scooped up all the diet pills on the shelves."

"What in the hell is wrong with these kids today?" Kincaid said. "A six-pack of Bud isn't good enough for them anymore?"

There was a knock at the door. The men turned and saw an elderly woman standing in the doorway. Her long gray hair was braided in pigtails, and she was wearing a blue and white checkered pinafore over a white blouse. On her feet were white anklets and a pair of burgundy patent leather shoes. She was holding a picnic basket.

44
———

Katie knelt beside her bicycle and squeezed the rear tire. It was completely flat. *No sense turning back now,* she thought. *At least it's downhill the rest of the way.* She grabbed the handlebars, disgustedly slammed the kickstand up with the side of her foot, and started out across the bridge, pushing the bike.

Almost immediately she heard her mother's voice. *That's not very ladylike, Katherine May, taking your anger out on inanimate objects. Only little children and immature adults do that sort of thing.*

In this particular instance, her mother would have been right. That insensitive hunk of tempered steel had triumphed. Her foot was bruised and already beginning to throb. She glanced down at the boots. She had gone to a half-dozen yard sales before she found them. *They were the perfect accessory to her costume,* she thought, *but maybe not so perfect for a two-mile trek pushing a bicycle.*

She eased the bike off onto the shoulder and leaned it against the guardrail. She sat down and removed the boots, pulled the gym shoes from her bag, and put them on.

Suddenly, there was the sound of a motor and the high-pitched whine of tires against the treads of the bridge. A pickup truck rolled past her and came to a stop at the edge of the highway ten yards from where she sat.

A man exited and walked to the rear of the truck.

45

———

"I must apologize for showing up without an appointment, Doctor," the woman in the pinafore said, "but I was on my way to the Ladies Auxiliary Halloween Party and thought I best stop." She placed the basket on the floor, reached in, and picked up the terrier, petting him as she cradled him in her arms.

"What can I do for you, Mrs. Reinhart," Doc said.

"Ajax has been sick to his little stomach all morning, Doctor, and I was hoping you could give me a new supply of those little pink pills you provided during our last visit. They seemed to do wonders for him. I could have left him at home with my housekeeper, but I was reluctant to do so. He gets even more anxious when I'm not around. Besides," she said, cocking her head to one side, and batting her eyes fervently, "what would Dorothy be without her little Toto?"

With the lavish blotches of rouge and eyeliner, the woman looked more like the scarecrow than Dorothy.

"That makes perfect sense, Mrs. Reinhart. We wouldn't want little Ajax upchucking all over the ladies, now would we?" Doc said. "Give me a minute." Doc disappeared briefly, returning with a small pill bottle. He held it up and shook it. "There's a dozen in here." Doc snatched Ajax from her arms, pried his jaws open, and tossed a couple of pills down his throat. "That ought to do the job for at least an hour. Give him another one as soon as you see him getting anxious." Mrs. Reinhart reached for her purse. "No, no, Mrs. Reinhart, uh . . . *Dorothy*, those are on the house." Doc put an arm around her and ushered her to the door.

"Why thank you, Doctor, you're too kind," she said and headed down the sidewalk toward her car, the basket draped over her arm.

"You be careful," Doc called after her. "We wouldn't want a house to drop on you on your way to the party!"

"That was the wicked witch, silly," she called over her shoulder and giggled.

"Oh, that's right," Doc said and grinned.

"Sorry for the interruption, gentlemen. Mrs. Reinhart is a bit eccentric, to say the least, but she's one of my best customers. Her husband died a few years ago and left her a small fortune," Doc said, sitting back down. "Anyway . . . where were we?"

"We were talking about the break-in. You had alluded to

some college students and the possibility they might have been involved," Traxler said.

"Oh, yes, that was actually a theory fostered by the newspapers. I don't know if there was any basis of truth to it. Never heard anything from the police directly," Doc said. "I wish I could help you more, but that's about all I know."

"We appreciate you taking the time, Doc," Traxler said as the men stood and walked toward the outer office. "Hope we didn't upset your day too much."

"Not at all. I'm planning to close up shop early today," Doc said. "Got a bushel of candy ready for the trick-or-treaters, and the grandchildren will be over later. Always leave early on Halloween. It's one of my favorite days of the year."

As they shook hands, Kincaid spotted the deer head mount hanging on the wall and said, "Twelve pointer. You bring that one down?"

"No, I'm not a hunter. Don't get me wrong, gentlemen, I'm not against it. You'd be surprised at the number of my colleagues who hunt. One of my best friends is a big hunting enthusiast, pheasant and quail."

"That's a beauty, Doc," Kincaid said, admiring the mount.

"A few years back, whitetail were thicker than fleas on a coon dog around these parts. The county commissioner had to bring in a team to cull the herd, get it down to a manageable number. They took some beautiful animals out of the woods just east of here. That fine specimen was given to me by a man named Conrad. He worked for the Federal Wildlife Services, as I recall. He was—"

Traxler interrupted. "The man's name was Conrad? Is that what you said, *Conrad?*"

"That's right, Stanley Conrad," Doc replied. "He lived about five miles west of here, near Greensboro."

"Do you know where the man is now?" Traxler said, apparently probing for details.

"I think he took a job as a game warden over in Illinois," Doc said. He thought for a few seconds, then looked at Kincaid. "Somewhere over in your neck of the woods, Deputy, I believe."

"Yeah, I know him, Doc," Kincaid said.

"He was a good man," Doc said, "always volunteering his time at the schools in the area. Tragedy what happened to the man's wife."

Traxler looked at Doc, his eyes widening. "What's that, Doc?"

"She died in an automobile accident just south of here on Beachum Road. She was diabetic and had some sort of seizure. Blacked out and flew off the road into a ravine. The car caught fire, and when the police arrived, all they found was a pile of smoldering rubble."

"Was Conrad living here at the time of the break-in?" Traxler said.

Doc thought for a few seconds. "As a matter of fact, he was. I talked to him that same morning . . ." A look of sheer astonishment crossed Doc's face. "You're not suggesting . . . surely Mr. Conrad wasn't involved in this horrific affair?"

Kincaid and Traxler looked at each other. "Maybe we

ought to sit back down, Doc. It seems we may have a few more questions for you," Traxler said.

46

The Pioneer Trading Post was located on Cumberland Road, about two miles from the Wabash River; a man named Avery Jackson owned the business.

When Avery purchased the fifteen acres ten years earlier, an old wood frame house, a silo, and a large sturdy barn stood on the property. Avery tore down the house and built a new one, then renovated the old barn, turning it into a roadhouse complete with restaurant and beer garden.

He also carved out spaces along the access road for merchant stands, a flea market of sorts. He thought it would be a good way to draw business to his establishment. Folks would stop to browse, have lunch or dinner, and hang around for a few beers and a little dancing to the bluegrass quartet that played on Friday and Saturday nights.

Avery and his wife were gearing up for a big weekend. In addition to the band, there would be a jack-o'-lantern carving contest, a three-legged race, and a prize awarded for best costume. They had high hopes for this Halloween weekend. Several of the merchants had already arrived and were in the process of setting up their stands.

"Keep on coming, Ernie, about another three feet. A little to the right," Zachary said, coaxing the man on the tractor slowly back with waves of his hand. The tractor's engine roared and belched a puff of smoke as Ernie eased the clutch out and nudged the wagon slowly back into a space between two large oak trees. It was a prime spot, only twenty yards from the entrance to the roadhouse. "Okay, stop! That should do it." He pointed to a small stack of bricks. "Wedge one of those on both sides of the back wheels, Evan. I'd do it myself, but this damn thing is giving me fits." He tugged at the strap around his neck, trying to reposition the sling, keep it out of his way.

"Don't worry, I've got it," Evan said, jammed the bricks into place, and stepped back. He watched as Zachary made one more pass around the wagon, inspecting it.

"Okay, Evan, yank that cotter pin when I step on this hitchamagig," Zachary said, bringing all his weight to bear on the wagon tongue. Evan yanked the pin, and the wagon broke free of the tractor. "Hey, we almost look like we know what we're doing here, son." Zachary turned and gave Ernie a thumbs-up. "I'd give you *two*, if I could, Ernie. I can't thank you enough. Don't know how I would have gotten this thing in here without you."

"My pleasure, Zach," Ernie said. "You know, I'd love to give my granddaughter one of those pretty little bracelets for her birthday. Any chance you could whip up one of those for me?" Ernie said.

"Consider it done. What's her name again?" Zachary said, trying hard to remember.

"Wendy . . . Wendy Lou," Ernie said as he pulled the tractor ahead several feet.

"I'll make one especially for her," Zachary said.

"Be mighty grateful," Ernie said and nodded as he turned the tractor around. "Have a good evening." He gave a little wave over his shoulder as the tractor sputtered off down the road.

Zachary turned to Evan. "Let's get this thing opened up and see if everything is still in one piece."

Zachary and Evan were standing under the raised side panel that formed a cozy little awning over the counter window of the wagon.

"Riley did a good job on the paint, Mr. Aiken. I like the colors," Evan said, running his fingers along the lower edge of the window frame.

"The man's handy with a paintbrush," Zachary said. "Great wrist action. You suppose he was some sort of athlete in a former life?" He winked at Evan.

Evan shot him a wide-eyed glance and said, *"You* know about Riley?"

"Of course. You're not the only one with connections.

My fourth great-granddaddy was a great chief, you know," Zachary said and grinned. "Okay, the door's on the backside. Get up in there, son, and we'll get this thing set up."

Evan walked around, opened the door, and climbed into the wagon. He looked around at the shelves and bins, then peered over the counter at Zachary. "Lots of room in here, Mr. Aiken."

"All the merchandise is in the storage area below the counter," Zachary said. "I'll tell you where everything goes. We'll get it all laid out, and maybe by the time Katie gets here we'll have a few customers."

"Well, hello there, little lady. Looks like the Halloween gremlins have worked a little of their mischief on you."

Katie cupped her hand beside her eyes and looked up at the man standing at the rear of the truck. "Oh, hi, Mr. Conrad. Couldn't see you at first. The sun was in my eyes."

Stanley Conrad wasn't surprised that Katie recognized him. He'd visited her class that morning, given a short lecture, and handed out fliers—SMOKEY'S SAFETY TIPS for the WINTER SEASON.

It wasn't the first time Stanley had visited the school. In fact, he had become a familiar face at many of the schools in the valley. As game warden, he had worked as a surrogate for the forest service, volunteering his time on several occasions during the forest fire prevention campaign. He would take the stage during school assemblies, usually accompanied by one of the school's janitors dressed in a Smokey Bear costume, introduce a short film on camping etiquette, toss out handfuls of I'm-Helping-Smokey buttons, and glad-hand the faculty on the way out. It had been the perfect charade, an ideal way for him to get to know his hunting ground.

His early victims had been strays, girls who had simply wandered into his web, but over time, his methods had evolved. Now, he preferred stalking his prey.

Truth was, the tactics were irrelevant. It was all about the end result. The voice in his head had made that perfectly clear. *You have to do your duty, Stanley. Rid the world of the scourge, those bitches who rip out a man's soul before casting him aside for a new model. Catch 'em while they're young, Stanley. It's a dirty job, but somebody has to do it.*

"Yeah, the tire's totally flat," Katie said. "Everything seemed fine until I got to the bridge. Brand new tires, too. I must have run over a nail or a piece of glass or something."

"Doesn't take much. Not much rubber on those tires. Most likely a nail. Sometimes it takes a little while for it to work its way into the inner tube," Conrad said, lighting a cigarette and taking a deep drag, knowing precisely what had caused the puncture. "So, where's this little cowgirl headed today?"

"Pioneer Trading Post. My friend and I are going to help with one of the roadside stands. You know, setting up things, selling stuff."

"Tell you what," he said, twirling the tip of his mustache and invoking a barely discernible impression of John Wayne, "why don't we load that hobbled steed of yours into my buckboard and I'll drive you down the trail to the trading post."

Katie laughed. "That would be great, Mr. Conrad, if it's not out of your way. My father is picking us up later, so that'll work out just fine."

"I was headed in that general direction anyway," Stanley said. He opened the door for her. "Jump on in there, little lady." He handed Katie her bag and hoisted the bicycle into the truck bed, wedging it in place with a twenty-five-pound bag of lime.

He leered at her out of the corner of his eye as they drove away. He wasn't sure why he had chosen her, why *she* had become the target of his vengeance—the object of his desire. It seemed he was much like the shark, the predator that relentlessly circles a group of swimmers, then launches a pinpoint attack, brushing aside a dozen other fortuitous souls to get to his targeted victim.

As he drove along, he heard the voice again, echoing in his brain. *Squelch the fire, Stanley, before these demons from hell set the whole world ablaze.*

48

—

Sophie Denton picked up the phone on the first ring. "FBI, Chicago Office, Miss Denton."

"Sophie, is Corey in the office today?"

"Oh, hi, Trax. Yeah, he's here. I just saw him in the break room. Is something wrong? More bodies?" she said.

"No, but we have a new lead. We're on the verge of busting this case wide open," Traxler said. "I need both of you in Laurenville, asap. I'm working on a search warrant for the residence of a local man, a guy by the name of Stanley Conrad. We're going to bring him in for questioning. Kincaid and I have about a three-hour drive back to Laurenville. I'll have more information for you when you arrive."

"We'll be on the road in thirty," Sophie said.

"Good. Give Jenkins a heads-up before you leave. I tried to reach him, but he's not answering."

"Will do. Oh, and one more thing . . ." There was silence. "Trax, you still there?" Sophie said.

"Yeah, I'm here."

"Be careful. You know the type of man we're dealing with here," she said.

Ten minutes later, Kincaid and Traxler were on the road just east of Indianapolis, heading west toward Illinois.

Kincaid pressed his leg against the steering wheel, jostling it slightly to keep the vehicle on the road while he lit a cigarette. He took a long drag and said, "I've known the man for a long time. He's the last person I would have suspected."

"Don't beat yourself up over it. Obviously, he wasn't at the top of my list, either," Traxler said.

"This is some sick shit we're dealing with here," Kincaid said.

"It's as sick as it gets, but when you analyze it, all the pieces fit," Traxler said. "Who would have more opportunity than a man in Conrad's job? He has freedom of movement. He knows every nook and cranny of the woods for miles around, and he's inconspicuous. Someone spots him roaming around in the woods, they think nothing of it. He's just doing his job."

"So, you're thinking this is all his handiwork. Markes had nothing to do with it?" Kincaid said.

"It's quite possible. Maybe Conrad was shaking Markes down on a regular basis. Markes couldn't go to the police, so he was the perfect patsy."

Kincaid nodded. His cigarette was clamped between his lips and he was puffing like a locomotive. "You think Conrad killed Markes, then planted that shit in his truck?"

"That would make sense, wouldn't it? Remember what Missy said about him being harassed? Conrad knew Markes was under suspicion. After all, he was the one who planted the seed," Traxler said. "I'm thinking, Conrad kills the Sanford girl and drives back into that marsh to dump the body. The stuff he confiscated from Markes is in the bed of his truck, and he ends up spilling some of it on the road. Probably doesn't think anything of it because he's not expecting anyone to be back in there digging with a backhoe a couple of days later. Then, when the shit hits the fan, he sees the perfect opportunity to push everything off onto Markes."

Kincaid thought for a few seconds and said, "Maybe his wife was his first victim."

Traxler nodded. "Could be how he came up with the idea of using the ACP. He'd seen Doc use it on animals often enough, so why not try it on the little woman? He could have shot her full of the drug and rolled her over the edge of that ravine. There wouldn't have been much left of her. Besides, she was diabetic, so everyone would have linked it to the disease."

"The man must have some loony thoughts rattling around in his head," Kincaid said.

"There are highly educated people who have spent their entire lives trying to understand the criminal mind. Personally, I think it's simply a manifestation of the most basic form of evil," Traxler said. "They can't help themselves. They were born with the evil gene."

49

———

Zachary was standing in the wagon, looking around at the merchandise on display. The row of bins along the front of the narrow counter was filled with bracelets, necklaces, flint arrowheads, and a variety of polished stones. On the back wall, on either side of the door, hung several breastplates made of beads, feathers, bones, and other material. There were a couple of framed photographs of Wapek Wanka hanging on the wall and a stack of autographed photos on a shelf below. Propped up on one end of the counter was a small cork-covered board with a colorful assortment of flies pinned to it.

"You did a good job, my boy," Zachary said. "There's a bit of everything, and it doesn't look cluttered." He lit his pipe, took a couple of puffs, struck another match, and lit one of the two kerosene lanterns hanging overhead at either end of the counter. "These will give us plenty of light," he said as he lit the second lantern, "and they'll help keep the mosquitos away . . . if there are any hardy specimens still hangin' around."

There was still daylight left, but the sun was low in the sky, and the woodland surrounding the Pioneer Trading Post, especially on the west side of the property where the wagon was situated, made it seem like dusk.

Evan was on a stepladder, using short strips of wire to attach a string of lights along the edge of the awning.

"I'm only going to use the green and orange ones," Evan said. "I don't think the red is very Halloweenish. What do you think, Mr. Aiken?"

"Makes sense to me. What do I know? Most of the time, my socks don't even match."

Evan folded the ladder and leaned it against one end of the wagon. There was a long extension cord coiled at the base of the lamp post a few feet away. He picked up the receptacle end, extended it to the wagon, and plugged in the lights.

Zachary had climbed down out of the wagon, holding two bottles of orange soda. He handed one to Evan, and they walked to a picnic table a short distance away. They sat there admiring the wagon.

"That's quite a sight," Zachary said.

Sitting in the grove of trees, freshly painted, the lanterns glowing inside, the wagon looked majestic, magical.

"When I first saw it," Evan said, "I thought it was falling apart. Now, look at it. How did you know, Mr. Aiken?"

"To tell you the truth, I wasn't so sure about it myself. Just goes to show you, anything can be fixed if it has a strong foundation."

A car rolled past them on the access road and parked beside the beer garden. Four men and a woman got out and began unloading guitar cases, a drum set, and amplifiers.

"Looks like the festivities will be underway before long. I'd better get in there and transform myself. Don't want the word to get out that Wapek Wanka may not be a *real* Indian," Zachary said and smiled. "How about you? What did you decide on for a costume?"

Evan unzipped the gym bag on the picnic table, reached in, and pulled out a coonskin cap. "Davy Crockett. I sent away for this a couple of years ago. When it arrived, it was about three sizes too big for me." He put it on. "Fits perfect now."

Zachary looked at him and smiled. "That's quite a lid. Better not wear it around Max. He might attack it."

Evan laughed. "It's kind of dorky, but it all looks pretty good together," he said, pulled out the pants and held them up. "It's not real rawhide, but it looks real. Mrs. Dobbins made them for me. She made Katie's costume out of the same stuff."

Zachary looked at his watch. "Katie should be here before long, shouldn't she?" He turned his wrist so Evan could see the time.

"Maybe I'll take a ride and meet her," Evan said and stuffed the pants and cap back into the bag. "She's probably on Cumberland Road by now."

"Good idea, son. I'll hold down the fort while you're gone," Zachary said, stood, and headed for the roadhouse.

Evan wheeled his bike around from behind the wagon, jumped on, and sprinted off along the access road toward the highway.

50

———

The truck was approaching the path that led to the Ghost Hill Mound when the deer shot from the grove of pines. It cleared the roadside ditch in one broad leap and slammed into the truck's left front fender. Stanley stomped on the brake pedal and yanked the steering wheel sharply, but the truck veered off the road traversing a ragged patch of ground, bouncing, reeling, and nearly overturning at one point before coming to rest atop a cluster of rocks protruding from the hard clay.

"What happened?" Katie said and looked around dazedly.

"Deer! Damn thing came out of nowhere!" Stanley said. There was a small cut over his right eye; blood was trickling down his face.

Katie's heart was pounding as she brushed her fingertips across her own forehead where it had smacked the windshield, then poked her head out the window and examined herself in the side mirror. No blood, just a lump.

As she ducked back in, a sharp pain shot from the point of her shoulder to the back of her neck; she cringed and turned to say something to Stanley, but he was gone.

She heard a loud wail, followed by bellowing. She turned and looked through the rear window. Stanley was standing over the buck. It was on the ground, pawing the air in a frenzy.

"Katie!"

She looked down Cumberland Road and saw Evan racing toward her. She slid across the seat, exited through the open driver-side door, and ran to meet him.

Evan jumped off his bike and hugged her. "Are you okay? I was worried when you didn't show up at the Pioneer," he said, looking around and spotting Stanley. "What happened?"

"I had a flat tire," Katie replied. "Mr. Conrad stopped to help me, and a deer . . ." She was struggling to catch her breath.

Evan glanced at the crumpled fender. "You hit a deer?"

Katie hesitated, took a deep breath and let it out slowly. "Actually . . . I think the deer hit us."

Evan put his arm around her to steady her as they walked back to the truck. "Sit here for a while," he said.

Katie sat on the running board, leaned forward and clutched her midsection, rocking back and forth. "I'm feeling a little sick."

The bellowing began again. Evan stepped to the rear of the truck. The tops of the tall pines along the river were beginning to eclipse the setting sun, casting daggerlike shadows across Cumberland Road. Evan could see Stanley standing in the shadows. The buck was lying at his feet, writhing, struggling to stand.

A gunshot rang out.

A hawk that had been sitting atop a telephone pole just a short distance down the road gave a loud screech and flew from its perch. Evan and Katie watched as it circled above the road several times, then banked off toward Spencer Bridge.

Stanley emerged from the shadows and walked toward the pickup, a rifle slung over his shoulder. As he approached he stoically said, "You the friend she mentioned?" There was no eye contact.

"Yes, Mr. Conrad, I'm Evan. I was worried about Katie and . . ." Evan paused when Stanley snubbed the conversation and walked to the front of the truck where he stood momentarily staring at the ground.

"I think I can get this thing out of here," Stanley mumbled.

On the sixth click of the jack handle, the front axle cleared the top of the rock. Stanley released the emergency brake, gave the truck a nudge with his shoulder, and watched as it rocked backward, slid off the jack stand, and slammed onto the ground. He started the engine and pulled onto the edge of the highway.

"Looks like we're good to go," Stanley said. He got out,

threw the jack into the truck bed, grabbed a coil of heavy rope, a pair of leather gloves, and dropped them onto the ground. "Wheel that bicycle over here. I'll get that carcass off the road, then I'll drive the two of you over to the Trading Post."

Evan rolled the bike over, and Stanley hoisted it into the truck.

"Do you need me to help?" Evan said.

"No, I'll handle it," he said and looked toward where the deer lay. "That's a bloody mess over there."

Katie sat back down on the running board, looked up and said, "Got to be hard seeing things like that all the time, Mr. Conrad."

He looked at her. "It's a nasty job, little lady, but somebody's got to do it." He slung the rope over his shoulder and headed down the road.

The sun was well below the tree line now. A northerly breeze had begun to stir as the unseasonably warm October day began to yield to the impending nightfall. Evan looked at Katie. "You're shivering," he said. "Do you have a jacket?"

"There's a sweater in my bag." She looked around. "Should be in the truck."

I'll get it," Evan said. He knelt beside her on the running board. The canvas bag was on the floor, nestled against the passenger door. He stretched across the floorboard, grabbed the bag and slid it toward Katie. As he backed out, something under the seat caught his eye, something shiny, gleaming, like a beacon in the night.

"What is it?" Katie said as she pulled the sweater on.

"Not sure, kind of dark under here," Evan said, knelt, and leaned in for a closer look. He wedged his hand into the narrow crevice between the floor liner and the seat base. He could see that there was a piece of heavy twine coiled around the object. He hooked his finger in one of the loops and gingerly eased it out.

Katie gasped when she saw it. "Connie Winters!" she said, the words sticking in her throat. The necklace was almost identical to the one she herself was wearing, but for the gold and onyx ring dangling amidst the cluster of beads.

They heard the sound of footsteps, turned, and saw Stanley walking toward them. With each stride, his pace seemed to quicken. As he moved in and out of the shadows, they could see that the gloves he wore were drenched in blood, and there was a spattering across his face.

"What you got there, kiddies?" Stanley said in a cold monotone. His thick walrus mustache separated his lower jaw from the rest of his face. When he spoke, he looked like one of those wooden dummies in a ventriloquist act.

Evan was trying his best to digest what was happening, put all the pieces together. He looked toward the road, hoping to see a car or truck approaching—*nothing*. "Come on, Katie!" he said, grabbing her hand and stuffing the necklace into his pocket. They took off running along Cumberland Road.

They heard the truck's engine roar to life. Evan looked

over his shoulder and saw the pickup lurch forward, its headlights glowing like the eyes of a beast—a beast intent on devouring them. He tugged on Katie's hand, urging her forward into an all-out sprint. "The mound," Evan said. "There's a place where we can hide."

Evan heard the harsh grinding of gears and the hollow sound of gravel pelting the fender wells. He didn't have to look back. He could sense that the truck was almost upon them. *Got to get off the road,* he thought. Katie was running beside him, just to his right. He grabbed her arm and veered toward the sloping shoulder, dragging Katie with him. "Jump!" They tumbled into the roadside ditch just as the truck flew by, its fender missing them by less than a foot.

Was he actually trying to kill us, run over us, mangle us like the buck lying beside the road? What kind of man could do that? The same kind of man who could rape and kill a young girl named Connie and dump her into a hole, Evan thought, as they climbed up out of the ditch, splattered with mucky clumps of mud and grass.

"You okay?" he said.

"I think so," Katie replied, wiping her face with her sleeve.

Evan glanced at her and pulled a big chunk of mud from her hair. "Let's go!" he said. They darted toward the tractor road that led to Sand Bottom Creek and the Ghost Hill Mound.

Just down the highway, gravel was flying as Stanley turned the truck around.

51

———

T*he pad of rubber Mr. Carver had attached to the pedal was working great,* Riley thought, balancing the force he was able to exert with his right leg and allowing him to maintain a smooth, steady pace as he breezed north on Juniper Street.

When he reached Gable Street, three young boys were standing on the corner in their Halloween costumes. They were waiting for the light to change so they could cross the street and make another pass at the little bungalow at the east end of the block. It would be their third visit, but for some reason, the old lady who lived there didn't seem to mind. She would simply give a little wink, smile pleasantly, and drop a Hershey bar into each of their bags while her army of cats sat in the bay window, peering out at the steady stream of trick-or-treaters making their way up the walk.

The boys waved and cheered as Riley made the turn onto Gable Street and rolled past them. Riley smiled and waved back, a feeling of exuberance washing over him; working at the school and being around Evan and Katie had given him a sense of purpose.

Clearly, Riley Winslow was still in there, and he seemed to be showing up more often of late. The hard part was getting him to stick around for a while.

52

Evan and Katie ran toward the mound. The dense woodland on either side of the path was stealing what little light remained in the day, and with each stride, it seemed to grow darker. When they reached the creek, they could see the mound rising like an island in the fog that had settled over the meadow below. Evan grabbed Katie's hand, and they started down the hill.

A minute later, they were clambering along the rock-strewn border at the east edge of the mound. The terrain had been easy to negotiate on that calm, sunny day with Zachary, but now every step was tenuous.

"Be careful," Evan said. "If one of these rocks shifts, you'll go down."

Katie looked around anxiously. "What are we looking for?"

"Two big boulders," Evan replied. "Should be an opening between them."

"Evan, I'm scared," Katie said, her voice weak and wavering.

"Me, too, Katie Blue. Hold on to me. We'll make it," he said.

They advanced another twenty feet, duck-waddled under some thorny low-hanging brush, and immediately spotted two massive pear-shaped boulders slumped against each other. They were closely abutted at the top but widened to about an eighteen-inch crevice at the bottom.

"There it is!" Evan said. They scrambled toward the opening. "You first, Katie. I'll be right behind you."

Katie turned sideways and pressed her head and shoulders through the opening, worming her way along until she was able to grip the inside edge of the cold, unyielding stone and pull herself the rest of the way through.

"I'm in!" Katie said as she surveyed her surroundings. There was a narrow corridor extending to the center of the mound; the rest was a tangled thorny web of gnarled tree limbs and vines. With the thick ivy canopy closing in from above, there was barely enough room to stand. "It's tight, Evan. Give me your hand. I can help you through."

Evan heard a noise, the grating sound of footsteps along the fringe of the mound. He turned and saw Stanley making his way toward him. He was holding a flashlight, and the rifle was slung over his shoulder.

"No time, Katie. He's here! Stay there," Evan said as he scrambled down off the rocks on all fours.

He would have been on me before I made it through. Not even sure if I would have fit, Evan thought. He glanced over his shoulder, then sprinted back up the path toward the truck. It was parked at the top of the hill, about a hundred yards away.

Think of something, Evan. You may be able to outrun him, but you can't outrun a bullet . . . and what about Katie?

Stanley had started after him, but after several strides, he halted and shouted, "I'm not going to play hide-and-seek with you, boy! That wouldn't be very smart. What I *am* planning to do is take this fine rifle and pump a few rounds into that cozy little nest where your little girlfriend is hold up. I might just get lucky."

Evan had reached the truck and was standing beside it, panting. "You wouldn't do that . . ." Evan shouted, trying to catch his breath, "someone would hear the shots!"

"Maybe, maybe not. Wouldn't be the first time someone fired off a shot back in these woods." Stanley turned and started back toward the mound.

"Don't hurt her, Mr. Conrad, please!" Evan said.

"That's up to you, boy. If you really care about her, you'll do the right thing," Stanley shouted over his shoulder.

When Stanley heard the horn, he stopped in mid-stride, turned slowly, and looked back at the truck. The blare came in prolonged bursts. To Stanley, it was a maddening sound like fingernails on a blackboard, the barking of a dog in the middle of the night. He stood motionless for several seconds, simply glaring, then clamped his hands over his ears, threw his head back and let out an ear-piercing scream.

Abruptly, he stopped screaming and charged up the path, the *voice* in his head speaking to him again, stoking his madness. *Do your duty, Stanley. Extinguish the fire. Smokey will be proud of you.*

<h1 style="text-align:center">53</h1>

It was almost dusk as Riley rolled across Spencer Bridge. Ahead, he could see a fog settling into the valley, obscuring a stretch of the road for a hundred yards or so.

He had promised Mr. Aiken he would be there to help with any last-minute things to be done with the wagon. He didn't want to be late. *When you have a job, you have to work hard, Riley. Being on time is important.* Mr. O had told him that on more than one occasion.

He leaned forward and bore down on the pedals. With every turn of the sprocket, a dull throbbing pain emanated from a spot just below his knee and traveled up the side of his leg to his hip joint, just as it had done at the end of almost every day since the accident.

Suddenly a hawk swept across the road directly in front of him, just a few feet off the pavement. Riley slammed down hard on the brakes. His bike fishtailed for several feet before coming to rest at the edge of the road.

His heart was racing as he watched the red-tail bank sharply toward the darkening October sky, then veer off toward a stand of pines that were drawn back a short distance from the road. The hawk hovered there, high above the treetops, while directly below, other birds were circling.

As Riley drew closer, he could see they were turkey vultures. Some were on the ground, picking at the carcass of the deer. The scavengers went voraciously about their business, seemingly undeterred by the aberrant sound echoing through the forest.

54

—

Evan stood beside the truck, leaning on the horn-ring. His actions weren't part of a calculated plan, but merely a visceral response, something he hoped would draw the monster away from the mound, away from Katie. His heart was pounding, his gaze fixed on Stanley, charging up the path. The stray light from the flashlight and that from the moon gave Stanley's face a chalky, cadaverous appearance.

Suddenly, Stanley stopped and unslung the rifle.

Evan darted to the rear of the truck.

The first bullet traveled completely through the open driver's door and lodged in the rear fender well. Stanley rammed another cartridge into the breech, took two steps forward and fired a second shot. It zinged through the cab, shattering the rear window.

Evan peered around from behind the truck. Stanley was on the move again. Evan looked around for a place to hide. He took a final glance over the top of the truck bed, then bolted toward a patch of tall fescue and cattails at the edge of Sand Bottom Creek. He ran a zig-zag route, his arms flailing to help maintain his balance on the squelchy ground.

He was about twenty strides from the creek when he saw the beam of the flashlight streak ahead of him. At that moment he felt like a convict making a run for the wall, caught in the light from the guard tower. His heart sank, and he clenched his jaw, preparing himself for what he sensed was about to happen.

He felt a burning sensation as the bullet tore through the outer part of his right thigh. He took three more agonizing steps before he went down at the edge of the creek.

Got to make it to the tall grass. At least I'll have a chance. Evan rolled onto his side, then to all fours, trying desperately to get to his feet. His head was spinning and he felt like he was going to vomit—or even pass out. He clutched at his leg and felt warm blood oozing through his fingers.

Stanley leaned the rifle against the fender of the truck, pulled the .32 Colt revolver from his holster, and advanced toward Evan, mumbling. The words were pure gibberish, but the inflection in his voice suggested it might very well be conversation.

Evan threw his hands in front of his eyes, the beam from the flashlight blinding him. Suddenly he heard a rushing sound and a noise like the flapping of a giant wing. Stanley must have heard it as well because he spun toward the path, instinctively casting the beam of the flashlight in that direction.

What they saw against the backdrop of a full rising moon was a figure clad entirely in black, rolling at breakneck speed down the hill. A long flowing cape trailed him, and a bolero hat was secured snugly in place with a chin cord. His eyes shone brightly through the slits of the black silk mask tied around his head.

Riley flew off the bicycle, lunging for Stanley like Night Train Lane going after a quarterback. Both men went down hard, rolled several times and tumbled over the edge of the bank that sloped nearly thirty feet to the creek below. Riley's bike rolled several more feet before slamming into a tree.

Need to do something to help! Evan thought. *The rifle!* He tore at the sleeve of his shirt, ripping most of it away up to the shoulder, then wrapped the shred of material tightly around his thigh and knotted it. He took a deep breath, climbed to his feet, and skip-hopped up the hill toward the truck. *Not broken,* he thought, *couldn't put weight on it.*

He took another couple of steps, tripped over a fallen branch, and went down into a pile of soggy leaves and debris. The burning in his thigh was intense. His knee was throbbing as though it were clamped in a vice and someone was slowly tightening the jaws.

The full moon was now well above the treetops, and the

light that shone from it illuminated the landscape like a streetlamp on Main Street.

"Evan!" Katie shouted.

Evan looked up from the ground and saw her running toward him. "The rifle, Katie. It should be near the truck!"

She disappeared into the shadows for a short time, then reappeared, holding the rifle in front of her like a soldier storming a beach. Evan could see that her hair was matted with splotches of mud and clumps of burrs. She was racing down the hill, and as she tried to slow, her feet flew from under her, sending her sprawling. Somehow, she managed to hold onto the rifle as she slid the last ten feet on her back.

She dropped the rifle, threw her arms around his neck and hugged him. "What's happening, Evan? I heard the shots, and . . ." She looked around anxiously. "Where is he?"

Evan nodded. "The creek," he said, grabbed the rifle and began yanking on the bolt lever. "Shit! Don't know anything about these things."

"When I heard the shots, I thought maybe—" She looked down at Evan's leg and saw the blood. "Oh, no! Evan, you've been shot!"

"I don't think it's that bad. Not much blood," he said. He continued fumbling with the rifle, pointing it toward the moon, looking into the breech; it was empty. "Damn!" He contemplated for a few more seconds, then tossed it into the tall weeds.

"We've got to run, Evan," Katie said and reached for him.

"I'll help you." She grabbed his arm, tears streaming down her face.

Evan clamped a hand on each of her shoulders and pulled her to him, hugging her tightly. "Riley's down there."

She pulled away and looked at him, eyes wide. "What are we going to do?"

"You've got to drag my bike out of the truck and ride as fast as you can . . . get help!"

"I can't leave you here!" she said, sobbing, her eyes pleading with him.

"I can't run!" Evan said. "I'll hide. Now, go, Katie . . . please!"

Evan watched Katie for a few seconds as she raced up the hill, then he stood and hobbled toward the creek.

He dropped to the ground and crawled under the low-hanging branches of a sycamore at the edge of the creek and peered down.

Both men were in the shallow water, about twenty yards apart. Riley limped forward a few steps, out of the shadows, stumbling over a submerged log.

Evan's mind was clouded, a jumble of sounds and images. None of it made any sense, but when he saw Riley standing there in the moonlight, a single thought came to mind—a line from the show they had watched the prior night—*I am known by many names . . . but you may call me Zorro.*

When Stanley looked down at the gray plastic sword

tucked into the sash around Riley's waist, the snarl on his face gave way to a broad smile and he began to laugh—a cynical laugh, like that of a man who had murdered his wife and gotten away with it.

"I know *you,*" Stanley said. "You're that retard who works at the high school." He let out another guttural laugh, then glanced down at the empty holster on his belt. He anxiously scanned the area, apparently searching for the revolver. When he realized it was nowhere in sight, he pulled the bone-handled knife from its sheath, and with a strange *Mortimer Snerd* grin, said, "Well . . . it looks like I'm gonna have to tangle with the Crippled Pimpernel."

"Run, Riley!" Evan shouted from above. "He'll kill you!"

Stanley snapped his head toward Evan. The snarl was there again. "You're damn right!" Stanley said, waving the knife like a man lecturing at the dinner table. "Then I'm coming after you and that pretty little girlfriend of yours!"

Riley glared at Stanley—his blood beginning to boil. He pulled the toy sword from his waistband and tossed it aside, then the hat and cape. He ripped off the mask. It caught on the edge of a jagged rock for a few seconds before the current whisked it toward the deeper water just fifty yards downstream. Finally, Riley reached down, pulled the rusty stub of fence pipe from the tangled pile of rubble at his feet, and trudged toward Stanley.

55

A behavioral scientist would contend that it's often a killer's nature to prey on the innocent: women, children, all those less equipped to defend themselves. That sort of behavior serves the killer's purposes well, quenching his lurid cravings while at the same time satisfying his need for power and control over his victims.

Ironically, it's often that same behavior that brings about his destruction by giving him a false sense of security and causing him to underestimate his adversaries.

Stanley Conrad gave further credence to that contention when on that moonlit night in October he made the ill-fated decision to engage Riley Winslow.

Stanley slashed and jabbed at Riley viciously. In the moonlight, the blade appeared in flashes, sparks flying as the tempered steel collided with the rusty hunk of pipe.

Suddenly, Stanley lunged at Riley, sweeping the knife in a wide arc toward his midsection. Riley took a step to his right and deflected the strike with his makeshift lance, the blade missing his upper thigh by mere inches.

Stanley flew by, off balance, landing on one knee in the shallow water. As he turned and struggled to his feet, Riley cocked the pipe above his shoulder, then slammed it into Stanley's rib cage.

Clutching his side, Stanley staggered backward and let out a howl that could have been heard in the next county. Riley swung the pipe again, catching Stanley's knife-wielding arm at the wrist. The bone-handled knife sailed out of his hand like a baseball yanked down the third baseline, burying itself in the muddy bank thirty yards downstream.

The force of the blow turned Stanley completely around. He began scrambling toward the bank—a look of sheer panic plastered across his face.

Riley dropped the pipe and rushed after him, threw his right arm around the man's neck, locking it in place with his left hand.

Stanley clawed at Riley's arm, trying to pry it away—struggling to breathe. With Riley draped across his back, Stanley stumbled sideways several strides, then fell face-first toward a cluster of rocks at the water's edge. There was a discernible sound, like a hammer striking a coconut. Stanley lay there motionless.

Riley released his grip, stood, and rolled the man over

onto his back. The two-inch gash in the center of Stanley's forehead was streaming blood.

"Are you there, Evan?" Riley called.

"I'm here, Riley," Evan said as he crawled from his nook under the sycamore, and shambled toward a fallen tree at the edge of the ravine. He stumbled over something in the tall grass, the flashlight. He picked it up, sat down on the log, and directed the beam of light at Riley, who was now making his way up the bank using the rusty pipe as a walking stick.

Riley limped over and sat next to Evan on the moss-covered log. He tossed the pipe aside, leaned back against an upright branch and closed his eyes. "Do you think he's dead?" Riley said.

Evan shone the beam on Stanley. Blood was collecting in the shallow pool of water around his head, and something that looked like egg whites was bubbling from the corner of his mouth.

"I'm not sure," Evan said, "but I don't think he's going to be getting up anytime soon." Evan switched off the flashlight. They sat quietly.

A few minutes later, headlight beams and flashes of red light danced on the branches above them.

Evan put his hand on Riley's shoulder. "They'll be here soon," Evan said.

Riley sighed deeply and looked at Evan, glancing down at the bloody makeshift bandage. "Evan, you're bleeding! I didn't know you were hurt!"

"I'll be okay," Evan said. "It's not nearly as bad as it looks."

"You could have been killed, Evan . . . Katie, too!" Riley said, his voice wavering.

"But we weren't. We're *both* okay," Evan said and patted Riley's shoulder. "You did great, Diego. I never saw anyone so brave."

Riley looked at Evan, smiled apologetically and shook his head. "I'm not Diego," he said, his face spattered with mud—a tear welling in the corner of one eye. "I'm just Riley Winslow."

56

Within minutes a small army of county and local police had arrived, along with three ambulances.

Katie rode with Evan in the first ambulance as it sped away toward Wabash Valley General Hospital. Minutes later, another left with Riley on board.

It was thirty minutes before that last vehicle departed with Stanley Conrad handcuffed to the stretcher. The official explanation for the delay was that the attendants wanted to be certain Stanley hadn't sustained a cervical injury before moving him, but some contended that "the crew had deliberately taken their sweet time in hauling Stanley's ass out of that woods," hoping that justice would be served and the man would have drawn his last breath right there in the muck along Sand Bottom Creek.

No one had given much credence to the latter contention, not until a few weeks later, that is, when during a Monday morning "bullshit session" at Will's Barber Shop, it was learned that Leroy Simms, the driver of the ambulance, had been a close relative of Connie Winters. At that point, the notion became a bit more plausible.

As it turned out, Stanley's injuries hadn't been particularly life-threatening. He was diagnosed with a concussion, two cracked ribs, a broken ulna, and mild tracheal damage, all injuries from which he would eventually recover completely.

An hour after the last ambulance departed, Agent Traxler and Deputy Kincaid were at the scene, followed shortly thereafter by the FBI forensic team from Chicago.

By nine o'clock that night, people from all over the Wabash Valley had converged on the Laurenville town square. Television crews and reporters from newspapers throughout the Midwest were on site to cover the events of the day.

Needless to say, no one got much sleep that cool moonlit Halloween night in '58.

57

———

Early December

O'Malley sat in his office drinking a cup of coffee, looking at the two photographs on the front page of the *Tribune* sports section. The larger photo was the one taken that day back in 1939, Riley in his White Sox uniform. He had a bat slung over his shoulder and was smiling his usual broad infectious smile. The bold headline above the photograph read:

A GOOD DAY FOR HEROES

The article below the photo provided details of Riley's life prior to the accident, his achievements, and accolades from those who had played baseball with him.

The smaller photo toward the bottom of the page pictured Riley, Evan, and Katie with Illinois Governor William Stratton. There were several state officials standing in the background, while the governor, centerstage, presented a gleaming new Schwinn bicycle to Riley to replace the one that had ended up in the shape of a pretzel at the edge of Sand Bottom Creek. Evan and Katie both had gold medallions hanging on ribbons around their necks. The text surrounding the photo chronicled the heroic actions of the trio that day at the Ghost Hill Indian Mound.

The *Tribune* wasn't the only paper carrying the article. Numerous newspapers across the country had picked it up and were running it as a human interest story.

O'Malley took another sip of coffee and stared at the newspaper spread across his desk. There was no need to read any of the copy on the page. He knew it almost verbatim. He had written it.

He removed his glasses, rubbed his eyes, and swiped his palm slowly down the length of his face as if he were trying to wipe away the wrinkles and age spots that had materialized over the years. He reclined in his chair, clasped his hands behind his head, and closed his eyes.

It's been a great run, he thought. A lifetime of memories began playing out in his mind, places he'd been, people who had crossed his path, the sheer excitement of his life as a sportswriter.

It's not over yet. Got to keep moving forward. Not ready to be propped up in the old recliner with a blanket tucked around me. He took a long deep breath and sighed. *Never will be ready for that,* he thought.

There was a knock at the door.

"Yes?" he called.

A woman pushed the door open and poked her head in. "There's a call for you, Mr. O'Malley, a young man. He said his name is Evan Mason."

"Put it through, Annie, please."

She smiled and nodded.

He leaned forward and stared at the phone. On the second ring, he picked it up. "Hello, Evan. Is everything okay?"

"Everything is fine," Evan said.

"Well, it's good to hear from you, son."

"I saw the newspaper, Mr. O. We all read it. I'm glad people will know about Riley, know who he really is, I mean."

"Everyone has a story, Evan. Sadly, for most people, their story is never told."

There was a short pause, then Evan said, "Grandma Bea is making a big dinner on Christmas Day. Everybody will be here. She thought maybe you'd like to come . . . if you're not doing anything special."

"I can't think of anything more special than that. I'll be there with bells on. I may even roll the top back on the old Sunliner . . . make the trip a bit more invigorating."

"Might be a little cold, Mr. O, and what if it snows?" Evan said.

"Well, that would make it even more of an adventure, wouldn't it, son."

They laughed.

Epilogue

Fall – 1999

Evan Mason had been sitting on the bench in front of the building for about thirty minutes, looking at the facade of the two-story brick colonial, with its broad porch and thick white pillars that extended almost to the row of second-floor windows.

The Oak Glen Senior Home was situated on Sand Bottom Creek two miles from the Ghost Hill Indian Mound. It was surrounded by giant oak trees that had probably been there when the native people were hunting the woodlands and burying their tribesmen on the sacred ground just a few miles away. The facility had been built ten years earlier, with funds from the foundation Evan had established for that very purpose.

It was a crisp October day, and a slight breeze carried leaves onto the porch. The leaves floated and swirled around the two elderly women sitting on cushioned high-backed rockers on either side of the large lattice French doors, the main entrance to the building. One woman was intently focused on her knitting, a hat or scarf, Evan couldn't tell from where he sat. The woman didn't look up, her thin, gnarled fingers laboring on the details of her work.

The other woman, her head resting against the wing of the chair in what looked to be a somewhat awkward and uncomfortable position, was slowly rocking. She wore a pair of thick-lens spectacles. She seemed to be looking at him, but Evan couldn't see her eyes, the glare of the morning sun prevented that, so for all he knew, her eyes may have been closed. Perhaps she was dreaming of her youth, oblivious to the fifty-three-year-old man sitting there on the bench watching her.

He glanced up at the second-floor window. *If only I could walk into the building,* he thought, *up the stairs into Riley's room and see the man with the broad smile and sparkling eyes. The once tall, strong, yet gentle man I had seen arriving that night in the summer of fifty-eight. The man who had come to the rescue that Halloween night.*

From the corner of his eye, he saw a woman coming around the side of the building. She stopped briefly, doused the half-smoked cigarette in the paper coffee cup she held and walked over to where he sat.

"Good morning, Mr. Mason. I'm Phyllis," she said.

Phyllis was the young nurse he had talked with on the phone earlier. Evan had never met her, but he knew the moment he spoke with her she had a caring nature about her.

One of those people whose sincerity shines through in the midst of tragedy and trying times, he thought.

"Good morning, Phyllis. I'm surprised you're still here. Didn't your shift end over an hour ago?"

"Yes, but I learned that the family of one of our residents wants to meet with me. They're driving all the way from New York. I have to make time for them," Phyllis said. "Are you okay? Did you get any sleep?"

"I was on my back for several hours. Dozed off and on. Not what you would call a *sound* sleep," he said.

"Where did you stay? I'm guessing the Holiday Inn on Route 1."

"No, the Dixmoore. It had nothing to do with the hotel. It was fine, clean and quiet. It was me. My brain was working overtime," Evan said.

"I checked on Mr. Winslow just a few minutes ago. He's stable but still weak. The heart attack has taken its toll. He was given a sedative, and it probably won't wear off for at least another hour."

"Thank you, Phyllis. I'm hoping he'll be lucid. I brought some pictures I thought he might enjoy." Evan nodded toward the leather-bound album lying beside him. "My wife will be here shortly. I need to prepare myself before I go in. I have an image of him in my mind, and I don't know if I'm quite ready to replace it with another."

"Is Mr. Winslow a relative?" Phyllis said.

"No, just a good friend. I met him when I was a boy."

Phyllis nodded and said, "I know this probably isn't the

time to be talking about it, Mr. Mason, but I must tell you how much I enjoy your music. My mother is an even bigger fan than I. We've seen both productions of *Mystic Garden*. We saw the Broadway production the very first day it opened. It was wonderful. Your music is so uplifting."

"Thank you, Phyllis, that means a lot to me . . . and I say that with all my heart."

"I hope to see you later, Mr. Mason, perhaps meet your wife."

Evan nodded and smiled.

Phyllis turned and walked up the sidewalk.

Abruptly, the wind began to gust, and the temperature dropped; a front was moving through.

Could be in for a storm, he thought, as he watched Phyllis hurriedly helping the two women gather their belongings. She had ahold of each of their arms as she escorted them through the door and down the hallway, a string of yarn trailing behind the one woman as she shuffled along.

Evan placed the album in his lap and began flipping through it. A few pages in was a photograph taken a week after the incident at the mound. Riley was on the stage of the Laurenville American Legion with the mayor, who was presenting him with a plaque. Katie was holding a bouquet of white roses, and Evan was beside her, a crutch tucked under his shoulder.

As he looked at the image, he remembered the moment he felt the bullet strike him. To this day, he believed that

Conrad had been intent on killing him with that shot, but it had simply missed the mark.

He'd been lucky. The bullet had passed completely through the outer part of his thigh, missing key blood vessels and bone. The wound had healed quickly, and there hadn't been much pain after the first week.

The *real* agony had come later, in the form of images, pernicious recollections of that horrific day that would, without warning, invade his mind and send a shudder throughout his entire body. Over time, he had learned how to give those images the bum's rush, shuffle them out before they had time to delude his brain with a false reality. After all, that's precisely what they were, visions of things that no longer existed, dispatched from some dark chamber of his brain. Of course, there were still the nightmares. He had no control over the things that came in the night.

In that same photograph, off to one side, was the FBI agent, Michael Traxler. He was standing beside Deputy Kincaid. Over the years, Evan had learned a lot about the case and the individuals associated with it. What he remembered about Traxler was that he had been involved throughout the investigation. He had met with Stanley numerous times while he awaited trial. During those sessions, Stanley Conrad had confessed to killing five other young women and girls, ranging in age from thirteen to nineteen. Their remains were found in shallow graves, three near Newcastle, Indiana and the other two at the southern edge of Bargetown. In late July 1960, Stanley was sentenced to three consecutive life terms to be served at the federal penitentiary in Terre Haute. He'd been spared the death penalty because of his cooperation during the investigation.

Many of the residents of the Wabash Valley were outraged with the sentence, but their anger turned to jubilation when, just two weeks after being transferred from isolation into the general prison population, Stanley Conrad was fatally stabbed by another inmate in the prison laundry.

Evan set the album aside, leaned back, closed his eyes and took a few deep breaths, trying to collect his thoughts.

He heard the sound of footsteps on the sidewalk behind him and knew, even without looking, who was approaching.

He turned, looked up, and said, "Hi, honey. Did you have a good flight?"

"I had to fly into O'Hare. There were no direct flights to Indy," Katie said.

"I'm glad you were able to get away. Riley will be happy to see you. What about Winnie and Zach? Did they get back to school okay?"

"Yes. They're both fine. They said to give you their love," Katie said. "Have you been inside?"

"No. He's been sedated. I thought I would wait for you."

Katie sat beside him and picked up the album. "Haven't seen this in years," she said. "I think the last time was just before Grandma Bea passed away."

"I'm not sure if it was a good idea," Evan said.

"There are a lot of good memories in here," Katie said, brushing her fingertips over the leather.

"Yes, and a lot of dead people. I can't believe they're all gone," he said and slowly shook his head.

A slight drizzle began to fall, and they could hear the soughing of the wind in the tall pines behind the building and the piercing call of a red-tailed hawk soaring somewhere high above Sand Bottom Creek. They stood, and Katie took his arm as they started up the sidewalk.

"They may be gone, but their spirits are still with us," Katie said. She stopped, looked up at the treetops and closed her eyes, the cool mist settling on her face. "Don't you feel them?"

Evan looked at her, smiled, and pulled her close. "I'm glad you're here, Katie Blue."

Katie put her arms around his neck, kissed him softly on the cheek, and whispered, "I'll love you 'til the day I die, Evan Mason."

About the Author

Michael E. Burge grew up in the Chicago suburbs and a small town on the Wabash River in Southern Illinois.

In the late sixties, he left college to serve on a U.S. Navy destroyer out of Norfolk, Virginia. Upon leaving the service, he transitioned to a career in the burgeoning computer industry, positions in product management and marketing.

He is now pursuing his lifelong interest in writing, publishing his debut novel, *Bryant's Gap*, in 2015. Michael also plays piano, paints, and is an avid golfer. He and his family currently live in Illinois.